"It's not your reputation I'm worried about,"

Beau said succinctly. "It's *my* reputation that would go up in flames!"

Elaine couldn't believe her ears. "What?" she asked, laughing in disbelief, then in anger. "What do you mean...*your* reputation?" she demanded indignantly. "How can being found alone with me hurt *your* reputation?" She clenched her jaw to keep her teeth from chattering. The jungle steam had vanished. Now she was enveloped in a damp, bone-chilling cold. The sense of comfort and protection she'd felt in his arms faded as his words reverberated in her head.

Beau was frowning as he answered her question. "It's very simple, Ms. Faust," he said grimly. "People don't like to hire men who seduce the woman of the household."

Dear Reader,

I hope you're now used to our new look, because this month's books certainly deserve to be found in the stores. First up is Kathleen Korbel's *The Ice Cream Man*, with a hero who isn't anything like he seems. After all, what self-respecting suburban mother could allow herself to fall in love with a man who delivers ice cream for a living? Not to worry. There's more here than meets the eye—all of it delicious!

Marilyn Pappano makes a welcome return with *Somebody's Baby*, a story that will break your heart, then mend it again. At fourteen months, Katie Ryan holds her adoring parents' hearts in her tiny hand, and she knows just what to do with them. She loves each one of them so much that they have no choice at all but to love each other just as much as they love her.

Lee Magner follows up her exciting *Master of the Hunt* with *Mistress of Foxgrove*, a sensuous, soul-stirring tale set in the beautiful Virginia hunt country. And new author Marilyn Tracy spins a Southwestern web to ensnare your heart as well as those of her hero and heroine in *Magic in the Air*.

In coming months you can look for books by more of your favorite authors: Nora Roberts (who has a special treat in store), Heather Graham Pozzessere, Kathleen Creighton, Barbara Faith and many, many more—as well as a few surprises. I hope you'll be part of the excitement.

Leslie J. Wainger
Senior Editor

Mistress of Foxgrove
LEE MAGNER

Silhouette Intimate Moments
Published by Silhouette Books New York
America's Publisher of Contemporary Romance

SILHOUETTE BOOKS
300 East 42nd St., New York, N.Y. 10017

Copyright © 1989 by Ellen Lee Magner Tatara

All rights reserved. Except for use in any review, the reproduction or utilization of this work in whole or in part in any form by any electronic, mechanical or other means, now known or hereafter invented, including xerography, photocopying and recording, or in any information storage or retrieval system, is forbidden without the permission of Silhouette Books, 300 E. 42nd St., New York, N.Y. 10017

ISBN: 0-373-07312-7

First Silhouette Books printing November 1989

All the characters in this book are fictitious. Any resemblance to actual persons, living or dead, is purely coincidental.

®: Trademark used under license and registered in the United States Patent and Trademark Office and in other countries.

Printed in the U.S.A.

Books by Lee Magner

Silhouette Intimate Moments

Mustang Man #246
Master of the Hunt #274
Mistress of Foxgrove #312

LEE MAGNER

is a versatile woman whose talents include speaking several foreign languages, raising a family—and writing. After stints as a social worker, an English teacher and a regional planner in the human-services area, she found herself at home with a small child and decided to start working on a romance. She has always been an avid reader of all kinds of novels, but especially love stories. Since beginning her writing career, she has become an an award-winning author and has published numerous contemporary romances.

Chapter 1

The man was frowning as he strode into the humid enclosure and the chrome-and-smoked-glass door noiselessly slid shut behind him. He surveyed the spacious room that housed the estate's indoor swimming pool; it took only a moment to locate the woman he was seeking. She was in the middle of the pool, swimming alone, so absorbed in what she was doing that she was oblivious to his arrival. Reluctantly he approached the poolside. The muted staccato of his boots hitting the stone floor was oddly compatible with the soft sounds of water slapping gently against her arms and body. That only made him more annoyed. He didn't wish to harmonize with her. Not in any way at all.

Broodingly he watched her lithe form glide through the clear water. He would have preferred to have this conversation elsewhere, but what he preferred was of minor importance. He was the hired help, and he did what he was paid to do, when he was paid to do it. He reminded himself that standing here admiring her swimming was not what he was getting money for. And a respectable amount of money, at that.

The sleek woman being washed by the rushing water wasn't paid by anyone, he reminded himself. She was the mistress of Foxgrove. Beyond his reach and his grasp.

A small spurt of anger surged through his veins. Anger at the fate that had stripped him of his wealth and his dignity. Anger at himself for not being able to prevent it. Anger at the position he now found himself in. With an effort, he forced the emotion back. Anger wouldn't change things. He knew that. He'd done reasonably well at not indulging in that particular feeling. Until recently, that was. Until she'd come home to Foxgrove.

Before her return, he'd considered coming to Foxgrove a clever move. It was a convenient location for some of the things he needed to do, personal matters that had nothing to do with the job. Now... he wasn't so sure. Maybe he'd made a mistake. There were other estates. Perhaps he should have chosen one of them, though none was the equal of this one.

Foxgrove had everything. He'd realized that when he'd applied for the job and eventually been hired by her brother. Foxgrove had a magnificent nineteenth-century mansion for a main residence, stone cottages for visiting friends, and log- or wood-frame cabins for a few fortunate employees. It had a large stable of fine horses, a famous kennel of pedigreed American foxhounds, and all the expertise in managing both that money could buy. He was now a principal part of that expertise. It had sprawling lands and elegant landscaping and a gracious and fascinating history, the kind that only a big Virginia estate could have. It had famous houseguests and storied neighbors and everything that wealthy life in the country was supposed to offer.

And it had the woman in the pool. She was like the rest of the place and its inhabitants: the finest that money could buy. Something curled in his stomach, and he grimly closed his mind against her. He'd known about all the other fine things here when he'd taken the job, but he hadn't known about her. Now he bitterly wished that he had.

He waited in silence for her to finish her laps, but while he waited, against his better judgment, he watched. Water glistened on her bare skin, and there was a lot of that. Her bathing suit looked like an expensive scraplet picked up from some exclusive European boutique. It didn't cover much, and it left the spectator wanting to touch her....

Elaine Faust sliced her right hand into the cool water with well-trained precision. As her palm hit the wall of watery resistance, she surged through the pool. She stroked steadily, building up speed for her last two laps. She'd been swimming for half an hour, and now she was beginning to tire. As she reached the wall, she flipped in a racing turn, pushing off against the hard blue-and-gold filigree tiles and hitting the rhythmic beat of the crawl at just the right moment.

It gave her satisfaction to feel that she was doing something right for a change. So much had gone wrong in her life in the past year. The simple laps served as confidence builders, although she knew most people would laugh if she told them that, so she didn't.

The indoor lap pool was heated, but the water felt cool against her skin. It washed over her slender body, cleansing her, and yet she still felt dirty. She knew it was psychological, but that didn't make the feeling any less real. Nor did it make the uncomfortable sensation go away.

Unpleasant memories poured into her mind. She lost her concentration and missed a stroke. She would have sworn out loud, but she couldn't without getting a mouthful of water, so she contented herself with thinking the oath with a vengeance. That didn't help much, either. Only time would make a difference, she supposed, time to forget her faithless late husband and the mess she had made of her life by naively marrying him.

Elaine smoothly turned and finished the lap with a backstroke, staring through hundred-and-thirty dollar swimming goggles at the skylight overhead. The November sky was a cool gray. Which was about her state of mind, she thought moodily. Gray.

The back of her hand touched the tiled edge of the pool, and she stopped, resting her hands on the smooth porcelain lip and floating on her back, relaxing as her breathing gradually returned to normal.

It was then that she realized she was not alone.

Not that she saw him, for she didn't. Not with her eyes, anyway. It was more like a primitive form of radar. Her sense of humor tickled away her gloomier thoughts, and a smile curved her soft lips. Maybe not radar, she thought, maybe sonar, like dolphins and whales.

She tilted her head backward and stared through green-tinted, shatterproof, diamond-frosted glass at the man standing upside down behind her. He wasn't dressed for swimming.

"Coming in for a swim, Beau?" she teased. He frowned down at her in exasperation, and she grinned up at him. "You work too hard," she proclaimed grandly, twisting around to stand in the breast-high water so she could see him more clearly. She whipped the goggles upward onto the tight yellow swim cap she was wearing and eyed him like the lady of the manor that technically, she was. She could see the annoyance in his gray-blue eyes, and she put up a hand to allay his irritation. "I know. You don't swim in the boss's pool. I guess that means you're here on pressing business." She paused and looked at him questioningly.

The annoyance in his eyes faded a little. He nodded and stared at her with the expression of sober amusement that she always found rather fascinating.

"Sorry to interrupt," he apologized, although he sounded more perfunctory than genuinely contrite. "I thought if I didn't catch you now, you'd be gone before I could talk to you. I understand you're going out to dinner tonight...." He let it hang like a question. His eyes were riveted to her face.

"Yes," she admitted. She put her hands on the poolside and pushed herself smoothly up and out. Water poured down her bikini-clad body and dripped onto the flat red-and-amber stone deck that artistically framed the three-lane twenty-five-meter lap pool. Since he was standing closer to her towel than she was, she asked, "Would you mind tossing me that?"

Beau handed her one of the thick, fluffy towels that hung discreetly in the midst of the giant potted palms and semitropical trees. He watched her impassively as she dried herself off, the water from her body leaving dark stains on the nearby redwood settee.

Elaine hung the goggles on a post provided for that purpose and pulled the tight elastic swim cap off her head, shaking loose her rich dark hair. She sighed with relief as the blood rushed back into her scalp. "That feels better," she murmured appreciatively.

She looked at Beau and found him, as usual, patiently waiting for her attention, his eyes on her face. Beau Lamond. She'd been told repeatedly that he was a handsome, charismatic man when you got to know him, but the way he treated her, she would never have guessed it. He was always polite, businesslike and a little bit aloof, though in the nicest possible way, of course, she had to admit. No, she hardly thought of him as handsome. Certainly not as charming. She thought of him as the Foxgrove stable manager. And that was obviously the way he wished her to think of him.

Normally Elaine wouldn't have given his status much thought. There were many people working at Foxgrove. Technically they were all hired and employed by her brother, Richard. He was much older and had stepped into the role of family financial manager after the death of their parents years ago. Most of the Foxgrove employees thought of Richard as their indisputable boss. At the same time, they looked upon Elaine with a respectful fondness that bordered on reverence.

But Beau treated her differently, and she wasn't quite sure whether she liked it or not. The more they had to come into contact, the more disconcerted she became. And she was beginning to feel that way again.

There he stood, waiting with growing impatience, in the familiar leather riding boots, jeans and flannel work shirt that smelled faintly of straw and horses and...Beau, she presumed. Elaine felt her cheeks grow warm. That wasn't the kind of thought that normally came to her, she thought uneasily. She hugged the towel to her midriff and tilted her head to one side a little defensively.

"What do you need me for?" she asked, a little more abruptly than was her style. She swallowed and tried to relax.

If he was aware of her uncharacteristic sharpness, he gave no indication of it.

"We're going to need two more hunters for the meet next weekend," he explained. "I thought I'd borrow them from Bradley File, if you don't mind."

"I don't mind at all. The question is, is it all right with Bradley?" she pointed out. She laughed as much to ease her sudden nervousness as out of amusement. Bradley File had been the Fausts' stable manager for over twenty years until he'd retired a little over a year ago. He'd been well-known for his outstanding judgment of horses and for his unpredictable, thoroughly irascible personality. Beau didn't look concerned in the least, she noticed. "Have you already talked to him?" she asked curiously as she crossed the smooth stone floor and headed toward her cover-up.

"Not yet."

He trailed along behind her and watched as she lifted the silky wrap from its rack. The loosely cut folds enveloped her upper body, but her shapely legs were well exposed. Belted, the white-and-gold garment only made it as far down as the middle of her bare thighs.

Beau didn't seem to notice. He appeared to be primarily interested in getting her okay and heading back to the stable.

"All right," she agreed. "Ask him. It's fine with me. As far as I know, no one will be bringing a horse to board with us for the weekend. There aren't going to be any visitors that you don't already know about."

Beau smiled the polite smile that he wore like a gun, and Elaine wondered whether she was more annoyed or impressed by his relentless neutrality where she was concerned. Respect and courtesy were fine, of course. But a little friendly conversation surely couldn't hurt. Besides, it was good for a person's ego. Especially if that person was a Southern girl. In the South—and northern Virginia was still in the South as far as she was concerned—men appreciated women. It was just normal social behavior. Not a come-on. Thinking of come-ons made her remember the deceptions of her deceased spouse. Her wandering thoughts came to an abrupt halt.

Mistress of Foxgrove

Elaine stood a little straighter, defiantly shaking out her hair and tightening her belt. She knew it was unfair to be annoyed at Beau for his total lack of awareness of her as an individual. She should be pleased, or at least indifferent. After all, polite social interest could sometimes slide into a more dangerous kind of awareness between a man and a woman. Elaine knew she didn't want that. At this point in her life, she wasn't sure she *ever* wanted to experience that particular feeling again.

However, she wasn't pleased, and she was definitely finding it difficult to be indifferent. No, she was annoyed. After all, they'd had the opportunity to get to know each other a little. It wasn't as if he had to treat her like a distant mistress of the manor.

Beau had been her bodyguard for a few tense days not so very long ago. Her brother had asked him to keep a close eye on her while a killer had been on the loose. Beau had been with her almost constantly, and she'd grown curious about him. Because of their constant proximity, he'd had to talk to her, but their exchanges had been remarkably lacking in information about him. She'd come to trust him, though, in spite of his constant circumspection. She'd known that her brother would never have asked Beau to protect her if he'd had any doubt that Beau could and would do it. She had felt safe with him. Safer than she'd felt in years. There had never been any doubt in her mind that she could count on Beau.

That was quite a feat after the dismal experience she'd had with her late husband. And it wasn't until the crisis had passed, and there had been no further need for a bodyguard, that she'd realized how much she'd come to enjoy Beau's company. She had hoped they could continue that quiet, peaceful acquaintance, but he had disappeared into his stable duties, studiously avoiding all but the most necessary contact with her.

He'd gone about his work, and she was to go about hers. Perhaps that was the problem, Elaine mused. She really didn't have any duties. She was at loose ends. She needed a new purpose in her life. Something meaningful. Beau's voice drew her back to the issue at hand.

"I think Bradley will be happy to lend us the horses," he drawled. "Last week he was complaining that he couldn't develop his hunters as thoroughly as he wanted because it was difficult getting them into the field enough. He'd probably pay us to hunt them for him."

Elaine was skeptical. "Really? That doesn't sound like the Bradley File I know."

Beau almost smiled. "Maybe you don't know him as well as you think."

Elaine thrust her feet into fine Italian leather. Irritation nibbled at her.

"How is it we can know the same people, Beau, and yet not see them in the same way at all?" she demanded.

It wasn't the first time this had happened, but it was disconcerting to find that her old mentor, Bradley, had shared a side of himself with Beau that he hadn't let her see in all these years.

"That's life, I guess," he muttered with a shrug. His eyes had cooled, and he glanced toward the door as if he were about to leave. "I'll get in touch with Bradley, then...."

Elaine stretched out her hand, but hesitated just short of touching him. He glanced down at her hovering fingers, then raised his eyes to hers. Something in his look made her withdraw immediately. He had looked...offended, she thought with a small sense of shock.

Beau frowned. "Are you all right?" he asked sharply. "You're pale."

Elaine swallowed and managed a moderate smile. "Too much staying at home," she demurred. She tried to inject some gaiety into her voice. "Which is why I can't stand around here talking...and why you were very wise to catch me while you could." She fluffed her hair a little more with her fingers and tried to forget Beau's reaction to her. "I'll be out late.... I trust your judgment, and Bradley's, too, of course. Do whatever the two of you can work out. Give me one of the hunt staff horses. I'm the second whipper-in, since Thomas is in Argentina this month." She gave Beau a smile worthy of a Vassar graduate. "And *please* use the lap pool. If you don't want to use it when I'm here, then use it when I'm not. Everyone else around here does. We're all family."

To her surprise, she thought she glimpsed a blue-white spark of pure anger in his eyes. He nodded, turned on his heel and strode out of the room, leaving Elaine wondering why he had reacted so strongly to her innocent remark. She had heard him mutter something under his breath, but she wasn't certain what. It had sounded like an expression of disgust, but that was so out of character for her courteous stable manager that she thought she must have misheard him.

Elaine stared through the ceiling-to-floor windows that formed one wall of the room, watching Beau as he crossed the courtyard between the estate house and the stable. It wasn't like him to be angered by a simple invitation to be part of the estate family. He was a loner, but he was generally easygoing. And it wasn't as if the offer was all that unique. The Fausts always tried to be friends of the people who worked for them. Surely he'd known that when he'd come. It was common knowledge that some of the staff had become family in nearly every sense of the word. Like Bradley File. Or Ambrose Whitley, the butler. Or Mrs. Adams, the cook. So what was bothering Beau?

Elaine wandered out of the room, leaving its lush flora and elegant sunny atmosphere, and climbed the curving walnut staircase at the back of the house. Her sandals were muffled against the plush carpeting as she passed through the silent halls. The eerie stillness echoed the emptiness of her life. She shook off the temptation to feel sorry for herself and concentrated on recalling a few snatches of information about the enigmatic horseman.

She knew that Beau had been the son of a wealthy Virginia family. They'd lived farther south somewhere. She vaguely recalled something about a scandal and that Beau's family had lost everything not so many years ago. Perhaps he was beginning to chafe at his loss, she mused. She could understand that. It couldn't be easy being employed by people who'd once been your social and financial peers.

On top of that, he'd had to put up with a lot of unexpected melodrama after she'd left her husband and come home earlier in the fall. She wondered what he'd thought of it all. He'd never said. Maybe he wanted to avoid any deeper involvement with the Fausts after what had happened. She couldn't really blame him for that. They'd been brushed by the hand of death in the form of a very evil woman.

Elaine shivered a little as she recalled her stepmother's sinister plotting and the remorseless way she'd arranged the murder of the people who could have unmasked her for what she was, including Elaine's husband, Cam. It was horrible, having had her so close, living intimately with them, sharing the Faust name, even though she had never had any real right to it.

There were times when Elaine fervently wished she could forget that it happened. Perhaps Beau wanted to forget, too, along with his own personal devils.... Her charitable feelings faded as she reached the end of the corridor. No matter what he was trying to get beyond, he didn't have to stick his head in the ground like an ostrich and pretend she wasn't even alive! Elaine could think of any number of other people whom he didn't treat so coolly. Why did he have to be so reserved with her?

Elaine yanked open the door to her suite of rooms and headed straight to the large bathroom, stripping off her pool clothes as she went. A few moments later she stepped inside the carnelian frosted glass of her shower stall and stood beneath its warm needlelike spray.

The soft-scented soap clung to her skin and her hair. It made her feel a little better. And she was going to need all the confidence she could muster for this evening. She was going to a dinner party, only she had the sinking suspicion that she might end up being the main course.

"If they're going to roast me alive, at least I'm going down in style," she muttered stubbornly as she pulled open the huge sliding doors to her walk-in closet a short while later.

Although she wasn't wild about going, no one would have thought it to look at her when she walked out of her suite. Her teal-and-silver-lamé slacks clung discreetly to the gentle curves of her hips and thighs. The matching teal silk shirt, stylishly slashed at the neck and neatly gathered at the wrists and shoulders, accentuated her delicate bone structure and the soft swell of her breasts. The subtle pastel colors she'd applied to her eyes and lips brought out their beautiful shape and the natural peach glow of her skin. Elaine Faust was a picture of elegant beauty, from her tinkling antique silver necklace down to her teal-dyed, hand-sewn, eel-skin pumps.

When she reached the front door, elderly Ambrose Whitley was waiting to open it for her. She slung the chain of a slim antique silver-mesh purse over her shoulder and gave the reserved butler a quick kiss a half inch away from his chin. He glared at her reprovingly, but Elaine laughed in affection. She knew he loved her, just as she loved him. He was more like a strict uncle than a servant.

"Jim brought the car around a few minutes ago, Miss Elaine," Ambrose noted, referring to the family chauffeur. The elderly butler was looking a little disturbed, which was unusual for him.

Elaine looked outside and saw the white Mercedes sedan, *sans* driver. The sound of male voices across the courtyard drew her attention. Jim Peterson was approaching with a none-too-pleased-looking Beau Lamond in tow. Car keys dangled from Beau's right hand, and the moment Beau's eyes met hers, she guessed what Jim was going to say.

"I'm sorry, Miss Faust," the chauffeur apologized as he stopped at the bottom of the great curving brick steps. "I've had an emergency...."

"I'm sorry," Elaine murmured sympathetically.

"My sister's boy hurt his arm. She's sure he broke it this time, and she's crying like you wouldn't believe. Her husband's out of town, and she just called. She wants me at the hospital when the doctor examines him. I told her I'd meet her at the emergency room...." He let the sentence trail off, but it was clear what he wanted from the look on his face.

"Go!" Elaine exclaimed without hesitation. "Take any car you need." She gave him a sympathetic smile. "Tell your sister she's welcome to stay here. And your nephew, too, if he doesn't have to stay at the hospital."

The relief on the chauffeur's face was immediate.

"Thanks, Miss Faust," Jim said sincerely. "I'll be surprised if the boy has to stay at the hospital. But...I may take them both back to their house and stay with them."

Elaine waved him toward the long garage.

"Do whatever you need to," she told him. "Don't worry about us." She glanced at Beau, who was still looking as if he wished he weren't standing there.

As he turned to go, Jim explained. "I asked Beau to drive you to the party." He grinned. "I figured he was a better choice than old Ambrose, here."

Ambrose sputtered an objection, but by then Jim was trotting across the driveway toward the garage. Beau looked mildly amused at being selected for driving duty primarily because he'd edged out antique Ambrose Whitley.

Elaine held out her hand, palm up, and her eyes met Beau's.

"I really don't need a driver," she said. That was true, but the greater truth was that she felt awkward having him drive her around. "It isn't your job." She laughed nervously although she knew that the fact that chauffeuring was outside his job description wasn't the real reason she didn't want him to drive her. After all, sometimes friends drove other friends around. But Beau wasn't willing to be friends, and she found it hard to think of him strictly as the hired help. If he'd been willing to be friends, perhaps it would have been different.

Beau shrugged. "No problem." He couldn't care less what he was being paid to do. Paid or unpaid, he was finding it increasingly difficult to be in Elaine's company, but that didn't mean he was going to be peevish and refuse to pitch in when his help was needed.

Elaine took a deep breath and tried to sound more commanding. She sincerely hoped she wasn't making a big mistake. She sensed that beneath his easygoing manner there was a core of go-to-hell independence that would be better left unaroused. She'd glimpsed it briefly once or twice, and she wasn't certain she was ready to deal with that hidden fire.

"It's really not necessary," she declared firmly, adding the best smile she could manage on such short notice. "I could drive to Margaret's in my sleep. Besides, when the party gets too dull to bear, I want to be able to make a discreet escape. Looking for one's chauffeur really puts a dent in 'discreet.'" She laughed. When no one else joined her, she fell silent.

Ambrose did not look particularly sympathetic. "It's not safe out on the roads alone, Miss Elaine. What if you have car trouble?"

Elaine smothered her laughter. "When is the last time any car of ours dared to break down?" she challenged. "Besides, there's a phone in the car." She eyed him affectionately. "Don't worry, Ambrose. I can take care of myself."

"You were going to let Jim drive you," Beau pointed out, reacting to the image of the beautiful Elaine being stranded alone on the lightless country road. Phone or no phone, he didn't care for it at all. His jaw snapped shut, though, as he realized what he'd said.

He was an idiot for opening his mouth. She'd given him the perfect out. He could have handed her the keys and saved himself a particularly distasteful experience. He loathed most of the people who doubtless would be attending tonight's bash. And he didn't relish being close to Elaine again. He'd had more than enough of that.

Elaine stared at him. She'd thought he wouldn't want to drive her, that he'd only been forced to, that she was letting him off the hook by offering to drive herself. His backhanded objection came as a surprise.

"I...thought you had other things to do," she said, honestly confused. The uneasiness was still with her, but she forced herself to be candid. "Weren't you going to talk to Bradley tonight?"

He was about to agree. That would be the easiest way to avoid her. He was on the verge of saying yes, ready to hand her the keys, when something happened to stop him. Elaine smiled. It was a gentle, brave smile, and it glowed like warm embers in her eyes, simmered like a tempting flavor on her lips. It drew him like honey, and he felt his whole body tighten in response. He held out his hand. To hell with the keys and his plans. He just wanted to touch her. Even if it was just her palm against his, her fingers entwined with his. Just for a moment.

Beau knew it was a bad sign, but he grimly told himself he could handle it. He could shake loose of her before it was too late. He was getting to be an expert at handling pain and frustration, he told himself. At least with her, there was pleasure, as well. He would take her wherever she needed to go. To hell with the pain.

Elaine was mesmerized by the shadowy mystery that had suddenly darkened his eyes. Unconsciously she relaxed, and something magical began to flow between them. It was an invisible chemistry that bound them together with the aching tenderness of a sigh. Without thinking, she put her hand in his and walked down the step. She thought she saw a glint of steel behind the soft gray blue of his eyes, but, as quickly as it had come, it melted away.

"Yeah," he admitted slowly. "I was just on my way to see Bradley when Peterson handed me the keys." He paused, and his eyes flicked over her casually. He cleared his throat and suggested, "How about if we compromise? I'll drop you off at the dinner party, then I'll go see Bradley about the horses. I'll pick you up on my way back to Foxgrove. That way, we'll both get what we want." Like hell, he thought. He knew what he wanted. But he wouldn't take it. Not this time. Not from Elaine.

"Yes," she murmured. "We'll both get what we want."

Nothing had ever sounded further from the truth, and for a second Elaine couldn't remember where she was, let alone what she wanted, other than Beau's company, that was. How could he do this to her? Was there some kind of subliminal hypnosis in the way he gazed at her? Straight into her, like an arrow piercing her heart...like a kiss...

He was standing there holding her hand as if he might lift it to his lips or draw her into his arms to dance. She felt his warmth like a warm tropical breeze. Male warmth. That was a contradiction in terms. Men were not warm. When she'd ached for warmth before, she'd been given derision. When she'd pleaded for loyalty, she'd been handed ridicule instead. When she'd cried for explanations, she'd been laughed at. A sliver of fear touched the back of her mind and pierced the recesses of her heart. It flashed into her eyes, and she knew he saw it, for he stiffened almost imperceptibly and then slowly released her hand. Steel closed over his eyes. The magic was broken.

"Let's go, then," Beau said abruptly.

"Be back by midnight, miss," Ambrose said with a fierce warning scowl. He glared reprovingly at Beau, then shot a disapproving glance at Beau's hands. "You haven't been out much since your return. I wouldn't want you to run into any...difficulties," he observed, glancing at Beau from beneath the bushy gray of his brows. "One never knows what to expect late at night," he told them pointedly.

Beau ignored Ambrose's fierce stare and headed toward the Mercedes. "Don't worry, Ambrose," he said as he opened the front door for Elaine. "I haven't lost a lady yet."

"Precisely my point," Ambrose grumbled.

Elaine looked from Ambrose to Beau in surprise. There had never been any friction between the two men before, but there definitely was now. It had materialized out of nowhere in the past few minutes. Elaine felt the way she had the first time a boy had taken her out on a date and her father had stood in the doorway, glaring at them. That was understandable. She'd been seventeen. *This* was ridiculous. She was thirty, for heaven's sake. And a widow.

"And this isn't a date, by any stretch of the imagination," she mumbled to herself as Beau came around and slid into the driver's seat. She wished she could point that out to her dear old friend.

But Ambrose was far away, standing on the aging red brick steps as they pulled down the driveway. And he was staring at Beau like a wizened shepherd who'd just glimpsed a wolf's tail flick beneath what he'd previously thought of as a sheep.

Chapter 2

It was awkward in the car at first. They were strangers again. Elaine nervously ran her fingertips over the silver-mesh purse on her lap. The rough metal texture was distracting, and gradually she managed to relax. Inside and out, all was dark.

The western horizon was still stained by the bleeding colors of twilight, but the rest of the sky was the indigo blue of nightfall. It wouldn't be long now before the last rays of sunset would be completely swallowed by glittering blackness.

"I always loved the sunsets here," she said softly. "The beautiful colors of the coming night. Rich reds and molten oranges all smeared across the skyline like a finger painting by some fearful giant."

She laughed nervously. She was telling him something he probably had no interest in knowing. She didn't care. She would try to break the ice between them anyway. After all, he didn't have to drive her. She'd given him a graceful means of declining, but he'd offered her his hand instead. So you're stuck with my company, like it or not, Beau Lamond, she thought defiantly.

"A giant's finger painting. That's what I thought when I was little," she explained. The wistfulness was hard to keep out of her voice. "My father even made up a story for me...all about my imaginary giant with finger paint on his hands...." She shook her head, adding pensively, "it's too bad things have to change. Sometimes it would be nice to believe in giants again."

She glanced at Beau. His profile didn't tell her much. He was staring straight ahead, his eyes on the road, as silent as a stone.

He had a lean, angular face. Maybe people were right about his good looks, she thought. In a very male sort of way, she supposed he was handsome. He had straight clean features and a way of lazily watching things that reminded her of a hawk biding his time before going after his prey. His dark blond hair had been bleached by the sun and was trimmed whenever he got around to it. Apparently he hadn't passed by a barbershop in several weeks. He looked like a battle-worn Viking.

Elaine smiled to herself at the image of a bare-chested Beau wearing leather breeches and swinging a Norse sword.

He glanced at her and caught her expression. "What's funny?" he asked bluntly.

"I..." Why not tell him the truth? she challenged her suddenly shy self. "I was imagining what you'd look like dressed as a conquering Norseman after a month plundering at sea." She giggled at his expression. "Sorry. My mind wanders..."

Beau's jaw tightened. "That's an understatement," he muttered. He normally would have asked why she'd been thinking something like that, but he wasn't sure that line of conversation would be neutral enough to suit him. He wanted to keep things strictly business between Elaine Faust and himself. A Norseman home from plundering wasn't his idea of a neutral topic.

The headlights washed a yellow swath across the curving two-lane road, momentarily blinding a deer grazing in a nearby glade. It was a young whitetail stag sporting a crown of two-pronged antlers, and he was frozen by the sudden brightness.

"Shut your eyes," Beau advised under his breath.

"What?" Elaine asked, surprised.

Beau grimaced. "Not you. The stag."

Elaine laughed. "Is that supposed to make more sense?"

Beau glanced in the rearview mirror in time to see the stag bounding across the open field. "If he'd shut his eyes, he could think clearly," Beau said. His gaze slid briefly to Elaine. "He wouldn't be blinded by the light."

"Typical," Elaine said.

"What's typical?"

"Loving what's bad. Males love bright lights and excitement. The stag couldn't help staring at it, even though it probably isn't the first time. It's part of his constitution. It gives him the thrill of being on the edge of an abyss and wondering if he's going to fall in."

Beau frowned. She wasn't talking about the deer, and they both knew it. "Men don't have a corner on risk-taking," he argued, taking issue with her. "Plenty of women do exactly the same thing."

Elaine tilted her head to one side and eyed him thoughtfully. "Are you speaking from personal experience?"

"What other kind of experience is there?" he growled, not the least interested in giving her his autobiography.

"There's vicarious experience...."

"That's not experience. That's imagination."

"So none of your experiences with women have been vicarious? They've all been personal?" She laughed.

He considered just falling silent. He'd done a lot of that with Elaine. But there was a sly, teasing challenge in her voice that piqued his pride. She was daring him to tell her something. So he turned down the lane that led to Margaret Innery's house, and then, when he pulled up in front, he looked at Elaine, prepared to give her what she wanted.

"My experiences with women have all been of the most personal and satisfying kind," he said pointedly. It wasn't exactly true, but it gave her the general picture. He reached across her to unlock the door, letting his arm brush her body lightly. He could feel her tense in surprise, although whether it was from their physical contact or from what he'd said, he didn't know. His eyes held hers. "Is there anything else you want to ask?"

His steady gray eyes had lost almost all traces of blue. They were hard and male and very experienced. Elaine shivered. He'd pulled back a mask and let her see a part of him that he'd kept hidden before. It was a part she hadn't expected.

"So you've led the life of a lady-killer?" she said.

She was trying to joke, to laugh it off, to humor her way past her sudden sense of dismay and disappointment. She didn't quite succeed. Her voice caught a little at the end. She'd known a lady-killer once. It still hurt.

Beau leaned back in his seat and nodded. "In the flesh."

A caterer assigned to greet arriving guests opened her door and helped her out. Elaine hastily took advantage of the opportunity to leave. Before the door closed, however, she told Beau, "Thank you for telling me that."

He shrugged and gave her an easy smile. "I figured you'd outgrown fairy tales."

"Like the finger painting giant?" she murmured.

The caterer looked at them as if they were out of their minds.

Beau nodded. "Yeah. Like him. What time shall I pick you up?"

Elaine bit her lip. "I'd like to say as soon as possible." She sighed. "But how about ten-thirty? I ought to be able to leave by then without hearing about it for the rest of the winter."

"Ten-thirty." He was tempted to wish her good luck, but he restrained himself. Distance. That was what he wanted. Describing himself as an experienced skirt chaser ought to help accomplish that. Her bastard of a husband had been chasing another woman when Elaine had left him.

Elaine watched him pull down the curving driveway and disappear into the night. Then she hitched her silver purse more securely on her shoulder and walked up the steps to the front door.

The dinner party was a cozy affair involving seventy-five of Margaret Innery's nearest and dearest friends. Margaret had been born with a silver spoon in her mouth, but it had been a rather small and thinly plated spoon, and she'd quickly had to learn to make her own way in life. She'd proceeded to do so with flamboyant success as a real estate agent.

She now lived in a late-nineteenth-century farmhouse that would easily go for three-quarters of a million dollars, if she was ever foolish enough to sell it, which was unlikely.

"Elaine!" trumpeted the hostess as she swept past the hors d'oeuvres and the wet bar to consume her newly arrived guest in a robust hug.

Margaret, gripping Elaine by the shoulders, leaned far back and peered at her in fascination.

"How *are* things going for you, my dear? I know that it's been *horrendous* for you, and for everyone in the family...." Margaret broke off her profuse expressions of sympathy long enough to smile at a pair of neatly dressed Japanese businessmen, who passed by with polite smiles.

"*Do* try the caviar," Margaret exhorted them, her red eyebrows raised. She turned to face Elaine as the men headed toward the hors d'oeuvres table. "They're looking for *real estate*." Her eyes lit up at the thought of the value of the yen.

Elaine tried to extricate herself, but Margaret merely firmed her grip and pulled her friend into the main action of the party. "My dear...after all you've been through, you really need to get out and mix," she cooed.

People were looking at them, and Elaine had the feeling that she was indeed to be part of the entertainment for the evening, just as she had feared. There was a subtle hushing, a lowering of voices, a suspension of conversation, as she passed people. She smiled brittlely and nodded, greeting the friends and neighbors she knew by name, and shaking hands with others as Margaret paused to make introductions.

By the time they crossed the room and reached the waiter who was serving drinks from a tray, Elaine was more than ready to take one. She smiled brilliantly as she deftly removed the last glass of champagne from his fingers. She finished half of it in one long, uninterrupted swallow. Mellow warmth spread through her like anesthesia.

Margaret stared. "My, my, honey. Marriage to Cam really gave you a certain...sophistication...didn't it?" she said admiringly.

Margaret's comment hit Elaine like a hard fist in her stomach. Sophistication wasn't among the legacies of her marriage to Cam Bennett. Disenchantment, distrust, dismay...yes.

"That's a terrible thing to say, Margaret!" she declared, shocked at the tactless comment. She eyed the older woman closely. "Is that what you really think?"

Margaret's somewhat puffy fifty-year-old cheeks turned a mild shade of pink, and she pursed her lips defensively. "Now, Elaine...we're all adults. I was just speaking frankly. I'm sorry if I offended you," she soothed perfunctorily.

Elaine looked around her. Eyes dropped; heads turned away; false smiles appeared at every turn. The sick feeling washed through her again. It was immediately followed by an even stronger surge of anger.

"This is the first time I've been anywhere since Cam's death," she reminded Margaret, smiling frostily back at them all. "I didn't realize that people would be *this* tactless." She glanced at Margaret. "Am I some sort of sideshow? The new piece of gossip for people to laugh over?"

Elaine recalled the dreadful scene when Cam had shown up unexpectedly at a lawn party on the evening he had been killed. She'd had her private life played out in front of her neighbors then, to her deep humiliation.

"Is this supposed to be the next episode in the continuing melodrama of my personal life?" she demanded angrily. "Honestly, I thought people would at least wait until dessert had been served before they started on me."

Margaret's eyes hardened, and she suddenly looked like the successful manipulator of people and source of community gossip that she was. "I know this is your first time out since Cam's death," she said firmly. "And believe me, you're doing the right thing. You can't avoid people forever. People are always going to get a...vicarious thrill, shall we say?...out of the problems of others. This time it's your problem, honey. You're just going to have to tough it out."

The slender glass in Elaine's hand felt very cool, and she hung on to it like a lifeline. She tried to remember why she'd ever thought coming was worth the pain. She remembered Beau's easygoing, parting grin and desperately wished she'd gone with him, even knowing the kind of man he'd said he'd been. She had the fleeting urge to run down the road after him, but it passed. Sooner or later, she would have to face these people. She would have to deal with their prying questions and insensitive comments. There was no way out of this but to face them. Running away wouldn't solve the problem; it would merely postpone the inevitable, as Margaret had said. Margaret might be a selfish, manipulative woman, but she was also quite shrewd about people. Elaine knew she really had no choice. She would indeed have to tough it out.

"So I'm their vicarious thrill, am I?" she murmured. Anger was burning away the sick feeling, and she smiled the elegant, polished smile of a woman who had the strength and the heart to stand up for herself. "Well, let's get on with it, then. The sooner we have it all out in the open, the sooner they'll leave me alone. Maybe they'll learn how to get *real* thrills, instead of pursuing imaginary ones at my expense."

Margaret nodded approvingly and patted Elaine on the shoulder with a plump mauve-nailed hand. "*That's* my girl! Your dear departed mother and father would be *so* proud of you," she cooed.

Elaine cooled. "Let's leave Mother and Father out of this, all right?" she asked with the smoothness of acid on glass. At least *they* could be left in peace, even if she wasn't going to be so fortunate!

Margaret's respect for Elaine increased. "My, my. You're goin' to be a regular little tigress tonight, aren't you?" she drawled. "My dear, you are going to be the *making* of my party!" The older woman laughed exuberantly and led Elaine into the lion's den of prurient interest.

Elaine downed her champagne and lifted another from a passing waiter without missing a step. With her most gorgeous smile fixed on her face, she held out her hand, waiting to be introduced.

Beau Lamond was sitting at a bar stool, nursing his third Budweiser, when Bradley File finally nodded and agreed to the terms for using his hunters in the Foxgrove Hunt's meets. Beau held out his hand, and the two men shook on it, lifting their bottles of beer to seal the bargain. It was as good as a written contract.

"Okay. Now that we've settled up on that score, tell me how Richard and Meg are doin'." Grizzled old Bradley File stared through seventy-year-old eyes that were known for piercing people to get to the truth.

Beau shrugged. "Okay, I guess."

The old man guffawed loudly and slapped his thigh. "Hell, Beau, that isn't the way you describe two people in love who're on their honeymoon!"

A reluctant grin spread across Beau's face, and he lifted his hands in apology. "Sorry. I wouldn't know."

Bradley eyed the younger man dubiously. "Don't give me that, Beau! I heard all about your escapades from your father. I heard you could smooth talk a girl outta anything within twelve hours, when you put your mind to it!"

Beau's unconvincing grin faded. "Yeah. Well, that was a long time ago," he said with another shrug.

Bradley took another swig of his beer and reached for a pretzel from the scarred plastic bowl on the bar in front of him. "It wasn't *that* long ago. Besides, no man forgets what it's like to be in love and get the girl he's been courtin'."

Beau lifted the brown bottle to his mouth and tipped it up, swallowing once, twice, three times. He put the bottle down and turned to watch a dart game in progress at the far end of the small falling-down bar. "Only *you* would call that courting, Brad," Beau observed with a wry grin.

Bradley ordered another drink and offered one to Beau, who shook his head.

"No, thanks, Brad. I've got to get back pretty soon. There's a lot of work waiting for me."

Bradley shook his head in clear disapproval. "You can't work yourself to death, Beau," the old man said sympathetically. "No matter how hard you work, no matter how much you deny yourself, you can't get a couple million dollars. You can't make good your old man's losses. You can't get back what your family had."

Beau's eyes were as cold as the North Sea, his face as hard as the arctic winter. "I didn't ask for your opinion, Brad. Leave it." Beau put some money on the bar and swung down off the stool. "Trailer the horses over any time in the next couple of days. We'll have some stalls ready for them. Someone's always in the stables."

Bradley nodded. He considered pursuing his previous line of advice, then decided to wait for another time. "Say, Beau..."

Beau hesitated.

"How's Elaine?"

Beau shrugged. "Better, I guess. She was going out tonight. To a big dinner party at Margaret Innery's."

Bradley swore and slammed his beer bottle on the bar top, causing the bartender to glare at him warningly. "That fool girl," he muttered. "She was always too naive, in spite of her brains! That bunch'll eat her alive. Damn it! I would have gone with her myself, if I'd known.... She needs someone beside her to stare down those vultures and keep them at bay."

Beau looked at the older man in amused surprise. "Don't you think you'd be a little out of place there with the upper crust?"

Bradley grumbled and glared. "Hell, no! I know 'em all, and they know me. A lot of 'em only got money on paper. If someone calls in their credit, they'll be washing my floors. Besides, some of 'em are just out-and-out clever crooks, or born to a clever crook! Why shouldn't I go? I'm just as good as any one of 'em!"

Beau put up his hands as if conceding the point. "Just making conversation, Brad," he said in amusement.

Bradley glowered at him in earnest then. "No, you're not, Beauregard Lamond! You believe it, damn it all! You think that because you were a devil-may-care kid, you let your family down. You think that because your daddy got caught with his hand in the till and went broke, it's somehow your fault. You think you've got to get it all back for them before you should be allowed any pleasure in life. You took all the blame, and you shouldn't have, damn it!"

Beau's face lost all trace of amusement. "You've said enough," he said with bone-chilling softness. There was nothing else soft about him at all. His eyes were chips of granite, and his body was taut. "You don't know a damn thing about it, Bradley. Not one damn thing."

Bradley sighed in frustration. He shut his eyes and rubbed a gnarled hand over his face. "Git on home, then, son," he said tiredly. "Just... don't punish yourself for something that wasn't your fault. Y'hear?"

"I never do," Beau said. He was tight-lipped as he shouldered past a staggering patron. The bar door creaked on its hinges and slammed shut.

Bradley File was one of the few men on the planet who could have offered him unsolicited advice on that particular subject without having his face flattened. Even so, Beau's fists were tense, and his stomach was knotted. He felt like a fighter bracing for a blow, or coiling himself to punch some other poor sucker's face in.

If only Bradley knew just how wrong he was.

Elaine looked at the grandfather clock in Margaret's cozy foyer for the third time in ten minutes. She was squinting to make the hands clear enough to read, when its deep, clear chimes sounded half past ten. Ten-thirty. She wistfully noted a foursome saying farewell to their hostess. If only she were leaving now, too.

"I've got to get out of here," she murmured unhappily.

"Afraid you'll turn into a pumpkin?"

Beau's deep tenor had been completely unexpected, and she nearly jumped in surprise as she turned to smile at him in welcome. "I thought you'd never get here!" she exclaimed in relief.

Beau raised his brows in surprise. "I'm right on time," he pointed out. She sounded mournful and grateful and a little sloshed. He eyed her narrowly. Her skin was flushed, and her eyes didn't appear to be focusing too well. "How much have you had to drink?" he muttered.

She clenched her teeth into a smile as a pair of curiosity seekers strolled by and slyly sized up Beau. "Of course I've been drinking. This has really been just one long cocktail party with a little dinner plopped in the middle of it," Elaine whispered in disgust. "Even when I asked for coffee, they slipped me liquor in it."

He nodded. "I see. Well, if you've had enough, let's go."

"Enough?" she repeated, flabbergasted that he could have any doubt. Her happy relief on seeing him disappeared entirely. She shot him an angry glance as he escorted her past the chattering party goers. Surely he didn't think she wanted any more, of the company or the drinks! "I've been ready to leave since you dropped me off," she whispered sharply.

Beau lightly touched her elbow and disregarded her exasperated comment. He'd never seen her drink more than a cocktail or a glass of wine with a meal, so he doubted that she had intentionally ended up in her present condition. Elaine had never been a lush, as far as he knew. However, she was clearly well oiled, and no one had poured the drinks down her throat. He glanced at the murmuring groups of silk- and wool-clad guests and found the most likely answer. The sly looks she was getting could easily have tempted her to take a couple more glasses than usual. And a hostess happy to lower Elaine's inhibitions a little would have insured that a dot of brandy was in everything possible.

Coldhearted, self-interested bastards. That was what they were. He'd seen crowds like this before. He'd hated them then, and he found himself hating them now, for Elaine's sake. Beau stared back at a couple of the more obviously catty onlookers, and they turned their heads away. Damn curiosity seekers, he thought angrily. Bradley had been right. They were like smiling vultures hanging around to pick at a wounded animal. It brought back bitter memories, and he had to make an effort to keep from showing his anger.

He had a tough hide. The vultures could circle him all they liked; he couldn't have cared less. But they'd dived and picked at his family, and they had been deeply wounded by the heartless attack. Beau had felt those wounds. And now he felt himself inclining toward protecting Elaine. He felt some of her pain, even though he didn't want to. Bradley had been right. Someone should have come with her. It was just too damn bad it had ended up being him, Beau thought grimly. But it was too late to back out now.

He coolly stared down another pair of hypocritical smiles. The elegantly groomed twosome melted away, their smiles slipping fast.

"The car's along the drive. We'll be out of here in a minute," he muttered. He thought he heard Elaine sigh, and he resisted the urge to squeeze her elbow in comfort. He was *not* going to get involved with her.

They had almost reached the wide-flung, butler-attended doors when Margaret Innery's sugary drawl brought them to a halt with one cooing word. "Elaine!"

Elaine felt her heart sink. "We almost made it," she murmured. She glanced at Beau and gave him a rueful smile. She thought she glimpsed a sliver of sympathy in his eyes. Then they turned back to face their hostess. Margaret was bearing down on them with a vengeance, and she had someone in tow. Elaine sensed Beau stiffen slightly the moment he saw the woman with Margaret.

"Don't go just yet, honey," Margaret called out melodiously. "Babs here was just telling me that she hadn't met you yet. Mr. Aboudi's nephews kept her cornered all evening, and she just couldn't get free."

Elaine took one look at the exquisitely turned out Babs and doubted that the woman had ever done anything she hadn't wanted to with men. The blonde had an air of experience about her that Elaine had no trouble in identifying. It was the kind of thing women saw easily in other women, but men never seemed to notice at all. Women like Babs dazzled men with their physical beauty, and a male with dazzled hormones was as blind as a bat, in Elaine's experience. Her resentment of such male idiocy began to simmer. Grimly she tried to find her smile one last time.

She noticed that Beau's hand had tightened slightly on her elbow. There was a subtle increase in tension in him that wasn't simply the result of having their escape interrupted. She glanced at him and was surprised at his expression. He looked as if he'd just been slapped in the face. There was a flash of cold fury in his eyes as he stared at the beautiful Babs. Then a shutter came down, and he was once again cool and unreadable. Beau the stable manager was gone. Beau the exasperating, semiwilling chauffeur-for-the-evening was gone. This was another Beau at her side. Her nervousness increased. She didn't need any more crises in her life. And no more horrendous surprises, either.

"Beau?" Elaine whispered softly. "Is something wrong?"

"We'll soon know," he muttered in cool measured tones.

He was keeping his eyes on the two approaching women. The blond beauty and he were looking at each other as though everyone else in the room had somehow faded away. There was an aura of building tension between Beau and the blonde that made Elaine feel even more uneasy. Under the circumstances, the woman's opening words didn't really come as a surprise.

"Hi, Beau," she said in a soft, melodious drawl. She held out one finely manicured hand. "It's been a long time...."

A slender gold bracelet dripped like a fine liquid strand around her wrist, and a large, luminescent emerald, nestled in flashing diamonds, winked on her ring finger.

He disregarded her outstretched hand. "Hello, Babs."

The blonde unhurriedly lowered her hand. She didn't seem offended or even particularly surprised that Beau had refused to take it. If anything, she appeared somewhat amused. Her eyes slid to Elaine.

"And you must be Elaine Bennett...." Babs said confidently. She looked at Elaine with mild curiosity, her eyes flickering quickly over the other woman from head to toe. As if completely satisfied that there was nothing more to note, Babs turned her attention to Beau again.

"Elaine *Faust*," Elaine corrected, lifting her chin. She had no intention of continuing to use her philandering late husband's last name. Nor did she intend to stand around and talk anymore, if there was a way to avoid it. She concentrated on clearly enunciating her words, since the effects of Margaret's libations were still numbing her. "If...you don't mind...we were just about to leave...."

Margaret had been surprised by the exchange between Beau and Babs, but she was clever enough to delay further introductions. She relished the little soap operas of daily life, and she had immediately recognized a hot one here. When Elaine began to try to leave again, Margaret intervened.

"Babs," Margaret declared severely. "Have you and Beau already met?"

Babs's red lips curved. "Guilty as charged, Margaret. Beau and I are...old friends. Aren't we, Beau?"

He stared at her. His eyes were an impenetrable gray when he finally replied. "We knew each other well."

Margaret's eyes glittered with curiosity. "Where did you two meet?" she demanded, always insatiable when it came to knowing the details of people's lives.

Babs laughed softly. "I can't answer that *here*, Margaret," she murmured in amusement. "It's a long story...."

Elaine glanced at Beau. He didn't appear to be worried about whether he stayed or went. He was standing there, sizing up the woman in front of him. Elaine frowned a little and turned her attention back to the blonde.

"Margaret, you still haven't properly introduced your friend," she pointed out. Since she obviously wasn't going to be allowed to leave just yet, she might as well find out who was holding her back.

Margaret laughed. "I'm afraid I haven't. Everything is getting confused now, isn't it? Elaine, this is Babsey Carlton. Babs to her friends." Margaret cast a speculative look at Beau. "She and her husband want to buy some land around here, and Babs is staying with friends while she looks around."

Elaine wasn't happy to hear it. Her first impression of Babs Carlton did not make her want to get to know the woman better. And the fact that Beau already knew her apparently quite well wasn't helping matters, for some unfathomable reason. Elaine was curious at the mention of a husband, however.

"Is your husband with you?" she asked as politely as she could while struggling to get her sluggish jaw and tongue to pronounce the consonants correctly.

Beau seemed unnaturally still at her side.

Babs looked at Beau for a moment before answering. In that fraction of a second, emotion burned in the woman's eyes. Then her silken smile covered the mysterious slip. "No," she said softly. "My husband is out of the country for a few weeks. I'm on my own." Her expression changed subtly. "Perhaps we can get together while I'm here, Elaine. Since you've lived here all your life, I'm sure you know the properties that are really worth having...." She gave Margaret a doubtful look. "Margaret here thinks every property is perfect...."

The last thing Elaine wanted was to see Babs Carlton again. What she did want—desperately—was to leave. If she didn't sit down soon, she would slide down in a heap at Beau's unimpressed feet. Grasping at the opportunity to go, she uttered the meaningless, socially correct words that one generally intoned at such times. "Fine. Give me a call." She kissed Margaret on the cheek and turned toward the front doors, with Beau silently following at her side.

"Let's go home," she pleaded in a whisper. "And if you see anyone *else* you know, duck."

"It's a little late to be giving me that advice," he muttered.

As he handed her into the sleek white sedan, he didn't have to look to know that Babs Carlton was standing in the house, watching them drive away, with a sadistic gleam in her beautiful eyes.

Chapter 3

The car swerved sharply, and Elaine's right shoulder rocked hard against the padded metal door. The violent motion jolted her back into consciousness, and she groggily opened her eyes to see what had happened. Everything looked bleary, and she knew it wasn't just because of the drinks that Margaret had skillfully supplied at the party. A steady drizzle was coming down, making a watery smear across the windshield in spite of the best efforts of the highly expensive windshield wipers to keep it clean.

Beau noticed her looking around. "Sorry," he said unapologetically. "Something ran across the road. I swerved to keep from running over it."

"A deer?" Elaine mumbled, blinking and trying to clear her brain of its fuzziness.

"Smaller. Big possum, maybe. Or a raccoon."

Beau smoothly negotiated another twist in the road and pulled sharply to the right, braking lightly to avoid a large branch that had broken off and fallen across the lane. The car skidded a little, and the tires squealed against the blacktop of the two-lane country road. It was hard to see the road, let alone the ditches on either side, in the rainy darkness. There were no lights, and the trees that dotted the countryside just added to the gloom. With the thick layer of clouds raining on them overhead, there wasn't even a little moonlight or starlight to help with the visibility.

Beau slowed the car to a crawl, and Elaine peered into the watery rural blackness, searching for the driveway that would take them to Foxgrove.

"It's got to be close," she said. She squinted just in time to make out the landmarks. The opening was marked by white-painted gates. They blossomed into view a few feet ahead on her right, looking dark gray in the night drizzle.

"I'm glad I didn't drive," she admitted with an embarrassed sigh.

Beau almost smiled. "That makes two of us."

He swung the car into the lane without saying anything else, but somehow the silence had become a little more companionable.

Elaine knew she was three sheets to the wind, and her only hope of getting upstairs unnoticed was to make it into the house with a minimum of noise.

"Take the driveway that goes to the garage," she ordered him. When he looked at her as if she'd lost her mind, she added, "I don't want the car to wake up Ambrose or Mrs. Adams or anybody...."

Beau looked less than enthusiastic, but he complied. When he had pulled into the garage and killed the engine, Elaine breathed a sigh of relief and gathered her strength for the task of getting to her rooms without waking anyone up.

"Thanks, Beau," she murmured hastily, then got out of the car and walked out into the driveway. She stretched her hands to the sky, purse dangling, a silly grin on her face, and pirouetted toward the house as the cool rain fell on her. She hugged herself giddily and began to giggle. "This is a dreadful way to try to sober up," she gasped as her chilly wet clothes began to cling to her skin.

"You're nowhere near sober," Beau observed critically.

His voice startled her. She'd thought he was still inside the garage, or on his way to his cabin to go to sleep. "Beau!" she exclaimed in a relieved whisper. "Thank goodness, it's you and not Ambrose...."

She started to giggle again and covered her mouth as if to muffle the sound. She would never hear the end of it if Ambrose caught her in this condition. Or anyone else, for that matter. Except Beau...

"What the hell do you think you're doing?" he growled, taking a step toward her. "You'll be soaked in another minute."

She leaned back and closed her eyes, enjoying the chilly caress of the rain against her face.

"I'm washing away the party. You see, I entertained my neighbors all evening," she replied in a conspiratorial whisper. "They have this terrible fascination with my personal life. I'm afraid they were a little disappointed, though. They must have been expecting to hear about some kind of wild, kinky sex escapades, or at least some knock-down-drag-out battles between my late husband... and me...."

She had started out with laughter in her voice, but in the end there were tears.

"Oh, Beau... why can't they just mind their own business and leave me alone?" she asked unhappily. "God, they make me feel so dirty. All I want to do is forget...."

She looked at him in mute appeal, and he stood absolutely still, not moving toward her in any way. Even in her rather muddled mental state, she could see that. She straightened up and wrapped her arms around herself, embarrassed.

"Sorry, Beau," she apologized awkwardly. "I forgot. You don't want to be friends. You don't want to be treated like family. N-naturally, that means the r-reverse is true, too. You d-don't want to be f-friendly with m-me or t-treat me like f-family... or l-like a f-friend...."

She forced herself to begin walking a straight line toward the front doors of the great estate house. She needed to get inside. She was feeling woozier by the minute. And she knew that tomorrow she was going to regret what she was saying to Beau tonight.

"I seem to be m-making a f-fool of m-myself again," she said in a very subdued voice. "It'll p-pass.... It's j-just a phase...."

She took one staggery step, and then she felt his arm come around her. He'd taken off his jacket and covered her with it; she could feel the heat from his body radiating from the material. She looked up at him and was startled to see something that looked very much like warmth in his normally cool eyes. She'd seen amusement there on occasion, or anger, or frustration. Never warmth... as if it were intended just for her. Of course, as blurry as he was, she couldn't be sure.

"Your teeth are chattering," he observed. He touched her face as he led her gently toward the house. "And you're getting cold." Under his breath, as if he didn't really intend her to hear it, he muttered, "You never should have gone there, you idiot."

When they reached the steps, she realized just how little strength she had left. Her feet and legs felt cold and wobbly, and by the top step, she had to hold on to Beau's arm for support.

"I don't th-think I sh-should have d-drunk that l-last glass of brandy...." she whispered mournfully.

She began to slide down, but Beau caught her and lifted her into his arms. Her head fell back against his shoulder, and she looked up at him. His face was wet with rain, and his dark blond hair was plastered against his head. He looked like a golden, avenging god.

"You know, you're a nice guy, Beau Lamond," she said, staring at him wide-eyed. And you're very good-looking, even soaked to the skin, she thought, but she managed to remember not to say that out loud, even if she was so well lit that she would have been entitled to such a slip.

He looked simultaneously amused and pained. "And you're as drunk as a skunk, Elaine Faust."

He hoisted her up against his chest a little as he opened the door and quietly took her inside. He was halfway up the great circular staircase with her when she realized that he'd called her by name—quite tenderly, really, for Beau. It made him seem warmer and kinder, she thought. Smiling dreamily, she closed her eyes and buried her face in his shoulder and made a contented sound deep in her throat.

"What am I going to do with you?" he muttered as he made his way down the hallway. "And where the hell is your room?"

At that point he heard Ambrose moving around downstairs, and he ducked into the first room that he came to, out of instinct.

Unfortunately, it wasn't the right one.

Beau pulled the door shut behind them, careful to hold the knob and not make a telltale click. It was pitch-dark inside, but he had seen the outlines of bookcases, a large desk, and a small table and chairs by the window before the light from the hallway had been doused by the closing door.

They were standing in Richard Faust's study.

"I wonder how Richard feels about uninvited visitors dripping all over his carpet," Beau muttered darkly. He shifted Elaine in his arms and was surprised to see her lashes lift. He had thought she was out for the count.

"He has them dr-drawn and qu-quartered," she swore in a solemn whisper.

Beau lifted one distinctly doubtful eyebrow. "Maybe that's only for little sisters," he pointed out in a whisper.

She grinned and nodded, snuggling more comfortably against him and wrapping her arms around his neck to ease her weight from his arms a bit. It was easy to relax with Beau, she thought. He was a rock, even if he didn't particularly like to admit it.

"You could be r-right," she whispered back. "Meg and I were the last ones he threatened with th-that." She paused. "We m-might also be the only ones," she further conceded with a giggle.

They could hear the sound of the front doors being rattled and Ambrose stomping around muttering about water on the carpet downstairs.

"Why'd we c-come in here?" Elaine asked in a conspiratorial undertone. "Are we hiding from s-someone?"

Beau looked mildly amazed that she'd asked, even if she *was* floating on alcohol vapors. "Yeah," he muttered. "Be quiet."

He turned his head so he could hear the sounds outside. Ambrose was grumbling and following the damp trail up the large circular staircase, apparently mopping with a cloth as he came, from what they could hear of his brittle comments.

Elaine had been trying unsuccessfully to gain Beau's attention through eye contact. Since he was flagrantly ignoring her efforts, she pulled herself up to his eye level and stared at him nose to nose, determined to gain an audience.

"Who're we hiding from?" she asked, wide-eyed. She was deadly serious. She was so close to her destination that she'd lost most of her fear that Ambrose would notice her inebriation. Especially since she didn't have to walk a straight line down the hall as long as Beau was carrying her.

"Shh!" he hissed, his muscles tightening.

His face was a few inches from hers, and she could feel his arms locked around her as if the two of them were glued together. They were both damp from the rain, and now their body heat was making the moisture evaporate a little. Instead of feeling chilled, however, Elaine felt as if jungle steam were enveloping her. It was producing a strange kind of sensuous lethargy that felt disconcertingly comforting, natural and good....

She opened her lips a little in surprise. It had been months since she'd felt this relaxed with anyone other than her brother and Meg. No, not months. More like years. Maybe never. It was a rather heartwarming discovery, even though made when she was less than perfectly sober.

She watched his gaze travel slowly down her face and come to a reluctant halt at her mouth. The effect of his slow visual scan was astonishing even to her inebriated senses. Her skin heated; her cheeks went hot, and her heart suddenly seemed to be pounding more audibly than it had been before. She held her breath, trying to shake off the wooziness that had nothing to do with what she'd had to drink earlier.

Beau was still staring at her parted lips as he answered, sounding a little strained. "We're hiding from Ambrose. Be quiet. He'll hear us whispering."

Elaine tried to listen for Ambrose, but it was hard to work up the concern that Beau obviously felt. She couldn't have cared less if Ambrose walked in on them. After all, if Beau

Mistress of Foxgrove 43

hadn't come along, she might be crawling up the front steps on her hands and knees, or slumped half-asleep on the great staircase. He'd saved her considerable humiliation, she thought with a grateful smile.

Since it seemed to matter so much to Beau, however, she bit back the next question that had come to mind. In deference to his help, it was the least she could do, she thought, feeling a deep upswelling of affection and generosity for her noble stable-manager-turned-savior.

The sound of Ambrose's footsteps halted outside the door. There was a long moment of hesitation, and Beau's face became set, like that of a man who was about to walk to his execution. There was a certain stoic resignation in him that made Elaine want to hug him reassuringly and soothe him with comforting words.

She shook her head slightly to try to chase away the effects of the alcohol she'd drunk. Then she laid her cheek against Beau's and mouthed encouraging words against his warm ear. "Don't worry," she whispered in her softest, lowest voice.

Beau flinched away from her, as if her lips had singed his flesh. His whole body had stiffened noticeably, although she couldn't tell whether it was from anger or alarm or some combination of the two. Ambrose shuffled away from the door and went back downstairs, muttering something about the stupidity of youth, and Elaine felt Beau relax again.

She looked at him sympathetically, although she still wasn't certain what he'd been so worried about. "Richard wouldn't really m-mind that much," she said apologetically. "I had no idea you'd t-take what I s-said so seriously."

He snorted and stared down at her in disbelief. "That wasn't what I was worried about, and you know it!"

She gave him a blank look. "Well, wh-what were you worried about?" she asked doubtfully.

He gave her a ferocious frown. "Being found upstairs with you in my arms," he declared bluntly.

Elaine laughed as if he had to be joking. "How p-perfectly ungallant of you!" she objected. "What's wrong with th-that?" she demanded to know. "You were j-just helping m-me out of a foolish s-situation I'd g-gotten myself into. No one w-would have th-thought really b-badly of me. You were just my errant kn-knight...."

She was smiling at him with tenderness now. It was touching for him to be concerned about her reputation, she thought. How very charming, how sweetly old-fashioned of him. She raised her hand to ruffle his damp hair where it curled a little around his ears, but he pulled his head back, and she dropped her hand away as if he'd struck it. She kept forgetting. He didn't want to be friends.

He then proceeded to crush her tender illusions without a second thought. "It's not *your* reputation I'm worried about," he said succinctly, his annoyance bordering on the sharp edge of real anger. "It's *my* reputation that would go up in flames!"

Elaine couldn't believe her ears. "What?" she asked, laughing first in disbelief, then in anger. She stared into his unsympathetic eyes. "You're serious...." she breathed. It was absolutely incredible!

She cleared her throat and shook her head, but the alcohol was beginning to pass its peak effect, and she found that she was seeing him more clearly by the minute.

"What do you mean...*your* reputation?" she demanded indignantly. "How can being found alone with me hurt *your* r-reputation?" She clenched her jaw to keep her teeth from chattering. The jungle steam had vanished. Now she was enveloped in a damp and bone-chilling cold. The sense of comfort and protection she'd felt in his arms faded as his words reverberated in her head. She pushed against him with the palms of her hands and wriggled her body. "Put me down, p-please."

"Gladly," he muttered. He dropped her like a hot stone. She stumbled, but regained her balance without clutching at him, even though she'd been tempted to. He was frowning at her as he answered her last question. "It's very simple. Ms. Faust," he said grimly. "People don't like to hire men who seduce the women of the household."

Elaine's cheeks went red. "No one would think that...." she protested angrily. "I don't have that kind of reputation, and neither do you."

He looked at her strangely, as if considering whether to spell it out further or not. "Believe me, that's what they would think." His mouth snapped closed, and his jaw took on a wired-shut look. He obviously did not intend to say another word on the subject.

Elaine's curiosity was aroused, and she tilted her head to one side, considering possible ways of extracting further information from him.

He reached toward her and lifted his dampened jacket from her shoulders. "Now, if you'll excuse me," he said, giving her a sardonic look and a rather rakish tip of his head, "I think I'd better let myself out before Ambrose comes back."

He reached into the pockets of his jeans and extracted his keys. The metallic jangle jarred uncomfortably in the utter quiet of the house. He opened the door, and soft yellow light flooded over them. The grandfather clock in the hall downstairs began to chime the hour, and Elaine remembered her jestful parting comment earlier in the evening, the one Beau had repeated to her when he'd picked her up at Margaret's.

"At least I made it back before I turned into a pumpkin," she said softly, wishing they weren't parting on such unpleasant terms. She'd liked the warmth, the closeness. She still felt he was needlessly worried, but she felt her irritation wilt as he prepared to leave her. She'd had such a perfectly miserable evening, and then he'd been there for her, and she'd felt... cared for... in a small way.

Beau turned to look at her, and his hand tightened fractionally on the keys in his hand. He saw all of her from head to toe without having to let his eyes travel over her. Her filmy blouse was plastered transparently against her flawless skin, and the rain-darkened lamé slacks were clinging to her shapely hips and legs like a sexy designer wet suit.

"No, a pumpkin you're not," he softly agreed. He expelled an angry sigh and shook his head. "I'm sorry I yelled at you." He rubbed a hand on the back of his neck and lifted his eyes apologetically to hers. There was a wary look on his face, though, and the tension between them was still palpable, in spite of their olive branch words.

Elaine cautiously held out her hand to him, and he took it. His was warm and strong, and she had the feeling they were joining in a way more profound than just the mere touching of palms and fingers. Her hand trembled slightly and his eyes darkened as he felt it.

"Thanks, Beau," she said softly, managing a shy smile.

He nodded and let her hand slip from his without a word. He watched in somber silence as she turned and hurried down the hall toward her room, alternately wrapping her arms around herself and rubbing her forearms to keep warm. Impulsively she turned at her door and smiled at him in farewell.

"It's cold," she said, her teeth starting to chatter.

"Yeah." He nodded, and his eyes traveled downward and then, slowly, upward once more.

Elaine glanced down and was shocked at the effect the rain had had on her clothing, not to mention the result her wet clothing had on her appearance. Her French lace bra was clearly visible beneath the delicate fabric of her wet blouse. And her nipples made two clearly defined points right in the middle of the lacy swirls. Her entire body looked as if it had been poured into her clothes. She looked much more provocative than she had standing in front of him dripping wet in her bikini, she thought. And though she felt a wild urge to flee, she had the savoir faire to stand her ground in spite of that.

She gave him a defiant look, mostly to mollify her own sense of embarrassment and buck up her courage. "You see a lot more than this on the Riviera...and a lot of other places, too," she argued defensively.

A glimmer of amusement dawned in his knowing eyes, and then, to her surprise, a smile touched his lips. "But it never looks much better than this," he said softly. There was a note of definite admiration in his voice. As if he regretted his candor, his smile vanished. "Go get warmed up before you catch pneumonia," he suggested evenly. He turned toward the staircase, not bothering to glance her way again as he said, "Good night."

She listened until she heard him reach the door, walk outside and lock it with the key. She kept her arms wrapped protectively around her body, but still she felt chilled to the bone and mildly bereft. When she was certain that he was truly gone, she walked into her suite of rooms.

"You're a strange one, Beau Lamond," she murmured as she searched with stiff cold fingers for a nightgown and a towel. "You're not quite the man you'd like us to think you are, are you? Who are you, deep down inside? Who is the real, true you?"

A need to discover him took hold of her, and she vowed she'd find out.

"Everyone needs a friend once in a while, Beau Lamond," she muttered. "It's not such a bad thing, friendship, once you get the hang of it.... You'll see."

A small sense of unease plagued her as she heard her own words. Maybe friendship with Beau wasn't such a great idea.... There was something about him that didn't quite fit the word "friend."

"Don't be melodramatic!" she told herself as she marched into the bathroom to drown in the pleasures of a hot shower and scented bath soap. "You're a grown-up woman. Don't act like a silly girl, for heaven's sake!"

That little pep talk cheered her up considerably, and by the time she fell exhausted into bed, she had a happy smile on her face. It was the first time she'd fallen asleep relaxed and smiling in a very long time.

Beau pulled his jacket on and bent his head against the gusting rain. Elaine's scent clung to his clothing, and he grimly told himself to forget the scent of Elaine Faust's body and everything else that had happened in the past few months. Saying it was one thing; doing it was something else again.

The stable was locked up, but he walked through one last time, telling himself it was a midnight check, just in case. The horses looked surprised, sleepy and even alarmed by his presence. He reached out and patted a couple of snorting, tossing heads, murmuring reassurances and apologies along the way.

They'd needed checking like he needed a walk in the midnight rain, he admitted with more than a little self-deprecation.

He knew he should have gone straight back to his cottage, rain or not, but he closed the stable door and turned to look at the Foxgrove estate house, not quite able to let go yet.

The big building of weathered red brick and great white pillars was imposing in the gray night rain. Here and there a yellow light glowed warmly at a window. Mostly downstairs. The household staff kept them burning all night long, partly for security reasons and partly out of practicality. One never knew when the master of the house would return... or when his sister, the mistress, might choose to go for a midnight prowl of the premises.

Unfortunately, he knew which room was hers now, and with a very uncharacteristic pang of guilt, he allowed his gaze to seek out her window. The lights were still on, and he could imagine her standing somewhere behind the curtained windowpanes, stripping off the wet clothes that had fit her like a second skin and stepping into the hot clean water of a shower in a bathroom no doubt as big as most people's bedrooms. Or maybe by now she'd be drying that glowing skin of hers with a towel the same peach color as she was, then blowing her beautiful wavy hair dry with a hot blast of air.

The rain came down steadily, drizzling across his face and eyelashes. He wiped the back of his hand across his eyes and stared across the broad darkened grass of the courtyard up at her windows and the muted white curtains that hid her from his view.

She had come back to Foxgrove a crushed and disillusioned woman, and at first he'd felt only the profoundest sympathy for her. He'd admired her determination to pick up the pieces and go on. He'd admired her resilience and her fierce loyalty to her brother when her ex-husband had been murdered and they'd charged Richard with the crime.

She'd been annoyed when Richard had asked him to keep an eye on her. That was when they'd had to start spending time with each other. He'd helped protect her from a murderer without letting her know what was happening, and she'd been vastly irritated, having him underfoot all the time when they flew off to settle her financial affairs with her battery of lawyers.

Maybe if Richard just hadn't asked him to do that...

Beau sighed in frustration. It was water under the bridge. It couldn't be undone. He'd just have to live with it and bite the bullet of unslaked lust.

That was what it was, of course. And was it ever getting to be a pain.

Once Richard had been cleared and had convinced their longtime friend and neighbor, Meg Hardesty, to marry him, Elaine had lifted her chin and told them she'd hold the fort while they enjoyed a well-deserved honeymoon, even if it *was* being squeezed in among some horse shows that Meg, a professional rider, had felt she couldn't plead free of.

Beau smiled ruefully and shook his head. He was glad he wasn't in Richard's shoes. Having to share honeymoon time with his wife's horses! He found it hard to imagine. Although Richard seemed to get as much time as he wanted, Beau had to admit. He grinned.

The thought of honeymoons made him think of beds and what happened in them when a man and a woman were naked in each other's arms. He stared at the windows and told himself he was too old to be standing there like an idiot. Hell, it was even raining! He didn't move, though. He stood, as if rooted.

The lights in Elaine's rooms winked out, one after another, until only one was left. He could visualize her climbing into bed and sliding down under the covers with a long, soft sigh.

He tipped up the back edges of his collar and lifted his face into the now-cold rain. The chilly rivulets that ran down his jaw and neck cooled him, and he badly needed cooling. If he didn't watch it, though, he'd end up with pneumonia himself, standing out here in the rain like a damn fool!

On the other hand, he could just as easily burn up, he thought in grim amusement. Burn with a fire that was getting stronger every day. The kind of fire that rain didn't touch. Damn it all.

He wiped the water from his face and looked over at her window again. The last light flicked off, and he turned and walked the half mile to his cottage at the edge of the woods. His boots sounded dull and hard on the old brick walkway. The rain had chased the animals into their lairs, and there was no other sound. Even the hounds were asleep down the road at the kennels.

Of course, there were the sounds he imagined he could hear...like the rustle of soft sheets as a woman turned in her bed...or the shivery whisper of silky dark hair as it rolled beneath her delicate head on the pillow...or the aching shimmer of a satin nightgown as it rubbed across her belly and breasts, or rode up her shapely thighs....

He jerked his door open. He generally figured that he had no use for a key, since he had nothing worth stealing, and tonight that just made things easier. He didn't have to fumble for his keys with fingers that were shaking with the need to touch something much, much softer than a small piece of carved metal.

Inside, it was dry, and Beau mechanically shed his wet clothes, dropping them onto the hooks on the wall to dry. He stood naked in the middle of the rustic wood room and, reluctantly, against his better judgment, he lifted his jacket one last time.

He brought the material to his face and closed his eyes. Memories filled his nostrils and eased the chill on his skin in the unheated cabin. He could still catch the scent of her...that elusive mixture of her body and her perfume.... His body tightened, and he clenched the material in his hand angrily. If he wasn't careful, he'd find himself becoming masochistic, he thought in disgust.

Wouldn't that be hard to believe? Beau Lamond, who'd had any woman he ever wanted within twenty-four hours from the moment he'd made up his mind that he wanted her, was standing here telling himself not to think about a woman, let alone touch her! And sniffing at the clothes she'd rubbed against, just like one of the Faust foxhounds!

"No," he swore to himself. "You're just another woman. You're just the boss's sister. You're my boss." The words came out sharp and hard, filled with venom, as if he would poison himself against her, end the deepening tug of desire, shore up his resolve to feel nothing for her but a kind of aloof friendship.

He hurled the jacket across the room. In spite of his blind anger, it hit the old wooden coatrack and hung there, dripping onto the floor.

It was cold in the room without heat, without her, and he reluctantly admitted he was human and needed some warmth, unless he intended to get sick, which he didn't.

Beau squatted in front of his fireplace and lit a small fire, tending it patiently until the logs he'd laid earlier were well caught and blazing. He stretched out on the bed and pulled the old worn quilt half over his body, but sleep was about the farthest thing from his thoughts at the moment, unfortunately. He laced his hands behind his head and grimly let the memories dance themselves out in front of him.

Elaine with the smile of summer... Elaine with the laughter of spring... Elaine with the eyes of sadness... Elaine rising from the pool like a mythic nymph... Elaine who loved everyone like an equal, until they proved themselves to be totally unlovable jerks...

He smiled against his better judgment at that thought. Meg had always told him that Elaine didn't have a snobbish bone in her body. That was true. It was one of her most endearing qualities, he thought.

She also didn't have an ugly or nasty bone in her body, as far as he could see, which brought his mind back to a very physical plane. The rest of her body was put together just right, from what he'd seen of it, which was much too much for his peace of mind.

Elaine...

His body ached, and he began to sweat as his pulse raced and blood poured through him, heating him, feeding his obsession with the woman he knew he shouldn't look at twice, shouldn't give a second thought to, and most certainly no erotic thoughts whatsoever....

"Damn it to hell and back," he swore between gritted teeth. "Why doesn't she find someplace else to go? Why does she have to hang around here and drive me crazy?"

He lay on the bed and stared at the amber firelight dancing on the bare wooden beams in the ceiling, and he imagined what it would feel like to have her there in his arms...her cool soft skin smooth and bare on his...her gentle arms around his neck...her kiss-swollen lips damp and yielding on his....

The fire crackled, and Beau groaned low and long.

At this rate, he'd never get to sleep, he thought in agonized disgust. Which was about right, because he lay on the rack of his bed for what seemed like hours, watching her rise out of the pool like a goddess...remembering her cradled in his arms, dripping wet...feeling her sprawled out against his body like a sweet, easing balm...seeing her face glowing in the moment of ecstasy....

He never knew when he fell asleep, because the intoxicating visions merely drifted along with him from his waking mind into his dreams, torturing him with unreachable pleasures all along the way.

Chapter 4

The dull throbbing ache in her head eventually dragged Elaine awake the next morning. Tentatively she opened her eyes, only to be stabbed by a blade of sunlight slicing through a crack in the draperies. She moaned and slowly forced her reluctant body to sit up.

"I will *never* drink champagne again," she vowed in a thready whisper as she carefully pressed her fingertips against her pounding temples. She crawled out of bed with a groan and cautiously felt her way to the bathroom in the hope of locating a bottle of aspirin and a container of mouthwash. "I will *never* drink champagne again," she repeated as she opened the medicine cabinet. "Never. Never. Never. Never."

Beau handed the groom his check and closed the ledger as the stable hand left the office. He'd accomplished a lot this morning. He'd paid the bills, calculated the feed requirements for the following quarter and placed his order with the local supplier. He'd paid the stable hands and balanced the books. He'd even spent an hour and a half schooling one of the green hunters.

He should feel more than ready for a break. So why didn't he? He grimaced. He knew damn well why.

Beau locked up the office and walked out to the paddock. It was past time for lunch. He was reluctant to go up to the house and eat, but he had too much work to do to leave the estate just to eat in the middle of the day. He hadn't bothered to stock fresh food in his cottage, so he couldn't very well go back there, and anyway, he'd take Mrs. Adams's cooking over his own any time. He just wished he knew if he was likely to run into anyone else in the kitchen at this hour. Especially anyone named Elaine Faust.

Richard's prize hunter stud was standing near the fence as Beau approached. The big bay stallion whickered softly, obviously hoping that Beau had brought along something tasty. Beau laughed and scratched the big horse's ears.

"Sorry. You're outta luck, pal," he drawled. The stallion swished his long black tail and tossed his head. "You'll have to eat at mealtimes. Just like me."

The mares in the field on the other side of the practice rings neighed and broke into a collective gallop. The stallion turned to watch, ears sharply forward, muscles rippling in expectation.

Beau patted the big horse on the neck in sympathy. "They can make you lose your appetite, can't they? And it sure is frustrating when they're on the other side of the fence," he murmured. "But who said life was going to be one roll in the hay after another, eh, big guy?"

The stallion snorted and, tossing his head, whirled to gallop across his field in the direction of the mares. He obviously wasn't going to stand around waiting for the next mare to be brought his way. Beau grinned. A horse after his own heart.

"It won't do you any good," he said softly. "That fence is too tall for you, big fella. You can't have 'em. Not today, anyway."

Beau rested his boot on the lower slat of the smooth white fence and watched the magnificent stud thunder around the field, snorting and prancing and generally showing off.

Mistress of Foxgrove 55

"You're making a fool of yourself, pal," he observed. "You kind of remind me of myself, too, I'm sorry to say," he added with a sigh.

He grimaced and turned away, recalling how hard and how successfully he had chased women in the past. He supposed it was amusing to see how different he'd become in the past few years. People who'd known him in the old days would probably have a hard time believing just how much he had changed. He certainly couldn't blame them.

Beau's stomach tightened in hunger, and he looked at his watch. If he missed lunch merely because he didn't relish bumping into Elaine Faust, he was going to be pretty damn disgusted with himself. For that matter, he already was pretty disgusted with himself. He'd never avoided a woman before in his life. He'd always been frank with them, and they'd always adored it. If he'd wanted a woman around, he'd told her so. If he'd wanted her to leave him alone, he'd said it straight out. The unvarnished truth, that was what he'd given them. And they'd lapped around him like puppy-eyed adolescents, begging for more of the same. Until now.

"I must be getting old," he muttered to himself. Not that he wanted to return to his old ways. But right now, it would have been helpful to be able to be a little more ruthless with Elaine Faust. He could think of the things to say, all right. He just couldn't bring himself to say them to her. Things like, *I want to take you to bed, lady, and if you keep hanging around me, you're going to end up there, so don't come near me unless you're ready to do just that.* Just when he'd get annoyed enough to say something to her, he'd remember the stricken look she'd had on her face when she'd run into her louse of a husband one night at a party. Beau knew he couldn't say something that coarse to her. He just couldn't bring himself to hurt a woman who'd been so poorly treated. "Face it," he told himself in disgust. "You've lost your touch. Right when you need to be a son of a bitch, you've turned into a soft touch with a conscience!"

He was only too well aware that Elaine was determined to disregard his off-putting messages. She kept talking to him as if she wanted to be his friend, as well as his employer.

He'd tried polite brush-offs, cool disinterest, maximum avoidance and a sort of courteous hostility. None of his strategies had helped. Elaine was unfailingly welcoming, always ready to start fresh, as if his boorish conduct hadn't meant a thing, and eager to get reinvolved with the stables... which were his special domain.

Beau wondered what would have happened if they'd met under different circumstances, say, before he'd been financially ruined. That was a new idea. Immediately he regretted even thinking about it. Why torture himself with the possibilities of what they could have had? Besides, when he'd been her social peer, he would have hustled her into the nearest bedroom and no doubt left her within a few weeks or months. He hated thinking about that. Elaine deserved better from a man. He would have been as rotten for her as her late husband had been.

He frowned. Maybe not quite that bad. Cam Bennett had been a smooth-talking liar. He'd wooed Elaine and wed her dishonestly, promising fidelity. Beau had never promised any woman that; he knew he would never have lied to Elaine.

He had no intention of lying to her now, either. He rubbed the bridge of his nose between his fingers. With any luck, he wouldn't even have to *talk* to her. That would solve things. For both of them.

He hoped that the excess of partying and the late hours that she'd kept the previous night would slow her down substantially for the better part of today. With that highly appealing possibility in mind, he turned away from the fence and headed through the stable and across the courtyard to the estate house.

He would just grab a quick bite to eat, and then he'd keep busy out in the fields with the horses until evening. With any luck, he wouldn't have to deal with Elaine Faust at all today.

He almost smiled.

Mrs. Adams was in the process of tasting her broth when she heard Elaine's tentative footsteps at the kitchen entryway. She held the big wooden spoon away and smiled cherubically, her round cheeks red from heat and nature's natural endowment.

"Good afternoon, Sleeping Beauty!" Mrs. Adams exclaimed cheerily.

Elaine groaned and gingerly stepped around the table and chairs. "It *can't* be afternoon," she protested in a plaintive tone. She pressed her eyes lightly with the backs of her hands. The pressure helped ease the ache a little. "It's *so bright*! The sunlight *has* to be shooting straight in the windows."

Mrs. Adams put her hands on her hips. Her sunny disposition clouded slightly as she examined the neatly attired young woman who was more like a niece than an employer. *"Elaine Faust,"* she scolded gently, "you have a hangover!" She sounded faintly alarmed but mostly astonished.

Elaine nodded sheepishly, careful not to rattle her sore brains. "I took some aspirin," she said. "How long should it take to work?" She walked gingerly over to the long butcher-block cutting table, where fresh vegetables lay scattered, freshly chopped by the jovial cook.

Mrs. Adams wrinkled her brow as if trying to recollect. "My late husband used to feel better in about twenty minutes...." she said doubtfully. "But it never completely fixed him up...and he was used to it...."

"I wish you hadn't said that," Elaine murmured regretfully. She managed a halfway convincing smile. "I thought maybe a cup of tea might help...."

Mrs. Adams was immediately wreathed in smiles. "Oh, yes! Tea is good for just about *everything*," she assured Elaine. She enthusiastically rattled about in search of a special brand of black tea leaves and her favorite silver infuser.

Elaine had thought she detected a slight lessening of her pain until the brittle clink of china caused her to revise her assessment. She had her fingers in her ears to deafen the shattering sound when the outside door was summarily yanked open, its bell tinkling shrilly. She briefly shut her eyes and bit back a moan.

Mrs. Adams exclaimed, "Well, it's about time! I was just about to give up on you, Beau!"

Elaine immediately forced open her eyes, only to wish she'd taken her time. She was assaulted by an unpleasant spinning sensation, the unforseen side effect of her hasty action. By the time the queasy dizziness passed and she'd turned her attention to the back door, Beau had entered the kitchen and was staring at her as if he couldn't believe that he'd actually had the misfortune to run into her. Elaine, stung by his attitude, had rarely felt less like being charming, but her many years of social training were not to be so easily defeated. It would take more than the grandmother of all hangovers and the disappointed look on Beau Lamond's face to demolish Elaine Faust's innate graciousness.

"Good morning, Beau," she said, forcing a sunny smile.

Mrs. Adams looked at Elaine in surprise, while Beau headed toward the sink to wash up.

"Good *afternoon*," Beau corrected softly as he passed her.

Elaine's smile became rueful. "Afternoon...I guess I gave myself away...." she murmured.

"The queen of the castle can sleep all day if she likes," Beau pointed out.

Elaine's smile faded. "That sounds like a useless kind of life to live," she observed. She followed Beau to the sink. Neither of them even noticed Mrs. Adams leave the room. "Is that the way I seem to you?" she asked. "A wealthy woman who has nothing important to do with her time and sleeps late every day?"

Beau methodically rolled up his sleeves. "That's not the kind of question you ask the people who work for you," he pointed out, his dark blond brows lowering to underscore the point.

Elaine leaned against the wall and stubbornly crossed her arms in front of her. "You're ducking the question," she pointed out.

He glanced at her in exasperation. "You're damn right I am," he said, laughing. He abruptly turned on the faucet and plunged his hands into the warm blast of water.

Elaine managed another smile. "All right. Go ahead and avoid it," she conceded. "I'll say it for you. Since I came back to Foxgrove, I haven't had any particular role to play, no job to do, and it's become easy to live the life of a pampered aristocrat."

He rubbed his arms and hands into a lather. "I didn't say that," he pointed out darkly.

Her smile warmed and broadened. "I know you didn't," she admitted. "But it's true, all the same," she said. She shrugged. "I guess you could say that I was one of the walking wounded." She added thoughtfully, "I crawled back into my castle and pulled the drawbridge closed after me." She laughed uncomfortably. "But it's time I crawled back out again, and that's what I'm going to do."

Beau wasn't sure he liked the sound of that. He finished rinsing off and grabbed a towel, thinking that her last words had had a peculiar ring to them.

He slung the towel back over its rack and turned to face her. "What are you planning to do?" he asked neutrally. He was hooking his thumbs through his leather belt loops when a thought occurred to him. Perhaps Elaine had decided to leave Foxgrove. That possibility should have cheered him up. It didn't.

She gestured toward her clay-colored jodhpurs and black riding boots. "I thought I'd take up one of my old interests." She smiled a little self-consciously. "I grew up riding," she explained. "I'm a little out of practice...." Her voice trailed off.

"Your husband didn't like horses?" Beau guessed.

She shook her head. "Horses were too slow for his taste," she replied. For a second, bitterness darkened her eyes. She blinked and shrugged off the memory. "He liked high speeds."

Beau watched her, wondering whether that was why she had become attracted to Cam Bennett. Had she wanted the risks? The excitement of life on the edge? It didn't quite quite fit his picture of her. Perhaps she had been different then.

"Anyway," Elaine continued, "I need something to do while I'm here, and I'd like to work with some of our horses." She hoped he would like the idea. She didn't relish walking into his domain without his agreement, even if the property was hers. Elaine had always preferred harmony.

Beau, while not antagonistic, was less than enthusiastic. "What kind of work did you have in mind?" he asked.

"Oh, helping with their training, showing, just about anything..."

Beau nodded and straightened. He unhooked his thumbs and looked straight at Elaine. "When did you want to start?"

Elaine was a little surprised at how easy it had been to convince him. She'd actually been expecting some kind of protest from him, comments that she wasn't a professional, or that he preferred to work with people he chose, or that he'd already laid out most of the training for the next few months. She wouldn't have blamed him if he had said something like that. After all, he didn't know whether she was a skilled rider or a hack.

"When did I want to start?" she echoed. "How about after lunch?"

His jaw was set like that of a man determined to make the best of an imperfect situation. He merely nodded and turned back toward Mrs. Adams.

The older woman was beaming cheerfully, her spirits soaring as she saw her last and favorite customers pulling up their chairs at the large rectangular table. She had set their places on either side of one corner of the old cherry dining table. Mason jars and canning equipment were taking up the far end, and the sweet aromas of cooking fruits were filling the air.

"There you are!" Mrs. Adams clucked contentedly. "Cozy as two peas in a pod." She smiled down on them beatifically and placed a serving plate of mouth-watering Salisbury steaks between bowls of tossed greens and a silver tea service. "Help yourselves," she urged them.

She wiped her hands on the skirt of her apron and pulled the linen cover off a basket of hot homemade yeast rolls near Beau. "I've got to call the greengrocer in town. You two look after one another, now, and I'll be back in a few minutes." She toddled off to the adjoining room that served as a pantry and food-storage area.

As her stodgy footsteps faded into the distance, an awkward silence enfolded the room. Elaine looked over the bowl of greens and the platter of succulent meat and met Beau's eyes. His face was as unreadable as a stone wall.

"Did you get up on the wrong side of the bed?" she asked, trying to laugh. She didn't quite succeed.

His granite expression flickered. "I beg your pardon?"

"You know...." She waved a gentle hand, her smile automatic. "Did you have a bad start to your day?"

"Not particularly."

"Surely you don't always turn to stone when you come in for lunch?" she teased.

Beau lifted one eyebrow slightly. "Do I look like stone to you?"

Elaine did laugh, then, and the laughter helped her relax a little. "Yes," she agreed with a sigh. "And annoyed." She picked up her napkin and shook it out. "Like you were last night when Jim Peterson handed you the keys and stuck you with being my driver."

Beau watched the pale green linen napkin delicately open and float down in the direction of Elaine's lap, grazing her blouse lightly.

"Sorry," he said evenly.

Elaine busied herself with the salad. "Don't be," she said lightly. "I value honesty in relationships. You've been very honest with me, and I appreciate it."

A frown began to gather on Beau's brow. "Is that so?"

She twirled a piece of Boston lettuce on the tines of her silver fork and nodded emphatically. "Yes. Now, we can work together and eat together and travel around together without worrying about any misunderstandings."

"I see."

There was an unsettling tone hidden beneath his words that made Elaine's eyes snap up. The granite was wearing a little thin, she thought. There was something beneath that facade of his... perhaps annoyance, or some other kind of uneasiness, she wasn't certain what.

She felt a small rush of satisfaction. She was getting somewhere with him. Good. She was sure she would feel more comfortable with him once whatever he was holding back from her was out in the open. It would clear the air between them. She had no doubt she could deal with whatever it was, as long as he just admitted it. Maybe it was working for a woman, or working for anyone. Or a misunderstanding of some sort.

She lifted her glass of water to her lips. Beau began cutting his steak with the vigorous single-mindedness of a man who wasn't planning to dawdle over lunch. He speared a piece of meat with his fork and raised it to his mouth. His gaze lifted, and so did Elaine's. Their eyes met, and suddenly everything spun to a standstill. Neither of them could swallow for a moment. Elaine, in desperation, dragged her eyes from his and tried to remember how to swallow, before she choked. Her throat worked as it should, and she sighed with relief. What was the matter with her, anyway?

Beau poured them each a cup of tea from the silver pot. He took one careful swallow, then stared over his delicate porcelain cup at Elaine's finishing-school smile.

"Just what kind of traveling did you have in mind?" he asked, picking up where she had left off.

Elaine shrugged. "Nothing in particular," she conceded. She glanced at him through downcast eyes. "Perhaps if you filled me in on what our horses are scheduled to be doing...?"

Beau tilted the teacup up and drained it. He set it down on the saucer with a slight clink and got up from the table.

Elaine looked up at him uncertainly. "You don't really mind this, do you, Beau?" she asked softly. "I mean..." Her smile was halfhearted but genuine. "If you really don't think I can be any help, I want you to tell me."

For the first time since he'd seen her, he almost smiled. There was a glint of amusement in his eyes along with the coolness. Not a muscle in his face gave anything else away, though. He leaned on the back of the chair and stared at her.

"Do you think I'm stupid enough to tell the lady who owns the place that she should stay away from her own horses?" he demanded.

Elaine nodded. "If someone else could do a better job with them, I want you to tell me so. And I don't think it's stupid. I think it's courageous."

The amusement in his eyes faded. He stared at her for a moment longer. "Courageous?" he murmured. "What kind of thing is that to say?"

"The truth." Elaine shrugged as if to emphasize that there could be no other interpretation.

Beau's eyes took on a cynical cast. He straightened and shoved his hands into the hip pockets of his jeans, then rocked back on his heels and shook his head. "You're still looking at the world through rose-colored glasses, aren't you?" he challenged softly.

She was surprised at first. She considered his comment for a moment and then shook her head. "I don't think so," she replied.

His jaw hardened. "I think you are," he countered. "And I'm not courageous," he argued. There was a note of self-derision there. "I'm not even particularly honest, for all you know. And don't kid yourself that you know me much, for that matter. I'm just a man who works for you. I do what you pay me to do. Or what your brother pays me to do." He considered her for a long moment, then decided to tell her something more. "Look, you've had a rough year. It's natural to want to ignore it and see things the way they were before all this happened to you. But you can't turn the clock back. The world isn't a particularly nice place, and it never was."

Elaine felt the warmth in her cheeks. She suddenly felt very much at a disadvantage sitting down, so she tossed her napkin onto the table and rose from her chair.

"You're very disillusioned, aren't you?" she said. She lifted her chin, and her eyes were clear. No hint of rose-colored glasses now.

Beau's stare was hard and unyielding. "'Disillusioned' is one of those rose-colored words," he said softly. "I'm not disillusioned. I'm realistic."

Elaine walked around the back of her chair and fingered the smooth wood. "Realistic," she murmured thoughtfully. She glanced at him a little less boldly than before. "Perhaps you're right," she said cautiously.

Beau was surprised to hear her say that.

Elaine caught her lower lip between her teeth for a split second, then smiled at him with a burst of renewed self-confidence.

He looked on uneasily as she picked up her riding hat and crop and marched resolutely toward the door. He held it for her, and she smiled up at him as she brushed by him on her way out.

"Maybe you could show me what it's like to see the world 'realistically,'" she suggested. "And I can occasionally loan you my rose-colored glasses, if I happen to see them lying around...."

Two of the grounds men were walking nearby and greeted them in passing. Elaine smiled and said hello. Beau nodded and tried to keep his eyes off Elaine's graceful back. He didn't need rose-colored glasses. What he needed was a good set of blinders. And maybe some saltpeter added to his diet.

Elaine glanced over her shoulder at him. "Where shall we begin?" she asked.

He dragged his eyes from her hips and guided her through the stable to the paddock. He walked into one of the hunter's stalls and saddled and bridled the gelding without saying a word. Then he cupped his hand to give Elaine a leg up. She felt light. A wisp of something provocative hit him. The perfume she used. Beau stepped out of the paddock and into the training ring, crossed his arms over his chest and nodded in the direction of the first jump. "Put him through his paces."

Elaine gathered the reins and laughed. "Yes, boss," she said with a jaunty tilt of her head.

She lightly touched her heels to the big Hanoverian's flanks, and he obediently cantered toward the first hurdle, ears pricked alertly. Elaine relaxed in the saddle. The horse had obviously been through this course before and was willing to take direction from his rider without any arguments. The reins felt familiarly smooth and flat in her hands, a solid connection with the gelding's mouth. When they were a few short strides from the first jump of stacked white bars, she urged him forward with her knees, but in her mind they were already over the jump. The gelding gathered his hindquarters and pushed off. His neatly tucked forelegs cleared the top bar with room to spare. Horse and rider soared for a brief glorious moment. Then they were on the other side with a one-two landing and it was over.

Elaine grinned as she felt the slight shock of land beneath her mount's hooves again. She was already looking ahead, concentrating on the next hurdle, holding the big horse to a steady canter. The second was a wider jump than the first, with a broad hedge in the front and a white crossbar behind. The hunter did as he was asked and took it as easily as he had the first, turning immediately across the course to the next obstacle. Elaine praised him and kept her eye on the next jump. Never look back. She'd learned that early in life. A part of her realized it had implications for many things besides jumping a horse over a fence. She let go of a little more of the legacy of bitterness from her disastrous marriage and soared through the cool fall air.

Beau watched her guide the hunter over one jump after another. She had obviously done this before. That was a pity, he thought. It meant that he couldn't refuse her offer of help. He was going to be stuck working with her nearly every day. So much for his plans to steer clear of her as much as possible. His jaw tightened.

Elaine was wreathed in smiles as she trotted away from the last fence, walking once around the ring and then heading the horse straight toward him. She saw the thin-lipped expression on his face, and her smile faltered.

"Did I do that badly?" she asked in surprise. She tried to be offhand, but it wasn't easy. His reaction unsettled her.

Beau shook his head and automatically reached for the gelding's bridle as she halted in front of him. She looked dismayed and uncertain, he thought. Surely she knew her own abilities well enough to know he wasn't grim faced because of her performance. His expression softened slightly.

"You passed," he said neutrally. "With high marks. You obviously enjoy jumping. Have you ever competed?"

Elaine breathed a sigh of relief and slid her boots out of the stirrup irons. She looked down at him, surprised at the relief she was feeling at his approval. She hadn't expected that. "Locally," she admitted a little reluctantly.

Beau looked at her curiously. "Why just around here? You're good enough to compete at any level. Lack of money or horses obviously wasn't a problem," he pointed out.

Elaine laughed. "You don't beat around the bush, do you?"

He shrugged. "I believe in calling a spade, a spade," he said.

He was waiting for her to answer his question, but she wasn't sure she wanted to tell him the real reason why she'd avoided show rings in the past. He would probably think it was ridiculous. Or silly. And she wasn't really interested in defending her thinking to him. Besides, she'd never told anybody the real reason, so why start now? She fingered the reins and gave him part of the answer. The usual answer. The one she'd given everyone else over the years.

"I chose to spend my time in other ways. It takes a lot of work, a lot of dedication, to be successful in the show ring." She smiled, as if she were a little embarrassed at her next admission. "I guess I was more interested in being a social butterfly than in being a dedicated equestrienne."

A small frown gathered on Beau's brow. "A social butterfly," he echoed. He'd known a few of those in his day. "You don't strike me as that kind of woman."

Their eyes met, and there was an odd stillness around them that made Elaine feel strange. She swallowed and smiled awkwardly. "I guess looks can be deceiving," she murmured uncomfortably.

"Hmm," Beau grunted, unconvinced. He tore his eyes away from her face and tried to recall what needed improving in her riding. "You looked a little stiff," he observed. "That shouldn't be too hard to cure."

Elaine stretched her legs, refound the irons with her boots and stood up in the stirrups, trying out a few limbering-up exercises in the saddle.

"Practice will take care of that," she promised. She eyed him cautiously. "Do you have any holes in your schedule that I could fill for you?"

He nodded. It would mean taking himself off a few horses, but that was no problem. It would also mean not having to recruit anyone for a couple of the others, if Elaine was interested in handling them.

"We're planning to enter three of the hunters in some one-day and three-day events. Almost all the horses need to be hunted throughout the winter. A couple of them are being trained for some of the shows next spring. We've got one that should do well in dressage, another has potential as a show jumper...." He ticked them off one after another while Elaine listened attentively. "And then there are the point-to-points and timber races...."

She was sitting in the saddle, thinking he sounded very professional and very neutral. She doubted he would tell her who was being knocked off a horse for her benefit, and she wanted to be careful about that. She'd never exercised her rights as mistress of the estate in a ruthless manner. She'd taken care to be considerate and respectful of others, and she certainly wasn't going to change her style now.

"Maybe I could start off as an exercise girl?" she suggested with an easy smile. "And fill in wherever there's a vacancy that you think I'm qualified to handle."

Beau smiled slightly. "You're treading very lightly, aren't you?" he asked.

She shrugged. "I don't want to take anyone off a horse," she pointed off reasonably. "I'm just asking for a chance with the ones that need a rider."

She patted the gelding on the neck and vaulted off, leading the horse back into the stable as Beau followed along without further comment. She busied herself taking the tack off before he could do it for her.

"How about giving my dressage a once-over?" she suggested. She'd been itching to try her brother's newest purchase, an Irish Thoroughbred mare. She glanced over her shoulder at Beau.

He saw the glint in her eyes and couldn't resist smiling slightly. "You want a crack at Irish Mist," he guessed.

She closed the hunter's stall door and turned to look up at the enigmatic stable manager. She laughed. "I'm pretty transparent, aren't I?"

"Sometimes."

He led her to the coal-black beauty, then saddled and bridled the mare for her. When he handed her the reins, their hands touched, and Elaine felt his heat. There was no particular warmth in his eyes, though, when she glanced at him, and she ignored a small stab of annoyance at that. She mounted the mare before he could offer her a leg up and rode the Thoroughbred into the dressage ring.

"Show me your stuff," she murmured as she collected the mare and began a simple series of dressage steps. She resisted the temptation to gauge Beau's reaction. "And try to help me not look like a fool," she added under her breath. By the time she'd finished, she was breathing a sigh of relief. The mare had made it easy. She was a gem, a champion if ever Elaine had seen one.

"I always knew my brother had a keen eye for a good horse," she told Beau as she dismounted and dropped lightly to the ground next to him. She patted the mare affectionately on the neck and shoulder. "She can make even a rusty old rider like me look passable."

Beau raised an eyebrow. "You're a little stiff, a little out of practice," he conceded. "But you're more than passable."

Elaine gave him a grateful look. "Thanks, Beau."

He seemed surprised. "Did you think I'd tell you you weren't good enough to ride?"

She looked away. "I didn't know what you'd say."

She remembered being told how bad she was at things, in subtle ways, for the last few months of her marriage. She straightened a little, determined not to let the past cow her. "But I'm glad you said what you did." She rested her hand against the smooth leather of the English saddle and inhaled the scent of horse, leather and the clean, fresh dirt of the riding ring. "I've been away too long. I'd forgotten how much I loved all this."

She looked more relaxed than she had all day, he thought. He understood what she was feeling. He enjoyed handling and riding horses. And he knew what it was to love the land and the property that went with them. Under other circumstances, he might have taken pleasure in sharing their common interests with her day after day.

But these weren't other circumstances. These were the same lousy circumstances he'd been in since before she arrived. The same ones that he was likely to be in for the indefinite future. And he knew what being in her company day after day was going to be like.

Not pleasant. And a little worse each day. He needed to find a way to deal with that. The obvious way, taking her, was not an option. So what else was there? He couldn't think of a damn thing. He felt like hitting the fence with his fist, but then she would have wondered what was bothering him, and he wasn't about to explain.

He heard the phone ringing in the stable office. Never had a sound been so sweet. "Would you take care of Irish Mist?" he asked bluntly. "It can be your first job."

Elaine was surprised at the hardness underlying his voice. He sounded eager to leave. "Sure," she agreed readily.

"Good."

He strode inside to answer the phone, leaving her to ponder his attitude.

When she went to look for him after finishing with the mare, he had already gone. She didn't see him again for the rest of the day.

She was standing at her window that night when she saw him walking in the direction of his cabin. "Well, well, you're back. Where did you go, I wonder?" she mused.

She pulled her curtains closed and crawled between her soft clean sheets. Tomorrow. She would ask him where he'd gone. Not that it mattered, of course. She just...wanted to know. Out of curiosity. Nothing personal.

Chapter 5

Elaine was happily surprised the following morning at how easily old habits began coming back to her. Habits like waking in the early light and looking forward to what the rest of the day would bring. Or walking to the stable so lightly that she felt as if she were treading on air. She felt healthy and full of life, itching to get her hands on a fine horse and gallop across the countryside with the wind whipping at her clothes. Lord, she hadn't felt so good in months.

Her thoughts brought a smile to her face as she lifted a saddle off its rack in the tack room and carried it through the cleanly swept aisle toward one of their best hunter's stall. A stable hand touched the brim of his baseball cap and wished her a good day as she passed him, offering to help her. Elaine returned his greeting and cheerily declined his offer before disappearing into the box stall that held the horse she wanted.

As she finished saddling the elegant chestnut, she sensed the hand watching her. He was relatively new to Foxgrove, having been hired while she was living abroad during her ill-fated marriage. His name was Eddie, but his regard didn't make her feel uneasy, because she had talked to him a few times recently. He'd always been polite and eager to please. Then, too, he had been the one to tell her that Beau had left the estate the previous afternoon. He'd given her the message that Beau had been called away on personal business and wouldn't be back until late. She wondered whimsically if Eddie was about to give her another such message. She led the clean-limbed Thoroughbred hunter out of his stall and smiled reassuringly at the young man staring alternately at her and her horse.

"Is something wrong?" she asked gently. Eddie was a shy man who might fear a raised voice from the mistress of the estate, so she tried not to make things worse for him.

He cleared his throat and shifted uncomfortably from one booted foot to the other. "No, ma'am..."

Elaine struggled to hold back her amusement. If ever a man seemed to be at odds with his words, Eddie was. She looked at him expectantly. "Are you sure?" she prodded encouragingly.

His cheeks reddened a little, and his eyes batted from Elaine to the horse to the floor and reluctantly back to Elaine. He swallowed and gathered his courage.

"Uh...Beau wanted that hunter worked out, ma'am," he said, the words coming out in a stumbling rush. "He was going to take him out over the timber trail in a little while...."

She breathed a sigh of relief. So that was it. That wouldn't be a problem. She led the horse toward the open paddock. "Don't worry about it, Eddie. I don't think Beau will mind if I take Mystic out for him." Elaine smiled at him reassuringly. "I'm helping him out with a lot of them now, you know." She gave Eddie a conspiratorial wink. "Besides, Mystic belongs to me, remember?"

Eddie's sigh of relief was audible even over the rhythmic thudding of Mystic's hoofs on the hard stable floor. He belatedly hurried after her, recalling one of the duties expected of him when riders were about.

"Uh...sorry, ma'am. Would you like a leg up?" he offered, sounding for all the world like a puppy eager to make amends for some infraction of the rules.

Elaine shook her head and lifted her foot to the stirrup. She hadn't mounted a horse this tall in a couple of years, and her thigh muscles ached a little with the effort it required to stretch so high. In a moment, though, she was up and sitting down lightly on the saddle. She gathered the reins and extended a last reassuring look toward Eddie.

"I'll be back in an hour," she told him. "If you see Beau, tell him where I've gone."

"Yes, ma'am. You're a real nice lady," Eddie said as he watched her ride away.

He turned back into the stable, happy that things were still working out well for him here at Foxgrove. It was a relief to work for such nice people. Some owners weren't. That Mrs. Carlton he'd worked for not so long ago, for example. He was glad he wasn't working for *her* anymore. Nothing pleased her. She was always angry with him.

It was lucky for him that Beau hadn't believed the nasty things that woman had said about him. Of course, he *was* a little slow, and he *did* get nervous about things, but she didn't have to fire him for that. It had been awful hard finding a job afterward. He didn't know much besides grooming horses. And word had gotten around Charlottesville that he wasn't reliable. That Mrs. Carlton had sure tarred him with her nasty talk. And he'd been so ashamed that people had believed her.

Eddie shook his head in an effort to rid himself of unpleasant memories. He located a pitchfork and concentrated hard on mucking out a stall. Dirty straw began to pile up in a wheelbarrow nearby. Soon the entire stable smelled of sweet, clean straw, freshly strewn. Eddie put up the pitchfork and wiped his youthful brow, thinking how pleased Beau would be with him. Working for Beau had really changed him. Why, he was hardly nervous at all anymore. And he could work a lot faster when he wasn't always scared someone would start finding fault with him.

He smiled secretly. Miss Faust would probably be pleased with him, too, he thought.

His chest swelled with pride. He would do his best for them. Yes, sir. His very best. And if he were lucky, he'd be working here forever.

Mistress of Foxgrove

* * *

Elaine trotted Mystic out to the edge of the forest, warming up both of them with the gentle gait. The late November air was crisp and cool, and the ground was hard with the hint of a frost. There was no one else in sight, now that she was away from the stables and the adjoining fields. She heard only the occasional sharp caw of a crow and the soft flapping of geese flying high over the desolate ridges behind her.

She urged Mystic to a canter and headed him toward a fence leading to the forest trails.

"Here we go, Mystic," she murmured to him. Gentleman that he was, he unhesitatingly cleared the jump for her and cantered down the bare winding trail, ready and eager for more.

Beau glimpsed a small flash of chestnut color through the sea of leafless trees and slowed his horse to a walk. Even squinting, he couldn't quite make out the small figure on the horse's back at first, but, it took his practiced eye less than a blink to recognize Mystic's coloring and stride.

Then he realized that the rider was a woman—which left him in no doubt as to who she was.

He touched his heels lightly to his mount's flanks and cantered toward the meadow to the west. At least he'd have a lot of space around him when their paths crossed, he thought, feeling a sudden surge of black humor. Space. How much would be enough to keep his resolve? he wondered darkly.

The stallion he rode tossed his head in a burst of excess energy. Beau sighed. He knew just how the stallion felt.

"Easy, boy," he soothed the animal roughly. The wind had shifted, and the stallion could scent the pasture full of brood mares on the other side of the hill. "You've got to remember that we're just passing through here. You're a guest. Forget about them. They're not yours."

The stallion rolled his eyes and snorted loudly, and Beau urged him into a gallop. If the stallion couldn't forget the mares, maybe some more exercise would at least make him too tired to do anything about them for a little while. And it wouldn't hurt him, either, Beau thought.

Elaine rode Mystic through the woodland trail and into the open valley beyond. She saw the man on the horse coming toward her and automatically slowed Mystic to a trot.

She recognized Beau immediately. His dark blond hair looked like burnished gold in the morning sun. He rode with the relaxed ease of a centaur. She didn't recognize the horse he was on, though, and that aroused her curiosity. She thought she'd seen all the horses on the estate. So where had Beau been keeping this one?

She waved at him when they were just beyond hailing distance, and when they finally reached each other, she greeted him aloud. "How long have you been out?" she asked as he drew his horse to a halt.

"Since a little after dawn." He wasn't smiling, but he didn't look displeased, either. "I'm surprised to see you up this early."

Elaine laughed. "That makes two of us," she conceded. She dropped her feet from the stirrups and stretched her legs a little, easing the stiffness in her calves and thighs. She glanced around the countryside and then, almost shyly, at Beau. "I used to go riding almost every morning. When Meg and I were in school, we'd saddle our horses as soon as it was light and ride for as long as we could."

"You don't have to squeeze it in before classes now," he pointed out, beginning to look a little amused.

Elaine lifted her shoulders, as if she couldn't help that. "True. School was out a long time ago." A small shadow crossed her face as bitter memories threatened to remind her of what her life had become as an adult. She refused to have her wonderful morning spoiled by it and pushed the ugliness away, focusing instead on Beau. "And what brings you out at the crack of dawn?"

She smiled to soften the question. She wasn't sure whether he would think she was needlessly prying. Recently he'd been touchy about innocent questions like that.

Beau patted his horse's neck. He didn't appear annoyed. "It's about the only time I have to work with Rapier."

Rapier, recognizing his name, tossed his head, nostrils flaring. He wasn't a particularly big horse, standing half a hand shorter than Elaine's Thoroughbred, but what he lacked in height he more than made up for in every other way. There was a rippling strength in him that she recognized immediately. Hard, tensile strength. He was sinewy and sound, a brown so dark he was nearly black. His elegant legs were shadowed with black stripes, like those of many wild mustangs. There was a suggestion of delicacy about his flaring nostrils, and the hint of a dishlike curve beneath his eyes, attesting to some Arab blood somewhere among his forebears.

Elaine turned her attention from the horse back to his rider. "I've never seen him before." There was a question embedded in her statement.

"I don't keep him in the stable most of the time. He runs free."

Elaine heard the undertone of determination in his voice and knew Beau would have preferred to be able to say the same thing about himself. She wondered what he was working with the horse for.

"He must be tough," she observed with a note of admiration.

Beau shrugged. "Tough enough," he conceded.

"Are you entering him in anything?" Elaine asked curiously.

He wasn't eager to tell her. He hadn't told anyone his plans. Not even Bradley. "I doubt he'd let me ride him into a show ring," Beau said dryly. The stallion pawed the ground and flicked his tail nervously, as if in agreement. "It's too boring. And he doesn't tolerate boredom."

Elaine wasn't about to be put off the scent so easily, however. His mention of the horse's toughness had already given her the clue she needed. She tipped her head to one side and hazarded a guess, since Beau was showing no inclination to clarify himself. "I'll bet the two of you would make rugged competition in an endurance race... or a steeplechase at the end of hunt season."

She was watching his face and just managed to catch the flicker of annoyance in his eyes, the stiffening of his back.

She grinned at him, pleased that she'd guessed accurately. And she would give him something he obviously wanted: secrecy.

"Don't worry," she said with a laugh. "I won't tell a soul. Just let me place a bet on you when the time comes. You can be the dark horse who wins the day."

Beau's eyes snapped to hers then. "I didn't say I was racing Rapier," he reminded her.

She found her irons with her toes and shrugged. "You didn't have to." She gathered her reins and squinted her eyes. "Is that old wagon trail still good for the length of the valley?" she asked him.

Beau nodded. "Yes." He eyed her warily. "Why?"

"How about a race?" she challenged. She looked from her horse to his. "Show me what Rapier's got as a flat racer."

Her eyes were bright with excitement, and her cheeks were pink from the chilly air. Beau felt the heat build in his blood, and his will to deny her faded away. He laughed and looked her over skeptically.

"I know what Rapier's got," he said. "And I know what Mystic's got. The only question is what *you* have."

Elaine laughed, and Mystic began to dance in anticipation. "If you want to see what I've got, Beau Lamond," she declared, "call it."

He pulled Rapier alongside her and murmured, "Go."

Elaine touched Mystic with her heels, and the Thoroughbred bolted forward. Beau gave her a one-stride head start before permitting Rapier to bound forward. They raced across the dead grass, neck and neck half the way. Mystic had longer legs and a Thoroughbred's advantage of having been bred for speed, but Rapier possessed the one quality that every winner had to have: the overwhelming determination to win. And win he did. By an impressive margin. Without working up a sweat.

Elaine laughed as they drew the horses up and turned to trot them back, cooling the animals down.

"Where did you get him?" she asked.

"An old friend of mine in Nevada found him as a colt. He was running with the mustangs, and he got left behind."

"Why didn't your friend keep him?" she asked curiously. She'd never thought of Beau knowing people that far away. He'd always managed to keep his life a blank, so much so that she thought of him as knowing no one outside the state of Virginia.

He didn't seem perturbed by her inquiry, but he certainly didn't rush to fill in the gaps about himself, either. "Jonathan had all the horses he could handle at the time. Besides, he was trying to get away from mustanging so he could prospect more." He glanced at her and was entertained by the look of surprise on her face. "You don't like prospectors?"

Elaine didn't think it sounded very promising, but she tried to be fair. "Has he ever found anything?" she inquired cautiously.

Beau laughed. "He did not too long ago. A sizable lode of opals and a very pretty woman who for some reason decided she was willing to marry him."

Elaine slowed Mystic to a walk. "I guess I admire his skill as a prospector, then," she said. "When did you meet him...this Jonathan?"

"I was out West at an endurance race...years ago."

She looked at him curiously. "And the acquaintance stuck...all this time?"

He didn't look at her. "Yes." When she remained silent, he found he didn't like it. He wondered what she was thinking. What ideas about him was she turning over behind her carefully blank expression. He told himself that he didn't care what she thought, whether she believed him or not, but he knew he was feeding himself a line.

"Let's get back," he said rather sharply. "If you meant what you said about wanting to take on some of the training of your horses, there are plenty more waiting for you."

Elaine was surprised at the sudden edge to his voice. They'd been relaxed, talking companionably, and she'd been lulled into a sense of easiness with him. She'd actually been wondering whether he would mind if she asked him more about his old friend when suddenly he'd thrown up a wall between them. She didn't know if it was because he didn't want to talk about his old friend, or if he didn't want to talk about himself, or if he didn't want to talk to her at all.

She told herself it didn't matter. She told herself it certainly *shouldn't* matter. Unfortunately, it did. At least she wouldn't let it show. Pride lifted her chin.

"Of course I meant what I said," she retorted softly. Her eyes flashed, and she looked away from him as soon as she realized he'd seen her anger. She didn't want him to see her anger. She didn't want to *be* angry. But, darn it, she was. "Mystic went well over the timber trail. He seems sound and eager. Do you want him to do any work in the dressage ring today?"

He knew she was offended at the way he'd cut her off, and he couldn't help but admire how she buried the hurt and tried to ignore it. She made no effort to pull rank or demand he be servile. That was just as well, because he couldn't have been servile if his life depended on it, and then the fur would really have begun to fly. That wouldn't have done either of them any good in the long run. He tried to repress his sudden feeling of admiration for her and concentrated on the business at hand.

"No," he told her. "Mystic's had enough for today. You can work on his dressage tomorrow."

They rode over the crest of the hill and saw the buildings of Foxgrove sprawling across the fields.

"What else can I do today?" she asked a little stiffly.

"You can work on Irish Mist," he offered, having thought it over for a moment before replying.

Elaine lit up like a Christmas tree, and Beau felt like a man fighting a losing battle. How could he steel himself against her when she looked like that?

"If that's my punishment for treading on your sacred private life, punish me anytime, Beau," she teased in relief.

He was exasperated by her candor. He'd given her a treat in offering her Irish Mist. He knew it. She knew it. So why did she have to point it out? That opened the possibility of more communication between them. More shared confidences. Friendship. An innocent yet potentially threatening intimacy between them. He swallowed his exasperation with a growl.

Elaine glanced at his annoyed countenance in amusement. He was a stubborn man. Beneath all that reserve and the distance he put between them, she had the feeling he wanted to help her. Why did he keep making it so difficult for them to get along, then? Perhaps another teasing little prod would help scratch his glacial surface....

"I'm grateful you're not the type to lick your wounds in silence and get even by withholding things," she said.

The look of disgruntled disbelief that he shot her was almost her undoing. It was all she could do not to laugh, and she didn't think he would appreciate her laughing at him. Beneath his visible annoyance, she thought he looked torn, as if debating whether or not to abandon his aloofness. His ambivalence made her feel more warmly toward him. She didn't know why he was so uncomfortable with her, but she wanted to make it easy for him to throw off whatever was bothering him.

His exasperation melted into a moderately fierce glare. "That tends to be a female solution to problems," he growled. "I'm a man." He held her with his cool gray-blue gaze. "If I ever want to punish you for something, you'll know it."

The sound of the horses' hooves on the hard-packed dirt made them both aware of the sudden silence that had fallen between them after his comment.

From the unwavering look that Beau had given her, Elaine felt the force of his personality. Beneath that smooth, courteous facade beat the heart of a lion. He had an iron will and a tenacity that for the briefest moment alarmed her just a little.

She passed her tongue over suddenly dry lips. Strength in a man could be comforting, but it could also be frightening. She remembered his loyalty and dedication in looking out for her when her brother had asked him to do so, and she pushed the frisson of fear away. Beau would never turn that strength against her. He was an honest man, she thought, trying to reassure herself. But the view she'd tried to hold of Beau as courteous, slightly distant brother figure was beginning to crack. He was courteous and slightly distant, all right, but he was definitely not brother material.

They reached the pasture gate, and Beau leaned down to open it. Elaine rode through, giving him a soft thank-you and smiling at him with an effort. His eyes bore into her, and she looked away first. If he wanted to intimidate her, she thought, he was going about it quite well.

He latched the gate after them and touched his heels to Rapier's flanks. Elaine followed suit, and they headed toward home at a gentle canter.

Needing to ease the tension between them, Elaine cast about for something to break the silence. "To Irish Mist," she exclaimed as optimistically as she could. She glanced at Beau. "And to your success at teaching me how to handle her."

He resisted the temptation to let his face soften. She was as tenacious as a terrier when she put her mind on something, and she obviously intended for them to get along. He'd let her glimpse what she was risking, and she'd screwed up her courage and carried on anyway. That was the problem with Elaine. She was basically too courageous and optimistic for her own good.

He slowed to a trot, musing how far he was willing to go to keep her at a distance. If he made a serious pass at her, she would back off in a hurry. He was reluctant to do it, though. The thought of coldly doing something like that made him uncomfortable. He didn't want to treat her that way, even if it probably would solve his problem and get her out of his hair.

He repressed a cynical smile. It would also probably land him in the unemployment line, but that really wasn't what held him back. What held him back was that he didn't want her to look at him with contempt. He didn't want her to feel humiliated or hurt at his hands. And then, too, if he put his hands on her, he wasn't sure he could play the cool cad with her. He would run the risk of her finding out how genuine his attraction to her was.

And he would be the vulnerable one then.

They walked the horses into the paddock, and Eddie and one of the other stablehands came out to take them.

Beau headed toward Irish Mist's stall, hearing Elaine's booted steps falling in quickly behind him. So she wanted to ride her own horses for a while. So she wanted to joke and laugh with him. So she was licking her wounds and healing after a hell of a year. Sooner or later, she would get over it. She would tire of the routine, the monotony, the hard work, of keeping her horses fit. He would let her have her fun. He'd have to. He really didn't have much choice in the matter, under the circumstances.

He only hoped that she got it all out of her system in a hurry and went back to the rest of her life before he did something that they both would eventually regret.

He brought the saddle and bridle from the tack room and found Elaine busy removing the mare's blanket. She turned to him with a smile that brought an odd warmth to his chest and an answering, if also reluctant, softness to his eyes.

"Okay, boss," she said a little breathlessly. "Just tell me what you want me to do." She reached for the bridle and proceeded to slip it onto the mare's head.

Beau lifted the saddle onto the horse's back, hoping that the luck of the Irish would indeed be with them. Or, at the very least, with him.

"First take her out into the dressage ring and limber her up a little."

He gave her a leg up, stepping back as soon as she dropped into the saddle. His face was expressionless as he led the way to the ring.

The first time Elaine had taken Irish Mist out, she'd been stiff from lack of practice and so fascinated with her brother's newest acquisition that she hadn't done as well as she was capable of as a rider.

Today was different. She was limbered up, relatively relaxed and interested in thoroughly reviewing her own knowledge of dressage. She gradually forgot that Beau was leaning against the fence, as she became more and more immersed in signaling Irish Mist to execute one move after another. The more she did, the more deeply impressed she was with the mare's level of training. She had already recognized the horse's impeccable conformation and sweet temperament. One look told anyone with eyes to see that the Thoroughbred was a graceful beauty. But it took expert horsemanship to uncover the mare's exquisite sense of timing, footing and obedience.

Elaine felt a glow in her heart that she thought had been extinguished when the horse she'd learned to ride on had died years ago. "Beauty, beauty, you are a beauty," she murmured.

The mare zigzagged from one corner of the ring to the other in a delicate half pass, and Elaine felt as if she were floating on air. She glanced at Beau and grinned from ear to ear. Then she concentrated on coming up with some complicated patterns for the horse to try.

Thirty minutes later, she rode Irish Mist to the edge of the ring as Beau opened the gate to let her pass through. She held her breath, wondering whether he'd feel she was good enough to work with the mare regularly. Irish Mist was clearly destined to be a champion if she had the right rider on her back.

Beau watched Elaine dismount and smiled slightly. "You don't have to look like I'm about to announce your execution," he said.

She rolled her eyes. "I hate suspense," she said. "How bad was I?"

He almost laughed. "Not bad at all. You need to work on your seat a bit, and a few of your aids are rough around the edges and could be made a little more subtle." He paused.

She saw him debate with himself whether to say something else. She gave him a threatening look and tilted her head to one side warningly. "Give it to me straight. All of it. You're the boss here. I'll accept what you say."

His cheeks darkened a little, and she saw a flash of annoyance in his eyes. "I always tell it straight," he growled. "And I'm completely aware that I'm in charge here."

Elaine took a deep breath and tried a different approach. In a more soothing tone she said, "Could I become good enough to show Irish Mist?"

He looked away from her, then turned back, looking straight at her. "Yes. As a matter of fact, you have a touch with her that I've only seen in one other rider."

"Really?" said Elaine, gratified to hear it. "Who was that?"

"Meg."

The open curiosity on Elaine's face gradually faded as his answer sank into her mind. She caught her lower lip between her teeth and looked at the mare. "Is Meg planning on showing Irish Mist?" she asked quietly.

Beau shrugged. "I don't know," he replied. He looked at Elaine curiously. "Does it bother you that Meg is a good match with Irish Mist?" he asked neutrally.

She shook her head a little too quickly. "No, no. Of course not." She led the mare into the stall and began removing the tack.

"You don't have to do that," he pointed out. "I'll have Eddie clean her up."

Elaine gave him a somewhat less than brilliant smile and hoisted the saddle off the mare's back.

"I don't have anything else to do," she argued. "Besides, I'd like to."

He couldn't very well argue with that, so he nodded and went off to dig through the pile of paperwork that had accumulated on his desk.

As the papers passed in front of him, he kept wondering why Elaine should be worried about Meg's interest in Irish Mist. Meg had more than enough horses to ride. She was actually too busy to take on the mare. She would probably only do it if Richard got down on bended knee and begged her to, which he might, considering how determined he'd been to get her to ride the horse.

There was no reason for Elaine not to take over, though. So why had she suddenly stopped dead in her tracks when he'd mentioned Meg's involvement?

He shook his head and told himself that he didn't want to know the answer. It was nothing to him. He didn't care what was going on in Elaine's stubborn little head or kind little heart.

The phone rang, and Beau yanked it up to his ear. "Lamond," he growled. "Sorry, Bradley," he said with a sigh, running a hand through his hair. "It's been a long morning.... What can I do for you?"

Chapter 6

The days slipped by peaceably enough.

Elaine found herself going to bed and rising early, enjoying working with the Faust horses again. Beau was unfailingly professional, offering astute criticism and advice. He observed her for ten or fifteen minutes with each of the horses she worked with, patiently commenting on her horsemanship or the personality of the mount she happened to be handling.

And occasionally she took a turn watching him work with a horse. He had a confident hand with them that the horses seemed to like. He managed to pull a little sparkle out of even the most stubborn nag.

She was smiling when he led one of the green hunters out of the ring after having spent thirty minutes jumping the animal over cavalletti with a lunge line. His hair had fallen across his forehead, and his cheeks were ruddy from the chilly air.

"I never thought he'd give in," she admitted, referring to the stubborn horse's habit of shying away from the low bars when he had to change leads at a canter.

Mistress of Foxgrove 85

Beau smiled faintly and patted the young horse on the neck. "He'll be okay. He just lacks confidence. Practice will take care of that."

She followed him into the stable. When he handed the horse to one of the grooms, she followed him into the office and sank down into the soft leather sofa. Beau stood behind his desk and looked at her questioningly, a slight frown on his brow. She didn't usually come into the office.

"The other day," she began hesitantly, "when you left for the afternoon on personal business..."

His look was not encouraging. "Yes?" he said. It sounded more as if he were daring her to pursue the subject rather than encouraging her to go on.

Elaine gathered her courage and continued anyway. "I hope it wasn't anything serious...."

He shrugged and shook his head, then dropped his gaze to the papers on his desk, as if there were nothing more to say.

She tilted her head against the back of the sofa and tried to pick her words diplomatically. "You know, you can take time off if you need it...."

He didn't lift his eyes. "I know."

"But..."

His cool eyes lifted. He stared at her, his mouth tightening almost imperceptibly. "But what?"

Elaine sighed and ran a hand through her dark hair. She'd left it loose for practice, and now it was like a cloud around her head, tousled from the wind and exertion. "I heard that you have family, but I've never known you to visit them.... If you wanted to... if they ever needed you..."

His face became even more unyielding. He stopped handling the papers and slid his hands into the front pockets of his worn jodhpurs. "I know..." he interjected evenly. "I'm just like family. I could go to them in a minute. You'll babysit all the horses and supervise all the stable hands for me in my absence. You'll even pack me a picnic lunch to see me on my way."

Elaine's cheeks darkened. His words had been unexpected. They'd been needlessly harsh. She was sure he knew that. But it hurt that he would speak to her so sarcastically.

Hurt, humiliation and surprise mingled for a moment on her face. Then she rose to her feet and returned his unwavering gaze.

"That's right," she said, lifting her chin just a little in prideful self-defense. "But please don't thank me for the offer. I've become accustomed to having them thrown back in my teeth."

She crossed the room and was almost to the door when she felt him move. He blocked her way and closed his hands over her forearms. The heat from his body warmed her, and she looked at him in genuine surprise. What she saw in his eyes made her catch her breath. The fury, the heat, the anger, the roiling frustration. They were all there.

He blinked as if suddenly realizing what he was doing, and he slowly released his hold on her arms. But he didn't move away. He stood there, a foot away from her, and he closed his eyes, rubbing a hand over his face. "I'm sorry, Elaine...." he muttered.

The moment of alarm she'd felt when he'd grabbed her faded as soon as he'd let her go and closed his eyes in obvious self-condemnation. She moved a little away from him, just to be on the safe side, and decided his defenses might have weakened just enough to permit some truly honest answers for once.

"How sorry?" she asked gently.

He looked at her, and this time he was the one to look surprised.

"Sorry enough to answer my questions without taking my head off?" she went on softly. "Surely we've been through enough of my catastrophes in the past few months for you to trust me with some of yours?"

She asked him so gently, with such genuine kindness, and he felt so guilty at having grabbed her, that Beau decided it might be better just to tell her whatever it was she wanted to know.

He sat on the corner of his desk and crossed his arms over his chest. "All right," he said. "We might as well get this over with. What do you want to know?"

It was a strange way for him to put it, she thought, wondering what dark secrets he thought he was going to be forced to reveal. She caught her lower lip between her teeth and tried to pick questions that wouldn't hurt him. She felt like a blind woman feeling her way.

"Would you tell me where you went that afternoon that you disappeared?" She hurriedly added, "If you want to tell me it's none of my business, go right ahead." She laughed, although it almost hurt to do so, since she didn't feel at all amused and was laughing out of nervousness. "I've got plenty of other questions I could ask in its place."

He seemed amused by her carefully polite hedging. "I'll tell you. I went to jail."

Elaine couldn't have looked more surprised. When she didn't open her mouth to ask him why, he told her anyway.

"To visit my father."

Her cheeks reddened a little, and her eyes softened in spite of her determination to be casual and sophisticated about his revelation. "I'm sorry," she murmured. "I didn't know...."

He laughed, and it was harsh and humorless. "No? Then you're one of the few in the state who don't. Don't you want to know what he's in jail for?"

Elaine asked calmly, "What for?"

"Embezzlement." There was bitterness beneath his cold expression.

"That's why your family lost everything?" she asked softly.

He turned a furious look on her. "No. We lost everything because I went to bed with the wife of a man who was very influential and didn't care to be cuckolded by his accountant's son."

Elaine's face paled, but she tried not to make things worse for Beau. "Did you really do that?" she asked.

"Yes."

The silence was as rough as sandpaper for a long, painful moment. Elaine swallowed and wished she'd never begun this conversation. She remembered his comment the night he'd chauffeured her to Margaret Innery's party.

"Is that why you told me all your relations with women had been of the most satisfactory kind?"

He sucked in his breath. It was harder than he'd thought, having her illusions about him destroyed while he watched. He ran his hands through his hair roughly. "No," he muttered in annoyance. "That's not why. She wasn't at all satisfactory, as a matter of fact. She was a bitch. She still is."

Elaine walked across the room and forced down the rush of disappointment and dismay that was swamping her. She hadn't realized until that moment how much she'd begun to idolize Beau. She'd made him more perfect than he really was. She couldn't believe he was as heartless as he was trying to make himself seem, though. She pushed away the hurt and turned to face him. He seemed very far away, with the room between them. It made her feel... lonely.

"Somehow I missed a lot of the details, I'm afraid," she said as steadily as she could. "How did we get from the woman you... went to bed with to your father in jail."

He sighed and rested his hands on his knees. Maybe it would be just as well if she heard it from him rather than from someone else.

"The woman's husband knew he couldn't do much to me. Unless he killed me, which he's much too cool and calculating to bother with. So he framed my father for embezzlement. I don't know how. But somehow he did. My father stood trial and was convicted. He's been in jail for over a year." Beau's voice was tight, his face like the arctic, devoid of all light. "That was the coin he used to pay me back."

Elaine was shocked. "I'm so sorry," she whispered.

He looked at her in grim amusement, his mouth twisted in a humorless smile. "What? No more questions, Pandora? Have you heard enough evil for one day, then?"

She closed her eyes. "I deserved that."

"No, you didn't," he said bitingly. He stood and turned his back on her. "It isn't something I particularly relish talking about," he admitted.

Elaine walked across the room and laid her hand on his arm. The lean muscles felt tight beneath her fingers, but she didn't flinch away.

"If there's anything my brother and I can do to help, please tell us, Beau," she said softly. "We owe you a debt

Mistress of Foxgrove

of thanks. And my brother might be able to think of something. Richard is an expert when it comes to financial transactions, you know."

Beau shrugged off her arm and faced her with a look of icy dislike. "I'll take care of this in my own way," he said in a voice hard with anger and the taste for revenge.

Elaine, who thought his dislike was directed at her for offering to help, blushed in embarrassment. It never occurred to her that the object of his dislike was himself, or the frustrating position he was in.

"I'm sorry," she said, her voice barely rising above a strained whisper. "I keep forgetting that you don't want to have anything to do with us."

The hurt that she struggled unsuccessfully to keep from her eyes stabbed him, and he reached out for her without thinking, pulling her into his arms so suddenly that she was literally speechless with surprise. He buried one hand in her hair and pulled her body against him. Her lips were scant inches from his as his burning eyes roamed restlessly over her startled face.

"You don't understand," he said roughly. "That's not how I feel at all. I'm trying to protect you, damn it. Are you *blind*? Can't you see what I'd like to be doing with you?"

Not bothering to find out what she might reply, he demonstrated exactly what he meant by pulling her up and lowering his mouth to hers in a hard, hungry kiss. One steely arm held her immobile against him while the other controlled her head, forcing her to be still.

His mouth was angry and demanding, and the kiss ground against her lips until she felt nearly bruised. She tried to jerk her head to one side, opening her mouth in protest, trying to say no, but he used the moment against her, forcing his tongue ruthlessly inside her mouth.

Elaine felt her initial shock turn to horror, then to fear, then quickly to confusion. She sensed his anger and his frustration in every taut muscle that held her captive. Yet beneath it she heard him catch his breath, as if he truly wanted her. That was almost more terrifying than anything else, bringing back vivid memories of humiliation and desperation from her short-lived marriage.

She began to struggle in earnest, forcing one arm between them and pushing against his hard chest. His lips moved against hers, and to her dismay she felt an answering flame come to life within her. She thought she must be going mad. How could she respond to him? This wasn't an expression of love. It was a brutal demonstration of power and anger. She struggled all the harder, as much to free herself from her own response as to free herself from his unexpected ravishment.

Something got through to him, and gradually the pressure against her mouth lessened. He continued to hold her, but the anger was leaving him, and his hold was firm rather than harsh. He opened his eyes and stared down at her, his breath caressing her lips.

"Have you had enough?" he asked in a voice roughened and soft all at the same time.

Elaine kept her hand pressed against his chest and looked straight into his stormy eyes. "Enough talk?" she asked unsteadily. "Or enough kissing?"

He let go of her and sighed. "I wouldn't call that kissing," he admitted.

Was there a trace of sadness in his eyes? Maybe she was just kidding herself. Elaine swallowed and pushed her hair back into a semblance of order.

"No. I don't suppose that's kissing," she agreed when her voice steadied. She decided to try to be the lady of the manor about it. That approach was usually good for relieving embarrassment and awkwardness. And if ever she'd felt embarrassed and awkward, this was it. "Do you always jump on a woman when she tries to carry on a conversation?"

He was silent for so long that she had to look at him. A warm rush of feeling poured through her when she saw the lonely anger burning in his eyes.

"No," he said. He sighed. "You don't give up, do you?"

She smiled and shook her head. "No. It's a character trait. Runs in the family."

He walked over to the window and slid his hands into his pockets. His back was to her, and she couldn't tell from the set of his shoulders what he was thinking.

"Do you want me to resign?" he asked bluntly.

Elaine wet her lips. Part of her cried out yes. He was too real, too alive, too dangerously strong. But part of her cried out no. He was more genuine, more true, than almost all the men she'd known. Granted, she had no real proof of that, but she sensed it instinctively. She'd lost so much in her life. She didn't want the warmth and happiness that had been blooming around her recently to end. If he left...

She laughed as if he'd said something remarkable. "Leave?" she echoed in disbelief. "Over a kiss?" She made a distasteful sound. "What kind of woman do you take me for, anyway? Forget it. I have." A lie, but it saved her pride. She swallowed and gathered her most elegant self. "You're too good a horseman to lose over a little lapse in control. Besides, if you're as successful a ladies' man as you've insinuated, I'm sure you'll turn to greener pastures and forget about me." She hesitated and added, a little more intensely, "Won't you?"

Beau lowered his head and rubbed the bridge of his nose with his fingers. He shouldn't let her off the hook so easily. He should keep after her and make himself a real bastard in her eyes. But he remembered the startled, nearly fearful look on her face when he'd pulled her to him, and he knew he couldn't do it. He couldn't scare her anymore.

"Damn," he murmured under his breath. He gritted his teeth and said more loudly, "You're absolutely right. Nothing like greener pastures to make a man forget."

Elaine ran her tongue over her lips. She should have felt relieved. She didn't. "Fine," she said. "We have an understanding, then?"

He glanced at her over his shoulder. "I'll find my... outlets elsewhere."

"Yes." She could hardly say it.

"Understood."

She walked out, leaving him staring at her back and burning to finish what the kiss had merely hinted at beginning.

Tears glittered on her eyelashes as Elaine walked stiffly back to the house. The gold had turned to ashes in her hand. Did she bring out the worst in all men, for heaven's sake?

She'd liked Beau... but then, she'd liked Cam in the beginning, too. Not that they were particularly alike. Except that they were both quite popular with the ladies, of course.

She ran up the circular staircase, taking the steps as fast as she could. She hated for people to see her crying. And they'd seen much too much of that in the past few months.

"I'm not letting you do this, Beau," she swore as she stomped into her room. "I'm going to be a happy person again no matter what!"

And with that she tossed off her clothes and headed for a long soak in the whirlpool.

Beau was examining one of the hunter's hooves when Elaine came into the stable the following morning. He handed Eddie a jar of ointment to take back to the medical supply cabinet, waiting until the stable hand had left to speak to Elaine.

"Good morning," she said. The words were light and cool, a perfect match for her elegant demeanor.

She knew that she probably appeared composed and in good spirits, and that helped buoy her confidence in handling this first meeting with Beau since the previous day's unexpectedly intimate confrontation. She wasn't so successful, however, in quelling the nervousness that had been plaguing her for the past two hours. She'd been angry and upset with him all afternoon and evening, and it wasn't until she'd been buttoning her blouse this morning that she'd admitted she wasn't going to be as aristocratically unmoved by him as she wanted to be.

Beau looked at her, his brows drawing together in a slight frown. "Good morning," he said quietly.

His eyes were on her face, but Elaine had the feeling that he was seeing all of her. The walls of the stable seemed to be much closer than before, the space between them much too confining. She was standing by the stall door, still ajar after Eddie's departure. She took a half step back, clasped her hands behind her back and dug her fingernails into her palms to shake herself loose from the cloak of warmth and intimacy that was swirling around them. It was his eyes, she realized. His gray-blue eyes like the end of a storm.

Mistress of Foxgrove

"We've got three horses that need dressage schooling, two that need some practice in the jumping ring and three that need work over the timber trail," he said carefully.

He came closer, walking slowly, deliberately. She reminded him of a skittish mare wary of getting too close to a rutting stallion, he thought grimly. An apt reaction for which he had only himself to thank.

He'd half hoped she wouldn't come today. That she would decide to do something else with her time. He'd told himself that would be better for both of them, but as soon as he'd seen her, he'd breathed a sigh of painful relief.

He'd worried about her for hours after she'd left him in the office. He'd gone into town for dinner, mainly to avoid her, but she'd haunted him constantly. He hadn't glimpsed her around the house or anywhere else on the estate after they'd parted. Granted, when she'd left him, she'd seemed to have been handling the situation well enough, but later he'd wondered whether that might have been a well-polished act. He had enough experience with women to see through most of their veils, but he'd needed to see Elaine again to reassure himself that she wasn't harboring some hurt from his action. In spite of her strength and resilience, he'd always sensed a vulnerability in her. And he remembered how Meg had said Elaine buried her feelings rather than burden others with her fears and disappointments.

He was surprised at how fiercely he wanted to avoid being the source of additional pain to her. Her emotional scars from the past year were barely healed as it was, without him adding to them. Perhaps he could undo some of the damage, if indeed there was any.

He closed the stall door and leaned negligently against it, noticing that she'd backed away and was holding her hands behind her back. So she was more nervous than she wanted to admit, he thought. His eyes narrowed thoughtfully. They couldn't very well work together if they couldn't get past what had happened. Since she obviously intended to keep to her original plan of working with the horses, the least he could do was make it as easy for her as possible. The fact that it would be hard as hell for him was probably just what he deserved.

His eyes softened, and the muscles at the corners of his mouth reluctantly tugged the grimness into the hint of a smile. "Are you going to shove a dagger into me?" he asked teasingly.

Elaine didn't understand. "I beg your pardon?"

The grin settled more comfortably, and he nodded toward her arms. "I thought maybe you were clutching a knife behind your back...."

She smiled a little awkwardly and held up her palms. "Not today."

He dipped his head as if in thanks. "After what happened yesterday, I wouldn't have blamed you," he said softly.

She lowered her eyes. His gaze was unnerving, although she knew he was trying to put them both at ease. She drew in a breath and said, "I don't think anything more needs to be said about that."

He shook his head. "I don't agree. There are several things that need to be said." The sound of a horse being led by one of the grooms drew his attention, and he frowned in the direction of the sound. "This isn't exactly the time or place, though, so it'll have to wait."

Elaine was relieved to hear that, and she mustered a cheerful look. "Do I have my choice of horses, or have you got a schedule worked out for me?"

Beau indicated that she should come with him as he headed through the maze of stalls. "I've got a schedule. You can veto the assignments, if you want."

She knew she wouldn't veto anything, and from the casual way he'd said it, she knew that he wasn't expecting her to. It had merely been a gesture of courtesy. Or perhaps a way of acknowledging her position as owner and his as a man in her employ. She hoped it wasn't the latter. Throwing that at her only seemed to complicate things, she thought.

"Why don't you start with the dressage...." he was saying as she followed him into one of the stalls. The saddle was waiting outside, and he'd brought the bridle in with him. "You can work your way up to those rides through the timber...."

She soon realized that he was trying to make it as easy for her as he could. He was completely professional when he stood in the dressage ring, giving her an occasional suggestion. There was no special intimacy in his eyes when he looked at her, no inappropriate staring, just a professional horseman sharing his knowledge. Just Beau who had been beside her on many days before this one. Gradually she relaxed.

By the time she'd finished with the first horse scheduled for the jumping ring, she was famished, and she didn't hesitate to say so. Beau grinned, and they walked together to share a meal at Mrs. Adams's kitchen table. Discussing the various problems each of the horses had presented kept the conversation going when they weren't both busy eating the tasty chicken-and-noodle casserole that Mrs. Adams was clearly so proud of.

As they were leaving to head back to the stables, the cook called out to Elaine, "By the way, your brother called a little while ago."

Her face lit up at the news. "Is he having a good time?" she asked with a laugh. Richard and Meg were supposed to be coming back sometime today, unless they'd changed their minds.

Mrs. Adams's rosy cheeks turned an even redder shade. "Shame on you, young lady! To ask me that about a man on his honeymoon!" She giggled a little and covered her mouth. "He did sound happier than I've heard him in a long, long time," she conceded with a romantic sigh. "I'm glad he realized how he felt about Meg." She looked a bit piqued at that. "It certainly took the man long enough!" she grumbled.

Elaine couldn't have agreed more. "Are they changing their travel plans?" It was the only reason that occurred to her why he might have called.

"Oh, no," Mrs. Adams hurriedly reassured her. "They'll be back late tonight."

"Well, I'm relieved to hear that!" Elaine exclaimed with feeling. "I'll be able to stop worrying about whether it's a fatal breach of etiquette to have a meet of the Foxgrove Hunt without its Master present!" Richard was certainly cutting it close. The hunt was meeting tomorrow. At least the horses would be ready for it, she thought in amusement, even if the people weren't.

Mrs. Adams wrinkled her brow. "Oh...there was another call for you, Elaine. Anita Darlington wondered if she could extend a special invitation to someone staying with the Longacres this week."

Elaine nodded. "I'll call her from the stable."

Beau was riding one of the green hunters over the field of hunting panels, and Elaine was alone in the stable office when she dialed Anita Darlington. Anita was the secretary of the Foxgrove Hunt and sent invitations to people at the Master's order. There were about twenty to thirty regulars, only two-thirds of whom usually showed up at any particular meet. Occasionally someone had a friend staying over, and a special invitation was generally extended by the Master as a courtesy to the regular member.

When Elaine reached Anita, the woman was already flustered.

"You can't imagine how many hours you need in the day to handle the social schedule of three teenaged girls!"

Elaine smiled. "I can imagine. I was one of them once...."

"You couldn't have been as exhausting to keep up with as my daughters are," Anita moaned.

Elaine twined the telephone cord around her finger and remembered with some fondness the affection between Anita and her three children. "Mrs. Adams said you have a last-minute request for an invitation?"

Anita, who had nearly forgotten about the hunt in the chaos of the day, let out an exhausted groan. "Yes...and since Richard is out of town, and I certainly didn't want to bother him with this on his honeymoon...."

Elaine laughed. "Yes, you did the right thing. Richard left me in charge. I can make the decision for him. Who is it?"

Anita rustled papers at the other end of the line and mumbled to herself for a moment. "Oh, here it is.... It's a woman who's staying with Pamela Longacre. You did know that Pamela is quietly trying to sell her estate, didn't you?"

"No," Elaine murmured in surprise. "I'm sorry to hear that. She's been a wonderful friend...."

"Yes." Anita sighed. "But since Roger died last winter, she just hasn't wanted to put the effort into the place that it needs.... You know, grounds keeping...parties...the open house in the spring for the garden club. I think she's planning on renting a villa on a beach somewhere for a few months to mull over what she wants to do with the rest of her life."

"I suppose it's understandable, but we'll all miss her here at Foxgrove." Elaine tried to get Anita back to the original subject. "About the guest...?"

Anita laughed. "Yes. Sorry, Elaine. I've been inundated with my girls' conversations for so long that I'm starting to babble and digress just like them. The guest is a Mrs. Carlton. Apparently she lives in Miami in the winter but has recently opened a second home in Charlottesville. Her husband is in commercial real estate development or handles financing for developments or something like that...."

Elaine hadn't heard much past the woman's name. "This wouldn't by any chance be Babsey Carlton who was at Margaret Innery's party last week?" she asked cautiously.

Anita sounded delighted. "Yes! That's the one. Well, it's all right, then. You must have met her. There isn't any problem in inviting her?"

There was, but Elaine knew she couldn't refuse simply because Babsey had known Beau, which bothered her, for some odd reason. That would sound utterly ridiculous.

Anita apparently took the silence as agreement and barreled onward. "She doesn't have a horse with her. Naturally." Anita laughed. "Who goes house hunting with their horse in tow?"

"No one, obviously," Elaine agreed with amusement. "We have a couple of extra hunters in residence. That won't be a problem." Too bad, she thought. That would have been an excellent reason for the beautiful Babs to take a long walk instead of a swift ride.

There was a female shriek in the background, and Anita begged off. "Lisbeth must have been asked to the dance by that long-haired moron she's so infatuated with," she said forlornly. "She'll be pleading for a new dress all evening. I can hear it now. And to think how much I used to enjoy shopping!"

Elaine laughed. "You will again someday, Anita."

"When they're grown and gone!"

"Bye, Anita. I've got to run."

"Of course. See you tomorrow morning."

Elaine hung up the phone. The traditional Foxgrove Hunt meet held on the Saturday before Thanksgiving was much enjoyed by its members. Elaine had looked forward to it many times in the past. Tomorrow's meet might well be a turning point, she thought with a sigh. She had the feeling that Beau wasn't going to appreciate having Babs Carlton around. And Elaine knew for a fact that she wasn't going to enjoy it much herself, either.

Chapter 7

Beau trotted the sleek Dutch warmblood back toward the stable. He'd worked the animal hard, and they were both sweating lightly in spite of the cool temperature. As the sun slowly slipped beneath the low mountain ridges to the west, the dropping temperature began to make both horse and rider uncomfortable and eager to be home.

Beau had been concentrating on breaking the green hunter of a couple of bad habits and had managed to temporarily forget about his own perplexing difficulties in dealing with Elaine Faust. His respite ended, however, the moment the big bay hunter rounded the last bend in the trees and broke into the open meadows that rolled toward the buildings of Foxgrove.

The first person he saw was Elaine. She was leading a horse around the ring nearest the paddock, stopping periodically to bend down and examine the animal's right knee and foreleg with her hand. Then she walked the horse again, studying the way he moved. She was totally absorbed in what she was doing.

He sensed for a moment what it would be like if she was there waiting for him. Waiting to welcome him home for the evening, opening her arms and her heart to comfort him. He quickly crushed the fantasy. He had more than enough trouble to deal with. He certainly didn't need to further blacken his family's name and his own slim chance of recovering their honor by letting himself succumb to a burning physical attraction to Elaine Faust. And she didn't need him at all.

He sat deeper in the saddle, and the big dark hunter slowed to a springy walk as they turned down the neatly maintained trail that led to the paddock. He knew the moment that Elaine heard his horse's hoofbeats, because she turned and looked in his direction. He was a little too far away to make out her expression in the fading light, but he sensed her welcome in the hand she lifted to wave at him, the way she tilted her head to one side as if she were smiling, the way she straightened her shoulders and stood a little more lightly on her feet.

Beau wondered for the hundredth time how her husband could ever have been such a fool as to have spurned her the way he had. Anger pulsed through him, and he automatically forced it away. He told himself that it didn't matter anymore. The man was dead and buried. Elaine was free to make a fresh start in life.

The idea of a fresh start brought him a renewed surge of annoyance. Beau visualized Elaine in the eager arms of a faceless other man, and his stomach curled into a hard knot. He refused to recognize the surge of jealousy that spiked him, choosing instead to turn his jealousy into anger at Elaine for having been victimized. She'd certainly made a poor choice with her first husband, he thought in disgust. He sincerely hoped she showed more sense the next time she let herself get involved with a man, and he most especially hoped that she'd take a very long time getting into any such relationship at all. Directing his anger at her was gratifying at first. He asked himself how she could have been such a blind idiot. How could she have fallen in love with such a completely worthless male as Cam Bennett? How could she have been so naive?

The pleasure of blaming Elaine gradually faded, however, and Beau recognized that he couldn't pin all the blame on her for accepting a silken snake like Cam Bennett as a mate. In all honesty, Beau was certain that she'd been victimized by Bennett's skillfully honed veneer of charm. Beau had never met Cam Bennett, but he'd gotten a very clear picture of the man from Bradley, Mrs. Adams and the few terse comments made by Elaine's brother on the subject. Beau had met a few people like Cam Bennett over the years. They were hard to recognize for what they were, at first. That, of course, was what made them so dangerous. He very much doubted that Elaine, protected by boarding schools and her brother, had ever been around someone like that long enough to recognize the few faint signs that could have given him away. She hadn't had a chance. Until it was too late, that was.

That thought brought Beau back to his original sense of fury at Cam Bennett, where his anger more properly belonged. His mouth tightened. There was no outlet for his rage. The man was dead. There wasn't anything Beau could do to exact revenge, so anger boiled in his belly, having nowhere else to go. And the anger showed on his face as he rode in.

When Elaine met him at the entrance to the paddock, she thought that he looked distinctly put out. She mustered a cheerful smile and wondered privately why he was in such an ill temper. She doubted it had anything to do with her, since she'd done only what he wanted and mostly in his absence. If she'd done something that didn't suit him, he wouldn't even know it yet. Therefore she assumed the horse he'd taken out must be the culprit. She restrained the inclination to give the hunter a sympathetic look. Beau would probably prefer to have any sympathy directed at him rather than the horse, she decided. Whatever the horse had done, or refused to do, must have really been something to put that dark look on his face.

"Did he give you a hard time?" Elaine asked innocently, nodding at the big hunter.

Beau dismounted and tried to figure out what she was talking about. He rarely had anyone ask him something like that. That was primarily because he never returned to the stable until the horse he was working with was doing what he wanted. The idea that he would ride home if the horse had won any battle of wills was almost incomprehensible to Beau.

"He's got a couple of bad habits," Beau explained, "but he's willing enough to do what he's told. This is one of Bradley's and Bradley wouldn't have him otherwise." He patted the horse on the neck. "Bad habits can take a while to break, though. That's just to be expected, I guess."

Elaine could tell from the easing of the expression on Beau's face that the horse wasn't the problem, so she accepted his explanation. Perhaps he was preoccupied with personal matters, or business, she thought. Since she didn't want to see that harsh look return to his face, she decided it might be wiser not to ask any more questions. She had no way of knowing what might trigger his anger again. She needed more information first. Instead of asking him about his afternoon, she decided to volunteer information about hers.

She rattled off the list of tasks she'd handled since they'd last spoken, including the problem with the horse she'd been examining as Beau returned. He listened without comment, bending down to feel the horse's leg and nodding his agreement with what she'd done. A stable hand took his horse in the midst of Elaine's debriefing, leaving him with no particular reason not to accompany her when she led the horse back into the stable a few moments later. She took advantage of that to continue talking about her day. She told herself that she just wanted to tell Beau everything while she could still remember the points she wanted to make. The fact that she enjoyed his company was merely a secondary consideration. A little icing on the cake.

Beau watched Elaine put the mare into the stall, hanging the lead outside on its hook when she came back out. Her hair was tousled, and her clothes were stained from riding all day, as were his. Yet he was sure he could scent the familiar sweetness that always clung to the air around her. He shook his head slightly to shake loose the image.

Inside the stable it was warmer, and since Beau was already warm from riding, he began to feel constricted by his clothes. He loosened the fastenings on his work-worn jacket and flexed his chill-stiffened shoulders while Elaine had her back half to him, examining with great interest the lead she'd just hung on the wall.

"Is there something else?" he asked, sensing she was gathering herself to say something unpleasant.

She turned to face him. Her eyes caught the motion of his hands just as he flipped open the lowest button on his jacket. She quickly looked at his face. She appeared composed except for a hint of unusually pink color in her cheeks. Beau wondered in amusement how pink she would have turned if his hand had been on his belt buckle instead.

"Surely it doesn't embarrass you to watch me unbutton my coat?" he said teasingly, trying not to actually laugh at her discomfort.

Her eyes were steady, but her cheeks were still a shade darker than normal. "Of course not," she said.

The breathless little laugh that accompanied her denial made a lie of her words. Their eyes met, and she knew that Beau saw through her hasty statement. Which only made her color deepen.

"It does bother you." He said it as a fact.

He frowned and moved a little away from her. So she was aware of him as a man, he thought. Hell. He didn't want to know that. He tried to remember what they'd been talking about. She'd been trying to figure out how to open a subject with him. He hoped like the devil that it wasn't anything to do with her susceptibility to his taking off his jacket.

"There's something else, isn't there?" He stared at her, frowning a little.

Elaine nodded. "Anita Darlington extended a special invitation to the hunt tomorrow to someone staying with one of our regular members...."

That didn't sound like a very thorny issue to him, and he shrugged. "What's the problem?"

"She'll need a horse...." Elaine began. She looked down at the toes of her boots and cursed her sudden faintheartedness. She had a bad feeling about this, though, and she knew she didn't want to see the look in Beau's eyes when she told him who it was.

"We've got a couple of extra hunters," he pointed out. "You know that."

"Yes..."

He could see that she was very uncomfortable, and he asked the obvious question. "Who is it?"

Elaine looked at him then, regret and apology in her soft eyes. "It's Babs Carlton."

The hardening of his expression and the cold anger in his eyes made her feel even more miserable than she'd expected. She wished it was her hunt, not Richard's, and she could have refused to issue the invitation. Even ordered a cancellation.

"I'm sorry, Beau," she said honestly. "After the other night at Margaret's, I didn't think you'd particularly look forward to her company, but... she's staying with Pamela Longacre, and I couldn't refuse. Richard would have asked why and..." She began to feel like a fool. She looked at Beau in exasperation. "I don't *know* why. I couldn't very well say it was an old girlfriend or something like that...."

Beau laughed, and the sound was painful for her to listen to. "An old girlfriend?" he echoed her words, speaking softly, as if he couldn't find a more repulsive expression if his life depended on it. He shrugged, and a cool shield closed over his eyes, shutting Elaine out. "Maybe that's as good a phrase as any," he said flatly.

"Is that what she was?" she asked after an awkward silence.

"No." He looked at Elaine as if weighing the advantages of one path over another. It was obvious from the look on his face when he came to a decision. "You might as well know exactly who she is," he said at last. "She'll be nothing but trouble, and you'll be fresh meat for her." Beau glanced around and added, "I'm not interested in discussing this in the middle of the stable, however."

"We could go someplace more private," she offered.

"Yes," he agreed. Their eyes met, and they both remembered the incident in the stable office. "I have a few things I've been wanting to say to you in private anyway," he added softly.

Elaine swallowed and gathered her years of social training around her like invisible armor to hold her up.

"The office is the closest place I can think of," she pointed out, as if it were perfectly reasonable and didn't bother her at all. Her dark blue eyes were clear and trusting. "Why don't we talk and then get cleaned up for dinner?"

Beau shook his head. "I don't think the stable office is...neutral ground...anymore."

Elaine looked away from him. She couldn't really argue with that. It wasn't difficult being in the office with him during the day with the door wide open and people coming in and out, but alone at night...she couldn't help feeling that it wasn't a place she wanted to be with him. Not alone, anyway. She thought her uneasiness would probably fade with time, but it had barely been twenty-four hours, which was hardly long enough.

"Well..." She glanced at him questioningly. "Would you come to the study in the main house?" She saw the odd, stubborn look come back into his eyes, and she laughed a little. "I'll feel very safe and confident there," she swore. "You'll be on my turf, Beau."

Beau's initial reaction had been that that was too public a place for them to be alone. The entire estate would see him close the door after them. The more he thought about it, the more willing he was to accept her suggestion, however. After all, Ambrose and half the household staff would be wandering around on the other side of the closed doors. And every place else he thought of was even more isolated or required a drive to get to. He didn't particularly want to find himself sitting next to Elaine in a car in the dark, discussing his peccadilloes—and hers.

"All right," he agreed. He brushed the palm of his hand against his riding clothes, knocking loose a light cloud of dust. "I think I'd better get cleaned up first." He grinned at her. "Ambrose wouldn't let me near the place, smelling like a horse."

Elaine laughed and welcomed the sense of relief his humor brought her. "Me, either," she agreed. She glanced at her wristwatch. "I'll see you at dinner. Then... afterward...we can talk."

She nodded at him as if it were all settled and walked out of the stable without a backward glance. She didn't have to look back to know that he was watching her leave. She just hoped that whatever he planned to say to her wouldn't make her feel more foolish than she already did.

"That wouldn't be too hard," she muttered to herself as she pushed open the front door. She seemed to be becoming an expert at making a fool of herself when Beau was around. She wished she could recapture her sense of self-confidence. Every time she thought she had a solid grip on it, something would happen, and she would let it slip from her grasp. The cold, shaking fear of humiliation and public ridicule would clasp her in its grip, and she would desperately search for the closest place to hide. "It'll come," Elaine told herself. She sighed, wondering how long it would take. "It'll come back...."

Stately Ambrose Whitley was walking through the main parlor off the foyer just as Elaine reached the bottom of the great staircase. He raised his bushy gray eyebrows in surprise. "Riding a bit late, aren't you, Miss Elaine? It's after dark. I hope there wasn't any trouble...?"

She tossed an affectionate smile at him over her shoulder as she ran up the stairs. "No trouble, Ambrose. I was just talking to Beau. Oh, Ambrose, could you tell Mrs. Adams I'll be down to dinner as soon as I get out of the shower? And Beau will be joining us later, too."

"Of course, miss," Ambrose said rather stiffly even for a man who prided himself on his formality.

Ambrose tut-tutted disapprovingly as he turned to carry out Elaine's request. Ambrose had liked Beau from the first. He still liked him, he supposed. He just didn't think he quite trusted him to have anything unchaperoned to do with Elaine Faust. She was a warmhearted, charming young woman who'd already had more than enough misery with the opposite sex. The poor girl didn't deserve a heated affair with a muscular Adonis with no portfolio and no visible chance of having anything to offer her in the foreseeable future. Ambrose had always rather inclined toward arranged marriages for that very reason. It rid the institution of the dreadful aftereffects of thinking with one's hormones. Marriage was much too serious a matter to be decided by some sort of glandular attack.

Ambrose walked toward the kitchen, mumbling to himself about the foolishness of pretty young women, the questionable motives of some of the males of the species and the urgent need for Elaine's brother, Richard, to take matters in hand before some additional hurt came to the young mistress of the estate. Poor thing, she was still a shadow of her former vivacious self. But she was getting better, Ambrose noted with pride. She was a thoroughbred at heart.

Ambrose was confident that Richard would soon arrive and see what was happening, then intervene in the way that only the inimitable Richard Faust could: decisively. Ambrose just wished he were already there.

Two hours later, as the grandfather clock in its rich mahogany cabinet chimed eight o'clock in round golden tones, Elaine led Beau through the open double doors to the quiet little study tucked away behind the stairwell in the center hall. Ambrose had just laid out an ornate silver tea service on a Queen Anne table, which had been pulled away from the wall just for that purpose. The heavy hunter-green-and-gold brocade curtains formed an elegant backdrop to the intimate tea-for-two setting. Otherwise, there was certainly nothing particularly romantic about the room at all.

The chairs were hardwood. Hand-embroidered cushions were the only concessions to creature comfort. The walls were lined from ceiling to floor with books. Unlike the Faust library and the first-edition books that were located in two other parts of the mansion, these books were frequently used in making operational and planning decisions affecting the estate. There were agricultural and legal tomes, books on local history, some of the estate records, and various books that didn't seem to fit anywhere else and were pushed out of the way here.

Ambrose withdrew to the door. He paused with his hands on the ornate turn-of-the-century doorknobs and directed a penetrating look at Beau. The butler's meaning would have been clear to a blind man. *Don't be anything less than a perfect gentleman to the gentle-hearted lady of the house.*

It was basically the same nonverbal message that Ambrose had sent him over dinner a little while earlier.

"Ring if you require anything further," Ambrose intoned. He left, closing the doors firmly after him.

Elaine poured the tea and handed Beau a delicate cup and silver teaspoon. She met his eyes as he took the fine bone china from her.

"Sorry about that," she murmured. Her cheeks were a warm shade of coral again.

"For what?" For a moment he had no idea what she was apologizing for. Then he glanced from her darkened cheeks to the doors Ambrose had just closed with such a clear warning. He leaned back in the stiff wooden chair and stretched out his legs, crossing them at the ankles in relaxation. He grinned wryly. "You're apologizing for Ambrose's warning me to behave myself?"

Elaine stirred a lump of sugar into her tea, but she made herself look at Beau when she answered him. "Yes."

He rested his teacup on his thigh. "Ambrose is very astute," he said.

Elaine put her teaspoon down and sipped the Prince of Wales tea, sorry she wasn't English and likely to be fortified by the drink.

"Ambrose is overprotective," she said smoothly. She looked at Beau again. "I don't need to be hovered over, you know." She fingered the teacup. "I made a mistake when I married Cam. I know it. Everybody knows it. Nothing is going to change that. It was a terrible shock to discover just how horrible a mistake it was, but..." She shrugged her shoulders a little. "The worst is long past now." She managed a small but very genuine smile. "Ambrose has loved me for a long time. He just can't accept that Cam, or anyone, would treat me the way he did. I don't think he realizes that I'm getting over it, either. But he'll believe it eventually. It's just going to take him some time."

Beau had been watching her as she spoke. When she fell silent, he lifted his teacup and took a swallow of his tea. "You inspire people to protect you, do you know that?" he asked at last.

Elaine sighed, and a smile glimmered on her lips. "Yes. I guess I do." She tilted her head to one side, and her eyes grew distant. "When I was very small, I was Father's little princess," she said softly, her face warm with love. "And then when I was a girl, my scowling brother, Richard, scared boys away left and right...." She laughed again, and some of her youthful happiness came through in the lightheartedness of the sound. She glanced across at Beau, and her laughter faded into the smile of a woman made wiser by life's tragedies. "Then Richard grew up and went away, and I, like an oversheltered lamb, walked right into Cam's matrimonial trap." She grimaced and rose to pour herself another cup of tea. "I rest my case against overprotection. Would you like another cup?"

Beau held out his cup, and she poured. "Since you don't want to be protected from life's earthier problems, you'll probably be happy to hear what I want to talk with you about," he said wryly.

She carefully put the tall silver teapot down on its silver tray, but he saw no sudden tensing in her fingers, no awkward stiffening of her spine. Perhaps the relaxed conversation at dinner and the relative safety of sitting in her own home were helping her, he thought. Or maybe she *was* recovering.

Elaine sat down again in the chair across from him. The soft wool sweater she was wearing enveloped her in a graceful swath of rich sea hues. Her loosely styled black slacks swung about her legs as she crossed them at the knee. She had dressed in a low-key, stylish fashion. Feminine without being provocative.

Except that anything she wore was equally provocative as far as Beau was concerned, simply because Elaine was wearing it.

"I'm listening," she prodded him cautiously. "You were going to tell me about Babs Carlton...."

"Yes," he agreed with distaste. "Her husband is Enoch Carlton." He waited, watching to see if the name meant anything to her.

She wrinkled her nose thoughtfully. "The name's familiar," she murmured, "but... I don't think I've ever met him." There was a tentative light of recognition in her eyes as she looked at Beau. "Isn't his name always appearing on those rich-and-famous lists?"

Beau nodded. "That's Carlton. His main business is basically a collection of holding companies. On paper he's worth quite a bit."

"Go on," Elaine encouraged him. Then she remembered what Beau had told her the other day... about the wife of a wealthy man and Beau's sleeping with her and the husband's having ruined Beau's father in revenge. She drew in a breath.

Beau nodded, and the grim smile on his lips grew hard and cynical.

"That's right," he said in a low, angry voice. "Babs Carlton was the woman I slept with."

He watched the delicate play of emotions across Elaine's face. First came embarrassment, quickly followed by a determined effort to take this information in her stride. He tried to steel himself against the protective feelings she aroused in him. Her father, brother and butler weren't the only ones she affected that way, he thought bitterly.

"I'm sorry, Elaine," he said tightly. "Would you rather I stayed away from the meet?"

She lowered her eyes and absently fingered the soft black fabric of her slacks. She saw Babs's cool, beautiful face swimming before her eyes. No wonder Beau had been attracted enough to... She forced the other images away. A rush of jealousy hit her, though she knew she had no right to be jealous of Beau's involvement with other women.

"No. I don't think it would help if you stayed away from the meet," she replied quietly. She raised her eyes to his, and they were the steady, deep blue of a woman who was sure of her path. "It never helps to run away from things." That was one lesson she'd learned beyond any doubt this past year.

There was a moment of silence broken only by the muffled ticking of the grandfather clock as they each kept to their own thoughts.

"Thinking of your own devils?" Beau finally asked.

She smiled wanly. "Yes. I can remember how horrible it was when Cam showed up at that lawn party and everyone knew what had been happening. They all just fell silent and watched us face each other down." She closed her eyes for just a moment. Then the pain subsided, more quickly than it used to, for which she was grateful. The steady look she gave Beau underscored what she was saying to him. "It's like my going to Margaret's party. It's better to confront your enemies. I think you should hunt with us tomorrow, just as we'd planned."

He moved his legs restlessly and frowned. "If it were just me, I wouldn't hesitate. That wasn't why I wanted to talk to you about her."

Elaine saw the toughness in him and realized he was telling the truth. "Why, then?" she asked. "Certainly scandal is nothing new to me or my brother," she pointed out with a rueful laugh. Then a thought occurred to her. Perhaps there was someone else he wanted to protect. "Does Meg know?" she asked uncertainly. She remembered how close Meg and Beau had seemed. Richard, she was sure, had even been jealous of Beau for a while. Another sliver of jealousy stabbed into her heart.

"Meg knows," Beau said, squashing that theory flat. "She heard the gossip a few months ago. I guessed what she'd heard and told her the truth one day."

"Oh," Elaine murmured. From the way he'd spoken, Meg had clearly remained a loyal friend to him in spite of the problem he'd gotten himself into. She forced herself to get on with the discussion. "What are you worried about, then?" she asked briskly.

"I don't want Babs to get her claws into you."

Her mouth opened in surprise. "Why would she do that?"

"To get at me."

She stared at him. "But how would she get at you that way? And how on earth could she do anything to me?"

"She's a very shrewd woman. If she sees us together, she'll realize there's something there...."

Elaine felt herself go cold, then hot. Her eyes clouded defensively, and she crossed her arms over her chest. "Something there?" she echoed distantly.

She stared at him, daring him to say what he was implying. She'd already urged him not to say things that couldn't be unsaid, and here he was on the brink of doing just that. After all the cold shoulders he'd given her, too. Was there no middle ground with the man? she wondered. And the moment she wondered it, she knew in her heart that there wasn't where he was concerned. She felt the heat rise in her cheeks, and she knew what he was going to say as surely as if he'd already said it. In her heart, she'd known it for some time. But her mind had carefully held it away, protecting her from the acknowledgment.

"Yes," he said softly. The grayness of his eyes had almost drowned out the blue now. "There's something between us. You know it as well as I do. If you hadn't been through such a hell of a time, you would have recognized it a long time ago. But you were too hurt, so I let you keep telling me it was your soft heart and your willingness to be friends with everyone in sight." He stopped and expelled a long, frustrated breath. "But that's not it. And Babs Carlton is a clever bitch. She'll take one look at you and me and know that I want you."

Elaine shut her eyes and put her hands over her ears. "Don't say that," she whispered desperately. "I told you not to say anything that couldn't be unsaid. Please...we were going to forget what happened the other day.... You promised...."

Regaining her sense of control, she let her hands drop back to her lap and reopened her eyes.

Beau nodded, recalling their conversation and appearing cynically amused by it.

"I was to turn my attentions to greener pastures, and you weren't going to be bothered by me again. We would politely act as if nothing happened. Everything would go on as usual."

"Yes," Elaine said quietly. Her look was almost pleading. "Is that so impossible to do? Is it asking so much?"

Beau laid his teacup aside and leaned forward in his chair, uncrossing his legs and resting his elbows on his knees.

"Oh, I can keep my hands off you," he assured her bluntly, his natural charm softening the words a little. "And I probably wouldn't have too much trouble finding all the greener pastures I had time for."

He noticed a small flash of fire and pain in Elaine's eyes and forced himself to ignore it. Under other circumstances he would have let himself believe she was jealous. He didn't want to even consider that as a possibility now.

"Well, then, for heaven's sake, what is the problem?" Elaine said, this time becoming angry herself. "Why are you bringing all this up?"

"I want you to be prepared," he said softly. "I don't want you to be hurt. If you know what kind of woman she is, and the kind of weapons she likes to use, maybe you can stay out of her range. Maybe her arrows will fall short."

The clock rang the hour. Elaine could only look at him, drowning in his eyes for a long moment. "You're not the tough son of a gun you make yourself out to be," she said softly.

He laughed harshly. "Oh, yes, I am," he retorted. "And if it weren't for the veneer of my Southern gentleman's upbringing, you'd see it more easily."

She smiled at him. "Your charm doesn't fool me a bit," she argued. "But... what weapons do you think she'll be using?" she asked, bringing him back to the topic at hand.

"I've been very successful with the ladies," he said flatly. "Babs will assume I've been successful with you."

Elaine ran her tongue nervously over her lips. "I see." It was all she could think of to say. "Well, let her talk," she declared, lifting her chin proudly. "I don't care."

Beau admired her courage. "I think it would be wiser if I just weren't around tomorrow," he said softly. "Why put yourself in that kind of situation if we can avoid it?"

Elaine rose and shook her head. "No. We need you tomorrow. Bradley's counting on you to ride one of his hunters. I'm counting on you to help keep an eye on the field." She suddenly realized how much she'd been looking forward to just having him there. Her mouth acquired a stubborn set. "You're supposed to be there. I won't let you back out because of something so inconsequential."

He rose to his feet and shoved his hands into the pockets of his corduroy slacks. "All right," he drawled. He looked her over from head to toe in a long, sweeping assessment. He wasn't too pleased at her choice, but at least he'd offered her an out. "Let me know if you change your mind."

He was going to walk by her and leave the room, but he found that he couldn't without touching her again. He reached out and cupped her face with one warm hand, bending to kiss her good-night.

It seemed so natural, it never occurred to her to flinch away. She let him kiss her cheek, and her eyes half closed as his firm lips touched her overheated skin. His breath caressed her, and she barely managed to swallow the moan in her throat before he could hear it.

She opened her eyes and stared at him. "Why did you do that?" she whispered.

He looked at her, studying her face as if committing it to memory. "I didn't want your only memory of me to be the kiss I forced on you in anger the other day," he admitted somewhat reluctantly. "Consider this my apology."

He walked out of the room, and Elaine stood with her fingers touching her cheek where his lips had been.

"Oh, no," she murmured, sinking down into her chair. "I can't fall in love with you," she whispered mournfully. "I mustn't. I *must not*...."

And there was Babs Carlton to face, as well. Dealing with Babs had to be easier than confronting her feelings for Beau. She almost looked forward to the other woman's arrival. Maybe it would take her mind off the feelings Beau was arousing in her.

Delicious, intoxicating, dangerous feelings...

Chapter 8

Beau was talking with huntsman John Luvell when he heard the approaching voices. It was early in the day, but the bustle around the stable was already considerable: horses' hooves clopped as they were led to the paddock for saddling; grooms did last-minute checks of the bridles and hunting gear; eager foxhounds whined and scrapped in the kennels down the road; tires ground against the driveway as cars and vans arrived. But over it all, Beau could still hear Elaine's soft, sweet voice. Two others were with her. He recognized Meg's laugh, then Richard greeting his staff and various members of the hunt.

"Okay, John." Beau turned his attention back to the dubious huntsman. "We'll try to keep the least experienced guests away from your prize babies if they lose the scent and you have to recast."

Luvell grumbled that he wasn't going to excuse *anyone*, no matter how green, if a horse kicked so much as a single hair on one of his precious young foxhounds. Then he mounted his horse with a slight grunt of exertion and rode toward the kennels to take charge of his barking four-legged children.

As Luvell left, a tall handsome man strode through the stable and into the paddock where Beau stood ready to greet him. He was dressed in a scarlet coat and pale breeches and walked with the iron confidence that was his due. He was Richard Faust, Master of the Foxgrove Hunt, and owner of the estate. He stopped a few feet from Beau and nodded pleasantly.

"Good morning, Beau. I see you've got everyone going."

Richard Faust's eyes were the same dark shade as his sister's. Where hers could be warm and tender, however, Richard's tended to be rakish and hard—except when his attention was focused on his lovely young wife, of course. When he looked at Meg, his eyes were as dark and tender as midnight on a midsummer's eve.

Beau nodded hello and led Richard's big gray hunter out of the box stall nearest them.

"Welcome back," Beau said. He grinned at Richard. "I won't ask if you had a good time."

Richard smiled wryly. "Thanks. You're about the only one who hasn't."

Beau laughed and checked the hunter's martingale. "I have great confidence in Meg," he explained in amusement.

Richard raised a dark eyebrow but ignored the teasing remark. He remembered the friendship between his wife and Beau, and he accepted Beau's comment in good humor. Even if he hadn't, he wouldn't have taken offense. He felt he owed Beau a great deal. The man had been an additional bodyguard for Elaine during a very tense couple of weeks. As far as Richard was concerned, Beau was part of the Foxgrove family for as long as he cared to stay.

"I'm glad to hear of your high opinion of my wife," Richard retorted, amused.

Beau handed Richard the reins and looked in the direction of the feminine voices just inside the stable. Someone had stopped Meg, and she and Elaine were answering questions and trying to extricate themselves without being rude.

"Meg's one of my favorite people," Beau agreed easily.

Richard patted the big gelding's head and neck, obliquely turning to study his stable manager's expression. "You seem thoughtful today," he observed. "Everything okay?" He hadn't really talked to Beau since he'd left on his somewhat unorthodox honeymoon.

Beau shrugged. "No problems at the stable. The accounts are in good condition. All the horses are coming along well. The vet was here last week to check on a bowed tendon that isn't improving fast enough to suit me, but other than that, I've got no complaints, I guess."

Elaine came into the area where Beau and Richard stood talking, and Richard noticed how Beau glanced at his sister, taking her in with one great, all-encompassing look, as if to make sure she was all right. Or to fill himself with the sight of her.

Richard's hand stilled on the big gray's shoulder. He looked at his sister. Elaine looked straight at Beau, unblinking, as if she were determined to be unmoved by him. Odd, Richard thought. His dark eyes went to his stable manager.

"No problems at all?" Faust repeated carefully.

Beau's jaw became noticeably solid, and his eyes were a little harder when he looked at Richard. "Nothing I can't handle."

Richard was tempted to draw Elaine aside right then and ask her what the hell was going on, but before he could, Meg threw herself into Richard's arms and kissed him full on the mouth. Automatically Richard's arm went around his auburn-haired wife, and he kissed her back.

She pulled away a little, laughing.

"You're not supposed to kiss the Master of the hunt," Richard declared in a tone of mock reprimand. He let his hand slide down her hunt jacket until it was dangerously near the top of her derriere. "Haven't you read the rules?" he murmured, his eyes glittering.

Meg laughingly slapped away his hand and audaciously kissed him soundly on the lips again. "I don't know what it says about kissing in the hunt regulations, but I know how to read between the lines of our marriage certificate, Richard," she retorted tenderly. She gazed adoringly at her tall, dark and handsome lover. Then she twisted a little away from him to grin conspiratorially at Beau and Elaine. "His bark's worse than his bite. Think of all the years I wasted being intimidated by this man!"

Richard laughed and pinched her lightly on the bottom, at which Meg softly squealed in protest. "Marriage certainly hasn't improved your respect for authority," he observed in amusement. He added softly, "But then, that wasn't why I married you, was it?"

Meg laughed and blushed prettily.

Elaine looked at her brother and sister-in-law and shook her head. "Look," she suggested half-seriously, "maybe you two should just retire to Richard's suite and forget about the hunt...."

Richard looked interested in the idea, but Meg shook her head energetically. "Oh, no! I won't have it said that I interfered with your duties," she swore nobly.

Richard managed to look stoic and said, "I don't mind." Then he whispered in Meg's ear, "I'm sure we could find some other duties that could be performed in my suite."

She blushed, kissed him soundly and murmured, "Don't tempt me, love." She grabbed Beau by the arm and said, "You'd better show me to my horse or we may never get this show on the road! Is Sinbad ready?"

Beau grinned and nodded, shrugging helplessly as Meg dragged him away. "I'll be back in a minute," he told Elaine.

She nodded, smiling a little stiffly. The teasing banter, with all its intimate undertones, had begun to make her feel a little uncomfortable. She wished that she hadn't had to stand there and listen to it, like some sort of fifth wheel. She knew that was ridiculously selfish of her, and from the pleased and contented look on her brother's face, she knew she would probably be hearing a lot more of the very same kind of repartee in the future. It wouldn't do for her to be a dog in the manger about it, she told herself. She'd get used to it.

Beau emerged leading Mystic. He was handing the reins to Elaine when Babs Carlton made her grand entrance. Elaine looked at Beau and saw the touch of grimness in his face that the woman's arrival had brought.

"Shall I throw her out?" Elaine asked through gritted teeth.

Beau relaxed a little and a half grin touched his lips. "Would you do that?" he asked softly.

"Yes. I would."

Their eyes met, and he felt desire twist in his belly. He laced his fingers and gave Elaine a leg up, letting his hands linger under the toe of her boot, all the while cursing himself for a fool.

"Thanks," he said quietly. "It's a generous offer."

Elaine looked over Beau's dusky blond head at the elegantly attired woman standing not too far behind him. Babs Carlton was chatting with Pamela Longacre, but from the occasional glances Babs was casting in Beau's direction, it clearly wouldn't be long before she ditched Pamela and made her way to Beau.

"No," Elaine said. "There's nothing generous about it. It's actually rather selfish of me, to tell you the truth."

He held Mystic's head while she double-checked her stirrup leathers. It wasn't necessary to hold the big chestnut hunter, but it was an excuse to be near her—and to avoid confronting Babs—for a few brief seconds more.

Babs tired of being ignored by him, however, and came forward, walking in a desultory way and tapping her hunting whip carelessly against her boot.

"Well, well, well," she murmured with great interest. "We meet again, Beau. It's certainly becoming a small world, isn't it?"

Beau released the reins as Elaine gathered them between her gloved fingers. He turned and faced Babs, his face impassive. "Good morning, Babs. I'd been told you would be hunting with us today."

Babs nodded. The smile on her lips was red and confident. She looked a little bit like a woman holding court with a vanquished enemy.

Beau ignored it. Elaine stiffened slightly, and a small flame lit her eyes. Babs smiled at her.

"Good morning. It's Elaine, isn't it? I believe we met at Margaret Innery's...perhaps you don't remember...." Babs let her sentence trail off apologetically.

The thinly veiled hint that she had been too drunk to remember rankled. Elaine smiled rather grandly. "Of course I recall," she said. "I believe you were house hunting."

"Yes." Babs let her eyes roam over the stable, over Elaine—and over Beau.

Elaine felt her lips threaten to turn hard with anger, and she forced herself to be as polite as possible. "Have you found anything yet?"

"No... but I have hope...."

The sound of horses and hounds gathering in the pasture drew Elaine's attention. She was one of the whippers-in, and she had to be there to help the huntsman. "Have you hunted before?" she asked courteously.

Babs laughed, and her eyes slid to Beau, who was standing there with his arms crossed and his face set. "Oh, yes. Beau and I have hunted together. I'm sure he knows just what kind of mount I like...." Her eyes slid back to Elaine.

Elaine couldn't keep the anger from her eyes. She knew Babs saw it. She also knew that she didn't care. "Then I'll leave you in his hands," she said carefully. She glanced at Beau as she turned Mystic toward the amassing riders. "See you later."

She touched her heels lightly to Mystic's chestnut flanks and joined her brother and the others.

Beau walked into the stable with Babs following along, her unspoken questions clogging the air between them. He had already had one of Bradley's hunters prepared for her. The horse was tied to a metal ring in the wall nearest the stable exit.

"Here you go, Babs," he said evenly, handing her the reins.

She smiled and let the horse outside. "Beau?" she called.

He came to the exit. In the distance he could see Elaine watching them. Everyone else was talking or looking in the direction of the kennels as the huntsman brought down the pack.

"What is it?" Beau asked coldly.

Babs gathered the reins and lifted her left foot a few inches off the ground, bending her knee.

"Could you give me a leg up?" she drawled. "For old times' sake?"

A couple of riders heard her comment, and their heads turned in surprise. Beau didn't want to see how much of a scene Babs was willing to create if he rejected her outright. The last time he'd rejected her, she'd ruined him and his entire family. He wasn't going to let her do that a second time. Beau went to her, laced his fingers and cupped his hand beneath her knee.

"One, two, three..." he said. On "three" she vaulted up, but on "one" and "two," her sultry eyes had been staring into his. He felt nauseated and infuriated.

She leaned down and murmured. "Thanks, darlin'."

Since Elaine was on the other side, she couldn't have seen that Babs hadn't come closer than a half dozen inches from his face. Beau realized that to Elaine it could easily appear that Babs had bent down and kissed him.

Angrily Beau looked at Babs and asked, "Tell me, Babs, how's your husband?"

Babs laughed softly and checked the strap on her hunting hat. "My husband is away, darlin'." She said in a soft voice so that the words didn't carry, "And he believes what I tell him. But then, you already knew that, didn't you?"

She turned the horse away and rode toward the gathering riders. And Beau cursed the day he had ever laid eyes on her.

Elaine was sitting quietly on Mystic, watching intently as the huntsman cast the hounds in a long semicircle through heavy cover, wishing her heart was in the day's hunting. She'd enjoyed it in the past...the excitement, the anticipation, the thrill of sighting the quarry, the challenge in pursuing the hounds over all kinds of terrain....

Her heart just wasn't in it today. She dutifully performed her role: keeping between the hounds and the field; shouting "halloa" when she sighted their first fox many miles earlier; urging the hounds on and generally doing what the huntsman or Richard needed to have done. But she kept wondering what was going on in the field. Not with all the riders, of course. Just with two riders in particular. Most especially Beau.

The hounds were snorting and tunneling and searching for a trace of scent in the heavy underbrush, and Elaine decided they probably wouldn't be helped by her plaintive staring at them. She turned a little and casually looked over the field of riders. They'd stopped a little ways away and were talking quietly or sitting in silence, hoping that the hounds would come across something soon.

Babs was smiling at Meg and trying to engage her in conversation. Elaine could tell that Meg was trying to be polite. Then Elaine found Beau and sighed. He was near the back of the field, surrounded by juvenile riders and green mounts, trying to keep them from doing any harm to themselves or anyone else.

He must have sensed her eyes on him, because he stopped in the middle of what he was saying and turned to look at her. Even over the distance separating them, Elaine felt the impact of his gaze.

"What have you done to me, Beau?" Elaine murmured to herself.

She felt uneasy all of a sudden and looked behind her to discover that Babs Carlton was studying her. Then Babs glanced in Beau's direction, and a strange smile illuminated the woman's face as her knowing gaze returned to Elaine.

Elaine felt faintly ill. Babs Carlton was a woman scorned, and Elaine had the distinct impression that she was still out for blood. It was a chilling thought. Beau had been realistic when he'd told her that he thought Babs might try to sink her claws into her. But what could Babs do to her? Elaine wondered. Considering the havoc Babs had already wreaked on Beau, Elaine didn't really want to let herself imagine the possibilities.

Before Elaine could think any longer about Babs's possible avenues of revenge, the foxhounds began to cry, and five couples tore out of the covert and dashed across a ditch into the field nearby, their tails feathering vigorously as they ran.

Elaine stood in her stirrups and pointed just as the huntsman blew his horn. There was no time to think about anything except the business at hand, and she turned her mount after the hounds.

She jumped Mystic over the first ditch and galloped him up the hill, taking a pair of fallen timbers with effortless ease. Behind her she could hear the thundering hooves of the rest of the hunt. She began to feel a certain sense of dread. If she took a spill, she wasn't sure how hard Babs Carlton would try to avoid trampling her. That thought had never seriously crossed her mind before. Members of the Foxgrove Hunt were always careful to give one another plenty of room. No one overrode their mounts or cut in front. If something like that did happen, the Master took the offending rider aside and thoroughly lectured him or her. The offense was never repeated.

The hounds had poured under, through and over a split rail fence, and Elaine rode her hunter straight toward it, riding far enough behind the hounds not to accidentally step on one if he lost his footing. Mystic gathered his hindquarters, tucked his forelegs and neatly cleared the paneling that the hunt had placed over the farmer's rustic fencing. As Mystic galloped freely across the open pasture on the other side, Elaine patted him on the neck. He wouldn't fail her. He was an experienced field hunter with a steady disposition, and he was always ready to obey her commands. Mystic would keep her in the saddle.

And then there was Beau. He was riding somewhere behind her, in the rear of the field. She knew he was paying very close attention to what she was doing, in order to keep the less experienced members from falling into harm's way. Considering the warning he'd given her last night, she imagined he was probably also keeping an eye on her for other, more personal, reasons, as well. For that she was now quite grateful.

She wished that he could be riding beside her, close enough for her to touch his hand. An unfamiliar ache squeezed her chest.

The hounds suddenly streaked off to the east, and Elaine had no further time to long for Beau. She turned Mystic and followed the baying hounds at a hard gallop. For once she prayed that the hounds would run the fox to ground quickly.

The hunt couldn't end too soon to suit her. Come on, fox, find your hole and dive into it....

The sun was falling in the western sky by the time the hunt turned toward home. The huntsman herded his panting hounds up over the rise that led to the kennel as the dusty and tired riders rode at a steady walk toward paddock or trailer. A few rode directly home across the fields, waving farewell as they departed.

Elaine was riding next to Richard and Meg, grateful that she could stop worrying about possible disasters in the hunting field involving Babs Carlton. Babs had ridden ahead and was already dismounting and handing her borrowed hunter to one of the grooms. Just when Elaine was cheerfully expecting to see her make a grand exit, the blonde stopped to talk with one of the unattached males standing nearby.

"Damn," Elaine muttered.

Richard and Meg both looked at her in surprise. They noted the direction of her gaze and looked at each other. It was Meg who asked the question that was hovering on both their tongues.

"What's going on, Elaine? The undercurrents between you and that woman are strong enough to wash a whale out to sea."

Elaine laughed. "Well said, Meg." She lowered her voice and glanced cautiously at her dearest and oldest friend. "Beau told me that you heard the rumors about him...."

Meg seemed startled at the sudden shift in the conversation. Then she glanced in genuine surprise at the willowy blonde chatting up the very flattered male standing next to her. She looked back at Elaine. "Do you mean that Babs Carlton is the woman?" she asked, shocked.

Elaine nodded grimly.

Richard cleared his throat in annoyance. "Will one of you ladies tell me what's going on?" he demanded. His dark brows formed a threatening line.

Meg hesitated and looked at Elaine. "Maybe you should tell him. After all, he's *your* brother...."

Elaine grimaced. "He's *your* husband. *You* tell him."

Richard laughed and managed to appear outraged at the same time. "Will you two stop passing me back and forth between you like a hot potato?" He shrewdly selected a new approach. "If neither of you has the courage to speak up, I'll just have to go inquire of Mrs. Carlton." He prepared to dismount.

"Richard!"

"Don't you dare!"

Elaine and Meg glared at him. Elaine gave Meg a pleading look.

"Meg can explain to you in private," Elaine suggested earnestly. She dismounted and led her horse to his stall before Meg could object.

Meg glanced at her husband and smiled gently. "I guess you're stuck with me."

The Master of the hunt removed his hat and leaned toward her, placing a warm kiss on her lips. Smiling, he murmured, "Just my luck..."

Elaine noticed Eddie as she led Mystic into the stall. "Eddie," she called out. "I thought you had the day off."

He hovered shyly near the corner for a moment, then carefully entered the stall after her. He closed and latched the door with the slow attention he always employed. Hesitantly, he smiled and shifted his weight from one foot to the other and then back again.

"Yeah," he admitted. "Beau told me to stay away. He said I could do whatever I want, said it was my day off, and I didn't have to work. Not a bit." Eddie's fractured smile fell a little. He looked embarrassed. "But I couldn't think of anything else to do. And I always kinda liked watching the people all dressed up in the fancy red jackets and shiny black boots with the foxhounds jumping all around and the horses so eager to go... I thought maybe Beau wouldn't mind if I just came and stood in the corner kind of quietly. Out of the way, I'll help, too, if anybody wants me to, if you don't think Beau'll mind." He frowned anxiously. "You don't think he'll be mad at me, do you, Miss Elaine?"

Elaine smiled at him reassuringly. "No, Eddie. Beau will understand." She lifted the saddle off and then the bridle.

Taking care of Mystic was relaxing, she thought. And the physical activity kept her out of the way, which wasn't so bad, either. Let Richard and Meg say goodbye to the guests. No one would really mind. Least of all her.

Babs's voice floated through the air, and Elaine grimaced, mimicking the saccharine tone as she mouthed the cloying words. Then she noticed the frozen look on poor Eddie's face, and she stopped.

"What's the matter, Eddie?" she asked gently. She stopped currying the hunter and stood looking at the young stable hand, who'd gone nearly white and was staring fearfully between the stall slats in the direction from which Babs's voice had come. Elaine went over to him and touched him lightly on the shoulder. "Eddie?"

He nearly cringed. When he looked up at her, Elaine thought she'd never seen him appear so upset.

"Is that...Mrs. Carlton?" he asked in a voice barely above a whisper.

Elaine nodded. "Yes."

His eyes became as round as saucers, and he slouched back against the stall, as if hoping he might sink into it and become invisible.

"She must be why Beau told me not to come," he murmured, staring at Elaine. He looked utterly miserable. "I sure wish I'd done what he said."

"She's leaving," Elaine pointed out quietly, perplexed at his reaction and trying to be reassuring. "Do you know her?" she asked, hoping the question wouldn't make him feel even worse.

He stared at her and nodded. "Yeah." He swallowed, and his Adam's apple bobbed painfully. "She sure hates me. Thinks I'm dumber than horse sh—" He glanced at Elaine and swallowed the word he'd been about to say, replacing it with another one he thought she wouldn't mind. "...manure." He wiped a trembling hand over his eyes. "If she tells you anything about me, don't believe it, would you?"

Elaine smiled at him reassuringly. Gently, she promised, "I wouldn't believe it if she engraved it on a silver plate, Eddie."

He breathed a sigh of relief and straightened out, trying to find his spine. He looked at her gratefully. "Thanks, Miss Elaine. You and Beau and everybody here sure have been good to me."

Elaine shrugged, as if it were only natural. "You've been a good worker, Eddie. Besides, we like you."

He looked as happy as a puppy then. "Thanks, ma'am." He looked nervously in the direction of the closest exit. "Do you think I'll miss her if I go that way now?"

Elaine grinned and nodded. "Yup. She'll never see you." Before he left, she asked curiously, "Did Beau know how you felt about her when he hired you?"

Eddie nodded. "Yeah. He was the only one willing to give me a chance. The only one who believed me, instead of her."

Elaine felt a lump form in her throat as she envisioned the scene. Beau had been able to help Eddie, even though he'd been unable to save himself from Babs Carlton's wrath. "I'm glad he did, Eddie," Elaine told him. "And if you would rather stay, I'll make sure she doesn't bother you."

Eddie looked at her as if she'd just dropped down from heaven. "Oh, thank you, Miss Elaine." He headed toward the stall door. "But if you don't mind, I think I'd feel better if I were somewhere else altogether."

"I understand," Elaine said with a smile as he ducked past her and slipped out of the stall.

He made a beeline to the nearest stable exit, leaving the same way he'd arrived, through the doors that no one else was using. Only a few people saw him leave, and they paid no attention. After all, it was only Eddie.

With so many horses to be taken care of, Elaine had no problem keeping busy for the next hour and a half. By the time she finished up with the last one, most of the members of the hunt had left. The stable hands were wandering away, pleased to have the rest of the day off.

Elaine stretched and reached for her hunting bowler, which she'd put down some time earlier. She sensed someone's presence and turned quickly to see who it was.

"Beau! It's you." She sighed in relief, clutching her hard hat tightly to her chest. "I thought you might have gone."

Beau was standing on the other side of the stall from her, leaning his forearms against the top slat, watching her. "No," he said. "I was just taking a last look at the horses. Are you about done?"

Elaine laughed, and she could feel her nervousness bubble up inside again. It was Beau, she knew, who was bringing on her edginess. Beau and the fact that he'd said he wanted her. And the realization that she was tempted to do something about that. She looked at the horse she'd just finished grooming, mainly to drag her eyes and thoughts away from Beau.

"Yes. I'm done." She glanced down at herself ruefully. "The horses may look clean now, but I got what they got rid of, I'm afraid." She moved toward the stall door and carefully slipped out. "Don't forget, after you get cleaned up, you're expected at the buffet we're having for everyone up at the house."

His eyebrows lifted. "Everyone?" He was looking at her as if he didn't particularly care what the answer was, even while he was questioning what she meant by it.

Elaine cleared her throat awkwardly. "Everyone at Foxgrove. It's a sort of family get-together...a welcome back for Richard and Meg." She couldn't seem to free her gaze from his. A little unsteadily she added, "Richard had it catered. Mrs. Adams didn't have to cook or anything. If you don't come, I'll have to bring your food to you...."

"That probably wouldn't be a good idea," he said reluctantly.

"No?" she said. "For you to come to the buffet? What harm can that do?"

He was shaking his head. "No. You bringing food to me," he explained. His eyes traveled over her as if he couldn't quite keep himself from it.

Elaine couldn't have agreed more. Bringing him food could well be disastrous. Especially considering the effect his merely looking at her was having on her temperature and heart rate. She wanted to close her eyes and groan. Instead,

FIRST-CLASS ROMANCE

Mail This Heart Today!

And We'll Deliver:

**4 FREE BOOKS
A FREE DIGITAL CLOCK/CALENDAR
PLUS
A SURPRISE MYSTERY BONUS
TO YOUR DOOR!**

See Inside For More Details

SILHOUETTE DELIVERS FIRST-CLASS ROMANCE— DIRECT TO YOUR DOOR

Mail the Heart sticker on the postpaid order card today and you'll receive:

—4 new Silhouette Intimate Moments® novels—FREE
—a lovely lucite digital clock/calendar—FREE
—and a surprise mystery bonus—FREE

But that's not all. You'll also get:

Free Home Delivery
When you subscribe to Silhouette Intimate Moments®, the excitement, romance and faraway adventures of these novels can be yours for previewing in the convenience of your own home. Every month we'll deliver 4 new books right to your door. If you decide to keep them, they'll be yours for only $2.74* each—that's 21 cents below the cover price, and there is *no* extra charge for postage and handling! There is no obligation to buy—you can cancel at any time simply by writing "cancel" on your statement or by returning a shipment of books to us at our cost.

Free Monthly Newsletter
It's the indispensable insider's look at our most popular writers and their upcoming novels. Now you can have a behind-the-scenes look at the fascinating world of Silhouette! It's an added bonus you'll look forward to every month!

Special Extras—FREE
Because our home subscribers are our most valued readers, we'll be sending you additional free gifts from time to time in your monthly book shipments as a token of our appreciation.

OPEN YOUR MAILBOX TO A WORLD OF LOVE AND ROMANCE EACH MONTH. JUST COMPLETE, DETACH AND MAIL YOUR FREE-OFFER CARD TODAY!

*Terms and prices subject to change without notice. Sales tax applicable in N.Y. and Iowa.
© 1989 HARLEQUIN ENTERPRISES LIMITED

FREE! lucite digital clock/calendar

You'll love your digital clock/calendar! The changeable month-at-a-glance calendar pops out and can be replaced with your favorite photograph. It is yours FREE as our gift of love!

Silhouette Intimate Moments®

FREE OFFER CARD

4 FREE BOOKS

FREE DIGITAL CLOCK/CALENDAR

FREE MYSTERY BONUS

PLACE HEART STICKER HERE

FREE HOME DELIVERY

FREE FACT-FILLED NEWSLETTER

MORE SURPRISES THROUGHOUT THE YEAR—FREE

☑ **YES!** Please send me four Silhouette Intimate Moments® novels, free, along with my free digital clock/calendar and my free mystery gift as explained on the opposite page.

240 CIS YAER
(U-S-IM-11/89)

NAME _____

ADDRESS _____ APT. _____

CITY _____ STATE _____

ZIP CODE _____

Offer limited to one per household and not valid to current Silhouette Intimate Moments® subscribers. All orders subject to approval. Terms and prices subject to change without notice.

SILHOUETTE "NO RISK" GUARANTEE
There is no obligation to buy—the free books and gifts remain yours to keep. You receive books before they're available in stores. You may end your subscription anytime—just write "cancel" on your statement or return your shipment of books at our cost.

© 1989 HARLEQUIN ENTERPRISES LIMITED

MAIL THE POSTPAID CARD TODAY!

PRINTED IN U.S.A.

Remember! To receive your free books, digital clock/calendar and mystery gift, return the postpaid card below. But don't delay!

DETACH AND MAIL CARD TODAY.

If offer card has been removed, write to:
Silhouette Books, 901 Fuhrmann Blvd., P.O. Box 1867, Buffalo, NY 14269-1867

MAIL THE POSTPAID CARD TODAY!

BUSINESS REPLY CARD

FIRST CLASS MAIL   PERMIT NO. 717   BUFFALO, NY

POSTAGE WILL BE PAID BY ADDRESSEE

SILHOUETTE BOOKS
901 FUHRMANN BLVD
PO BOX 1867
BUFFALO NY 14240-9952

NO POSTAGE
NECESSARY
IF MAILED
IN THE
UNITED STATES

she pleaded with him to come to the house. "Then come to the buffet. As a personal favor to me. To save me the trip."

She turned and fled. She didn't care how obvious it was that she didn't dare stay with him another minute. She'd certainly done more ridiculous things in her life. And in this case, she might have done something even more foolish if she'd stayed.

Like ask him to kiss her, for instance. She'd seen him looking at her with that barely concealed hunger in his eyes. All she'd wanted to do was step into his arms, raise her lips to his and close her eyes.

She could almost feel his arms enfolding her even now as she was running across the driveway to the house, with the cold November air biting into her skin.

One kiss. How dangerous could one kiss be? she wondered. She was crazy to even let herself wonder, she knew. She wouldn't wonder. She wouldn't.

Chapter 9

The formal dining room was full of relaxed conversation and the distinctive sounds of satisfied eaters. The long table was covered with a beige linen cloth and decorated at both ends and in the middle with rust and gold chrysanthemums and feathery green ferns. The hot and cold buffet items were spaced around the table, permitting everyone to take their time as they spooned food onto their plates.

Mrs. Adams was thoughtfully tasting a pudding at the dessert end of the spread. She'd insisted on tasting everything first to be sure it was acceptable. The other fifteen people present were trailing behind her, not paying the slightest attention to her pronouncements, they were all so famished.

There were chairs and small tables all around the room, but a few of the staff wandered into the kitchen to eat, feeling more comfortable in that setting.

Beau arrived a little while later. He had been too hungry to stay away, but he'd been about to take his plate into the kitchen in sheer self-defense when Meg caught his elbow.

"Come sit with us, Beau," she urged him cheerfully, obviously never considering that he might not want to.

He saw the destination she had in mind. Richard, Elaine, Ambrose and Mrs. Adams were sitting around a table in the corner near the French doors. And just joining them was their old friend, Bradley File.

Meg turned to look at Beau in surprise. "Is something wrong?" she asked, wondering why he wasn't following. Her plate teetered precariously, and she steadied it with her other hand.

Beau resigned himself to the inevitable. As long as he was working at Foxgrove, it seemed there was no way he could avoid Elaine. He'd been kidding himself to think it would be otherwise.

"No. Nothing's wrong. I'm coming," he replied.

Meg sat next to Richard, and with everyone else already seated, Beau had no choice but to sit next to Elaine. She smiled easily enough at him, but concentrated immediately on listening to what Ambrose and Mrs. Adams had been arguing about as Beau had sat down.

"No, they shouldn't have put nutmeg in it," Mrs. Adams was protesting, shaking her round face vigorously in objection.

Ambrose was clearing his throat of the last of the pudding and licked his lips appreciatively. He looked down his nose at the plumpish cook as if she hadn't the faintest notion how to spice a dessert. "I couldn't disagree more," he said archly.

Richard grinned and glanced at Bradley. "Your hunters got a fair workout," he told his old friend.

Bradley nodded. "So I hear. Catch any foxes?"

"One of the hounds had a mouth full of red fur," Richard said, laughing. His eyes narrowed a little, and he looked at Beau. "And we had some interesting wildlife in the field, too."

Bradley had been stuffing his mouth and chewing as fast as he could, but he caught Richard's meaning and glanced around the table, assessing expressions. Everyone looked as if they weren't sure what they could or couldn't say.

"Is that so?" Bradley said when he'd finally swallowed enough to be able to speak. "Anyone I know?"

"I don't know," Richard said blandly. "Babs Carlton. Have you heard of her?"

Bradley nearly choked on his slice of smoked turkey. After much clearing of his throat, he managed to regain his powers of speech. He looked at Beau. "What the hell is that witch doing here?" he demanded.

Beau stoically finished the slice of Virginia ham he'd been working on and shrugged noncommittally.

"She says she's house hunting," Elaine ventured softly. She laid her fork down. Talking about Babs Carlton wasn't helping her appetite a bit.

"House hunting!" Bradley sputtered the words. He looked genuinely horrified. "Well, the neighborhood is sure going to hell, if you ask me."

Richard laughed and offered to pour coffee for everyone. "I take it you don't care for her, Bradley," he observed mildly.

"You can take it a lot more negatively than that!" Bradley declared. He looked at Beau. "Did you talk to her?"

Beau nodded. "She rode one of your horses. I had to talk to her to give her the horse."

Bradley's cheeks were red with anger. "If I'd known she was coming, I would have forbidden you to give her one of my horses!"

Meg and Elaine concentrated on their coffee, and Ambrose and Mrs. Adams politely pretended great interest in their raspberry tarts.

Richard leaned back in his chair and looked straight at Beau. "From the way Bradley's talking, I take it you've met Mrs. Carlton before."

Beau wiped his mouth with the linen napkin, folded it carefully and laid it on the table. Then he looked across at Richard and nodded. "Yes. I know her."

Richard seemed to be considering whether to ask more, but Elaine couldn't bear to have him pick apart Beau's relationship with Babs Carlton with everyone listening. Even if Beau refused to answer, his refusal would cause as much titillation as a direct reply.

"I know her, too," Elaine interjected. "I met her at one of Margaret's parties. She's one of those people you just know you're not going to like."

Meg looked at Elaine strangely. "Are you kidding?" she asked, never having heard Elaine admit something like that before. "I thought you always bent over backwards to give people a second chance if you had a bad first impression."

"I've turned over a new leaf," Elaine said with forced cheerfulness. "I'm going to put more faith in my first impressions from now on."

Meg looked at Richard. He, in turn, was staring at Elaine. "I see," he said softly.

Beau had no doubt that Richard did indeed see, because the next thing he knew, Richard's blue eyes were studying him as if seeing him clearly for the first time.

Bradley cleared his throat and blundered onto the only topic that he'd thought about for days. "You know, before Meg got married, she had agreed to come over and work with me with my horses... be a partner in the business."

Meg smiled at him affectionately. "When I thought I was losing everything, you really came through for me, Bradley," she said.

Bradley grimaced. "Yeah. Well, you may be happy you married old Richard here, and your horses may have a fine time being fed and groomed by his people now, but where does that leave me? Up the hill with a stable full of horses and me by myself to manage it all."

Bradley glanced meaningfully at Beau. He knew he was being rude by trying to take Beau away from Richard while they were eating at Richard's table, but he wanted Beau to know just how serious he was. "I offered you the partnership before, Beau. It's still open, if you're interested."

Richard made a noise of protest. "And who'll manage Foxgrove's stables?" he demanded, mildly outraged and amused at Bradley's blatant recruiting.

Bradley mumbled that Richard could surely figure something out, and Beau looked at Meg and Elaine.

"Between the two of you, you could probably manage quite well," Beau said thoughtfully.

Meg laughed and shook her head, but Elaine went very still. "I certainly couldn't handle it," she admitted quietly. "I could help, but...there's a lot that I just don't know...."

She saw from his expression that Beau was seriously considering whether Meg and she could handle things. Something twisted inside her. If he left, he would stop thinking of her as his employer, which would be quite a pleasant change. On the other hand, he'd be across the valley and busy with Bradley and everyone else's business. How much time would he have for things involving Foxgrove—or her?

Elaine knew she would miss Beau. Very much.

Several other members of the staff were going back for seconds, and Ambrose and Mrs. Adams decided they'd had enough and excused themselves to go check on the situation in the kitchen.

"Any time," Bradley declared, leaning toward Beau. "Any time you're interested in going into business instead of working for Richard, just let me know." He got up and stretched. "I'm seventy years old. I can't wait forever, you know." He grinned at Richard. "Thank you for the supper. I think I'd better go say hello to a few of those folks who dove into the kitchen a while back."

Beau rose to leave. He'd eaten, as he'd planned. He'd sat around and endured the polite conversation. But he'd had enough. "If you'll excuse me..." He nodded at everyone. "Good night."

Elaine watched him leave.

"Elaine," Richard said softly, "I think we need to have a little talk."

She drew in her breath and stared at her older brother. She rose to her feet and went around to him, putting her arm on his shoulders and kissing him on the cheek before slowly shaking her head.

"Not yet, Richard," she said. She looked blindly through the French windows at the veranda. It was cold now.

"I like Beau," Richard said slowly. "But...if he's becoming more than a friend..." He frowned. He'd just been through hell with her disastrous marriage. He didn't relish watching anything like that happen again.

Elaine smiled gently. "I'm a lot wiser," she said. "And Beau isn't Cam." She laughed. "Beau isn't even my friend, which I'm sure he'd be only too happy to tell you if you'd ask...."

Richard was perplexed. "Well, what the hell is he to you?"

Elaine caught her lower lip between her teeth. "I don't know.... But when I find out, I'll tell you."

Richard threw up his hands, and Elaine started to leave.

"Good luck," Meg called after her softly. Meg was the only one of the three who was smiling. "Give Beau a kiss for me," she added with a twinkle in her eyes, then gave her growling husband a placating pat.

Elaine blushed and tried to protest, but Meg laughed. "That's the kind of advice you gave me about Richard," she explained, defending herself. "I just thought I'd return the favor. It was good advice, although I didn't think so at the time."

"This is altogether different," Elaine argued, but the soft blush stealing across her cheeks deepened.

"Oh, really?" Meg teased affectionately.

But Elaine had already left and mercifully didn't hear that last teasing jibe.

"What was all that about Elaine telling you to kiss me?" Richard said, leaning toward Meg with great interest.

She laughed and rose to go to him. He had gotten to his feet, and she looped her arm through his when she reached his side.

"Actually, she suggested I let you kiss me again...."

Richard, still intrigued, led her out of the dining room. "Let's find someplace where you can explain." He frowned a little and glanced in the direction Elaine had gone.

Meg ran her fingers soothingly over his forehead. "Elaine will be all right. Beau wouldn't hurt her," she told him softly.

Elaine was walking through one of the large rooms that faced the front driveway just as Beau pulled out of the garage in one of the estate cars. She hesitated, her fingertips on the delicate curtain, watching him disappear onto the country road. He was going in the direction of town.

She took her set of master keys and grabbed her down-filled riding jacket. It looked a little odd with her buffet clothes, but it had the advantage of being close by. She quietly let herself out and walked to the stable to do some investigating.

The stable was cool and deserted except for the horses resting quietly in their stalls. Their dark brown eyes followed her curiously as she passed. Elaine murmured greetings but didn't stop until she reached the office door, which was locked. She pulled out her set of keys, selected the one that would release the bolt and entered.

For a moment she just stood there, her hand on the curved brass door handle, leaning against the door. The office was a large square room paneled in red oak and Spartanly decorated. It reflected the male sense of comfortable surroundings, she thought fondly. Both Richard and Bradley had left their stamp here. Yet it also fit Beau, she realized. The three men, while very different, shared a certain quality that was hard for her to define.

It was easy to visualize Beau here.

Elaine walked around the room, her fingers trailing along a hard surface here, a solid fixture there, considering where to begin her search. She wanted to know exactly how complicated taking charge of the stable would actually be, if the need arose. She'd seen the look in Beau's eyes when Bradley had been urging Beau to leave Foxgrove, and she was afraid he might do just that.

His leaving would certainly solve the problem he seemed to have in working with her, she realized, but she ached to find some other solution. She didn't want him to leave. She forced herself to be realistic, however. She had to prepare for the strong possibility that he might very well do just that.

There were three walnut filing cabinets in one corner. Not far away was a large hickory desk with a computer and a business-size telephone console with an impressive array of buttons on it. Across the room were padded leather chairs assembled around a low-slung coffee table that had been cut from a single giant slab of Foxgrove oak. Along another wall stretched a leather upholstered couch beneath a captain's clock.

The clock reminded Elaine that she didn't have all the time in the world. It was getting dark outside already, and she had no idea how long it would take for her to get a sense of what needed to be done here. She stepped away from the door, dropped her coat onto a chair and headed for the filing cabinet.

She opened the top drawer and worked her way from the front to the back, methodically scanning the information as she went. Most of it was too detailed to merit spending much time on. It did give her a quick idea of the scope of the activities the stable manager oversaw, however, and that scope was awesome. Foxgrove had a lot of horses, and the amount of money, equipment, care and training they required was eye-opening even for her, and she'd grown up here.

By the time she'd been through the filing cabinet and the records in the desk, she knew she'd been correct earlier. This was beyond her experience. She could learn the job if she had to, but it would be a shame. She would make a lot of mistakes that would easily be avoided if someone with experience was there. While Meg would certainly be a tremendous help, since she'd comanaged her own small stable with her late father, the two of them would more than have their hands full. Assuming, of course, that Meg could juggle her competitive responsibilities with helping manage the stable.

Elaine laughed helplessly. She could see the storm on Richard's face already. He no doubt had plenty of ideas on how Meg should be spending her time, too. He wouldn't be thrilled at having to share her with something so mundane as the management of his horses.

Elaine sat at the desk and stared at the computer screen for the next two hours, perusing diskettes to glean further information, which turned out to be even more disturbing. One diskette in particular held her attention. In one file she found a list of winners of steeplechases, timber races and point-to-point events in the past year. Several Foxgrove horses were there, but the name that drew her attention was that of one of the winning riders: Beau Lamond. He'd ridden both Foxgrove horses and the horses of other owners. She totaled the purses listed next to the events and figured out the rider's share, then had to do it a second time just to make sure she hadn't made a mistake.

Beau had won a lot of money. He certainly didn't have to live the hair-shirt existence he seemed to. If he didn't want to work for Bradley, he could earn quite a chunk of change as a professional rider. Her heart sank further.

Elaine was so absorbed in what she was doing that she didn't hear anyone approach until the door opened. At the soft grating sound, she looked up quickly, as startled as a doe.

It was Beau.

"You're back." She blurted out the words without thinking.

He nodded soberly. "I saw the light. I thought I might have left it on. Or there might be a problem with one of the horses...."

She shook her head. "You didn't leave it on. The horses are fine."

He walked inside and came to stand next to her. He looked down at the computer screen.

"I was taking stock," she explained.

He unbuttoned his wool jacket and frowned. "Taking stock? Is something missing?"

"No. Nothing like that. It was what you said earlier...."

He thought back. "You mean Bradley's offer."

"Yes."

He moved away from her, walking around the room, as if reacquainting himself with it—or saying goodbye.

Elaine tapped out a few commands on the keyboard. The screen darkened, and she turned the equipment off. "Are you thinking of accepting Bradley's offer?" she asked, holding her breath.

Beau came back to the desk and faced her. "Yes."

She felt the blow to her heart and lowered her eyes to hide the feeling. "I see," she said quietly. She lifted her chin and rallied her pride. "I was afraid of that. That's why I came here. I wanted to see how much of a problem we'd have if you..." It was harder than she'd thought. She found she couldn't say it. *If you left*. She swallowed and rose to her feet, fidgeting nervously with the pencil she'd used to take notes. "I hope...I hope you aren't doing this because of me...." She couldn't quite look at him and say it, so she moved away and stared at the pencil. "Richard will really be furious with me if I've cost him the best stable manager he's ever found." She laughed, but the sound was far from light.

"Elaine."

She ignored his quietly stated command. She knew he wanted her to look at him, but she didn't want him to see the naked look in her eyes. Instead she wandered back to the filing cabinets and checked to make sure they were locked. She'd known they were, of course, but it was a way to rid herself of a little of her nervousness.

"You may be right, of course," she said, trying to sound light and reasonable. She put her hands on top of the file. The pencil dropped to the floor unheeded. "And it looks like you've got quite a knack for winning timber races and steeplechases.... Maybe you should skip Bradley's offer and just free-lance...."

He'd turned as she spoke. Now he closed half the distance between them, saying again, somewhat more forcefully, "Elaine. Look at me."

But she couldn't look at him, and she couldn't stand there in silence. It would make the pain harder to ignore. So she desperately concentrated on what she'd been saying.

"I had no idea the purses were that good," she said, laughing a little. "Richard really owes you a lot. His horses have never done so well."

His hands were on her shoulders, and he turned her to face him. He was a little rough, as if he were afraid she would resist and had used enough force to compensate for that. She closed her eyes. The slow dull agony was twisting in her.

"Elaine," he said, his voice almost unrecognizable to her, it was so dark and low and rough. "Open your eyes. Look at me."

She shook her head. "No. I don't want to." She turned her face away and felt him release one hand. Then his warm palm was against her cheek, pulling her back to him, and the ache inside her became even more acute. How she longed for his touch. How awful not to let him know how much.

"I can't stay here," he said in that rough, sandpaper voice. "You know what will happen if I do...."

She wanted to put her arms around him and beg him to hold her, but she couldn't throw herself at him like that. She opened her eyes a little and stared at his chest, broad and strong, covered with a clean beige cotton shirt.

"What will happen?" she asked, trying hard to sound in control of the situation, as if everything were normal, as if he weren't holding her and she wasn't standing a foot from him, completely tense, with her hands balled into fists at her side. She hurried to answer her own question, however, willing him to follow her lead. "If you stay, I'm sure Richard will be more than willing to renegotiate your contract to suit you. If you want more time to ride, he'll probably give it to you without even wanting to discuss it. If you want to keep more of the purses, you can probably get that, too...."

He pulled her chin upward, effectively shutting her mouth and forcing her to look into his eyes. At the same time he slid his other arm around her back, pulling her against him until their bodies were lightly touching.

"You can talk until you're out of breath," he said in that low, rough voice that hit her like a hot caress. "But it won't change a thing. You know what I'm talking about. If I stay, you know as well as I do what's going to happen between us."

She stared into his eyes helplessly. Her expression was unguarded, and her longing and humiliation were there for him to see.

"Why are you doing this?" she asked him in a ragged whisper. She closed her eyes in agony and then forced herself to open them. She wouldn't take the coward's way out. She couldn't pretend not to understand anymore. She ran her tongue over her lips. "Why couldn't you just pretend it wasn't there?" she cried out softly. "We could have ignored it, if you'd just...not said anything...." A small flame of anger lit her anguished eyes. "You told me you'd find greener pastures. You said you could keep your hands off me."

His eyes were as dark and bleak as the winter sky as he slowly shook his head. "I don't think I'm going to be able to." His jaw tightened, and his eyes clouded. "Every day I feel my control slipping a little more. One day it'll go completely. And I'll come after you and pursue you and do everything I can to convince you to let me have you." He lowered his jaw and rubbed his lips slowly over her cheek and jaw, sliding then down to her neck, then back up across her mouth, teasing... seducing.... "Believe me, I know all the ways there are. In the end, you'll say yes. And afterward... you'll hate me. You'll hate yourself. I don't want that to happen. Don't you understand?"

Elaine moaned softly and closed her eyes.

"I want you," he murmured harshly against the soft skin of her throat. "You're a burning fire that I can't put out."

She felt his mouth on her cool flesh, and fire raced through her like a hot summer wind. She knew just what he meant.

"I want you more than I've ever wanted a woman in my life," he swore, kissing her throat, her jaw, her cheek. "And I never learned to keep my hands off a woman that I wanted."

Elaine heard the warning and remembered his description of himself. A lady-killer. A careless seducer of women. A man who never tied himself down. She stiffened in fear, knowing how much it would hurt if he treated her so cavalierly. She knew he sensed her reaction from the odd way he sighed, the almost comforting way he held her. It bothered him, she thought with a small sense of triumph.

He lowered his warm firm lips to hers and kissed her. Sparkles of heat burst inside her mouth and spread outward. All of a sudden Elaine's world ceased to exist except for the exquisitely sensitive point where their lips were meeting. Beau slanted his mouth against hers, deepening the kiss and drawing her against his body by tightening his arm slightly.

Instinctively Elaine arched into him and slid her arms under his coat, around his waist. He was strong and lean and hot. She slid her hands up over his back. Touching him made her forget that there could be no undoing this, no pretending it hadn't happened. She hadn't realized how hungry she was to hold him until her palms splayed across the smooth muscles of his back. It made her ache to feel his bare skin against her, and she closed her eyes tightly, opening her mouth more to him, savoring every sweet sensation.

She could feel the buttons of his shirtfront pressing against her, marking her skin through the fine silk print blouse she wore. The buckle of his belt pressed against her stomach, and she pressed her body against him, feeling a soft surge of satisfaction as she heard him stifle a groan. Her nipples tightened, and she slid her hands up across his shoulder blades, pulling him as tightly as she could. Suddenly he was lifting her up against him, rubbing the fronts of their bodies slowly back and forth in a blatantly provocative movement. He tightened his hold on her, and the kiss became more demanding, harder, wetter, more deeply intimate.

Elaine moaned at the aching pleasure being born within her. She felt sensations blossoming inside that were fresh and new. He was like the spring rains bringing the earth to life at last, and her heart opened to him in gratitude. Nothing that felt so natural, so beautiful, could be wrong.

Beau broke the kiss suddenly, holding her tightly against him, breathing unevenly.

Elaine pulled her head back and studied him. He didn't look like a man playing with a woman. He looked like a man who was smothering his own desire. The heat in his eyes was warring with some tender feeling.

She swallowed and tried to get a grip on herself. That tender feeling was most likely her own wishful thinking, she knew. It was hard for her to accept that he might only be physically attracted to her. Especially since she knew she was attracted to him in so many other ways, as well. She knew that Meg trusted Beau, and she clung to that slender fact in the midst of her own chaotic emotions. No matter what he did or did not feel for her, he would not act the way her philandering husband had.

"I think you made your point very eloquently," she said unsteadily. She let her arms slide down until her hands rested lightly at his waist.

He wasn't smiling. He didn't say anything.

Elaine caught her lower lip between her teeth and searched for just the right words to say. "I don't think you should resign because of me."

He looked exasperated and, loosening himself from her, stepped away rather abruptly. He ran one hand roughly through his unruly dark blond hair, shaking his head as if he couldn't believe his ears. "What should I do then?" he exclaimed angrily. "Take you to bed?"

Elaine flinched as if he'd slapped her. "You needn't put it so bluntly," she said calmly.

A muscle in his jaw flexed as he gritted his teeth. He raked her from head to toe with a gaze intended to be insulting. "Are you selling yourself to me?" he demanded angrily. "You'll throw yourself on the pyre of my lust so I'll stick around? No sacrifice is too great to keep the family estate running smoothly, huh?" He snorted in disgust. "This isn't the Middle Ages, for God's sake!"

She lost half the color in her face, but she did not look away from him. He was trying to make her back down. But she wasn't going to. Not this time.

"No. I'm not selling myself. And I don't believe you mean any of the things you're saying."

He stuffed his hands into his coat pockets and laughed, throwing back his head. There was no joy in his eyes, however, and Elaine noted that fact, chalking it up as evidence to support her belief.

"I'm not going to whisper sweet nothings in your pretty ear," he said harshly. "I told you I wanted you. I think that's a damn good reason for me to leave, even if you don't. I've had enough scandal to last me a lifetime, and I don't care to see my name dragged through the mud again. Not even for the very great pleasure of making love to you."

Elaine recalled the night he'd carried her home and insisted that their being together would ruin his reputation. She smiled sadly, recognizing that he'd been telling her the truth, but only part of it. The other part was his desire to protect her from his black sheep past. If he'd been found with her, no one would have believed it was innocent. She remembered him telling her that she inspired men to protect her. She wondered if he'd been thinking of himself when he'd said that.

"You don't want to be thought of as a hired man who seduces the woman he works for," she said, as if stating a simple fact, not taking it personally.

His face hardened. "Precisely," he said. His eyes were bleak.

"I think I know how to solve that dilemma," she said quietly.

Beau gave her a long, searing look. He buttoned his coat and turned up the back of his collar. "So do I," he said harshly. "I'm going to leave." He headed toward the door, then hesitated. "Don't blame yourself, Elaine," he said, not looking at her. This time he sounded more in control. A man resigned to his decision. "It isn't your fault."

She listened to the sound of his boots against the stable floor until they were only a faded memory. Then picked up her coat, lifted her keys from the desk, locked the office and made her way out of the stable.

"You had your say, Beau," she said to herself. "Now I'm going to have mine." And she turned to walk resolutely in the direction of his cabin.

Chapter 10

Beau's cabin was a ten-minute walk from the stables. By the time Elaine reached it, she could see a thin ribbon of smoke rising from his chimney. The scent of a wood fire came to her as she reached his door. It gave the place a welcoming aura, which she was sure he'd be horrified to hear.

At the plank door, she hesitated. Would it be wiser to knock and risk being turned away, or should she simply take charge of the situation and just walk in? She wouldn't put it past him to literally shut the door in her face if she stood on his doorstep. However, she couldn't quite bring herself to burst in uninvited. She knocked.

The door swung open, and when Beau saw her, his jaw dropped.

She smiled cheerfully and walked past him. He was so surprised, he didn't make the slightest effort to stop her. She breathed a silent sigh of relief and walked over to warm her hands at his fire. She glanced over her shoulder when she didn't hear anything. Beau was still standing at his door, holding the knob, looking at her in complete disbelief.

"Close the door," she suggested. "It's getting cold outside."

She looked around the sparsely furnished room, half-holding her breath as she waited to see what his reaction would be. She heard the door close, and she exhaled softly as she realized he wasn't going to ask her to leave on the spot.

"I see you don't mind simple living," she observed wryly, nodding toward the few things around her.

There was a worn homespun rug spread on the floor in front of the fireplace, a plain wooden table with a tin cup and a plate on it, an aged chest of drawers shoved back against one wall and, near it, a simple wooden bed with a worn quilt. Nothing of his decorated the place, except his clothes hung on wall pegs and his boots by the door.

"Why are you here?" he asked bluntly.

There was no welcome in his voice, but there was no hostility, either, and Elaine counted herself lucky for that. She wandered over to the old coat tree near the front window, shrugged out of her jacket and hung it on one of the pegs.

"To finish our conversation." She went back to the fire and stood in the warmth. She was cold to the bone with nervousness.

"I thought everything had been said." He walked across the room to join her, although he kept a wary eye on her.

"You said everything you had to say. I still have a few things to add."

He looked distrustfully at her but leaned his shoulder against the wall and casually crossed one leg in front of the other. "And you have to say them tonight? Here?" he said incredulously. His hard eyes bored into her.

"Yes."

He raked her slowly from head to toe and back with a hard, knowing gaze, but Elaine suspected he was just trying to frighten her off.

"You're not going to scare me away, you know," she said.

"That's a pity."

She swallowed and gathered her courage.

"Well?" he prompted her coolly. "What is it?"

"I told you I had another solution to our dilemma."

If anything, his expression grew even less welcoming. "And I told you I had my own already and didn't give a damn what yours was."

She laughed and held her shaking hands out, fanning them against the warmth of the fire. "Well, that's too bad," she told him. "Because I intend to tell you anyway. Whether you want to hear it or not." She glanced at him from beneath half-shy lashes, then quickly lifted her gaze fully to his, forcing the shyness away with an act of sheer will. "I think we ought to be able to come up with something besides your running away."

He glared at her. "I'd hardly call it running away," he growled. "Any other woman would thank me for being a gentleman," he pointed out, sounding almost piqued.

Elaine shrugged. "Well, I'm not any other woman." She smiled at him. "But I do thank you for trying to be noble about it."

He exhaled his exasperation and closed his eyes. "Tell me your solution so I can reject it and send you home," he ordered curtly.

"I think we should put each other out of our misery," she suggested, amazed that she could sound so calm and collected while her heart was hammering inside her at about a hundred miles an hour.

Beau's eyes snapped open, and he straightened as if he'd been hit. "What did you say?"

Elaine bravely opened her mouth to repeat the words, but he immediately held his hand up to forestall her.

"No!" he exclaimed. "Don't say it! I heard you the first time."

She was relieved that he didn't even try to pretend he didn't know exactly what she'd meant. That saved her from having to say it even more baldly, which she would have found difficult, never having tried to seduce a man before in her life. She watched Beau as he paced across the cabin, running his hands through his hair, until he came to a halt in front of his bed. There he abruptly sat down and turned to glare balefully across the room at her. It was as far away as he could go and find someplace to sit, and apparently he needed to sit. He looked quite shaken, she thought.

She took a few steps in his direction, and he immediately held up his hand, telling her to stop.

"It really makes much more sense, I think," she said, hiding her own nervousness with words.

"You're out of your mind," he said hoarsely. He shook his head and closed his eyes. "Fine. I heard your idea. It stinks. Go home."

She saw him lower his head into his hands in despair, and her heart turned over. She walked as quietly as she could, so as not to raise any more objections, and crouched down in front of him.

"No," she whispered adamantly.

He was shaking his head, not looking at her. The firelight glinted and danced on his hair, casting his shadow against the wall behind him. He looked so alone that she ached for him.

"I won't go," she said softly. "I'm not some silly young girl, you know. And you're not taking advantage of me." She smiled a little sadly. "If anything, I'm taking advantage of you." She reached out to touch his arm, but he flinched, and she withdrew her shaking fingers. "You aren't seducing me," she said. "You never tried. Not in any way. I'm the one seducing you, so you have no reason to feel guilty about anything."

He lifted his eyes and stared at her. She could see the struggle going on within him, and for the first time since she'd come to him, she felt sure she was going to win this argument.

"You're wrong," he said in a rough, tortured voice. "I'll feel as guilty as hell. Don't you see? I don't want you involved with me."

Elaine had been sitting back on her heels, but now she rested her weight on her knees. Her eyes were level with his, and she could see the light playing across the smooth, strong planes of his face, could see the pain and desire at war in his storm-colored eyes. She raised her hands slowly to his face and slid her fingers gently through his soft hair. He was unnaturally still, but this time he didn't flinch away from her touch. She smiled at him tenderly.

"I'm thirty years old," she said softly. "I've been courted assiduously by a man who lied to me every day of our life together. I married him wearing those rose-colored glasses you accused me of having, and he eventually managed to shatter them for me. All my girlish illusions have already died, Beau. There's nothing left for you to crush."

He was listening, but she couldn't tell what he thought. Something had flickered in his eyes for a moment when she'd said there was nothing left for him to crush, but she wasn't sure what it had been. It didn't matter, she supposed. He was considering what she was saying. For that, she was grateful. He could have simply laughed at her, or ridiculed her. In spite of what she'd just told him, that would have hurt her. It would have hurt terribly.

"You don't know what you're asking," he said, speaking barely above a whisper.

She licked her lips and swallowed. "I do know. You said you want me. You pointed out that ... you know the feeling was mutual." She drew a breath. "You were right. I didn't realize it at first. I wasn't teasing you when I kept trying to be your friend. And afterward, I'd still like to be your friend. I know this won't be a ... a love affair or anything like that...." She drew another fortifying breath and forced herself to go on. "But we're both going to go crazy feeling like this and not doing anything about it. Don't you see? You can't just leave. That won't solve anything."

The fire crackled and hissed and spat.

Beau's face contorted, and he closed his eyes as if he were in agony. Elaine felt the tension radiating from him and sensed that he was marshaling himself for one last effort to send her away. Talking wasn't going to be enough, obviously. There was only one other way she could think of to persuade him to let her stay. She searched for the last vestige of her courage and braced herself to take it.

Leaning forward ever so slightly, she pressed her cool, trembling lips to his and kissed him with all her heart.

Beau was so shocked by the unexpected intimacy that he froze. Primitive instinct and endless weeks of aching for her undid him, however, and his first action was to open his mouth and kiss her back. Then, just as waves of pleasure began cascading through him, he realized exactly what he was doing.

He grabbed her shoulder to push her away, but before he could, Elaine slanted her mouth provocatively over his and ran her tongue softly over his lips. Her mouth softened as her tenderness and yearning welled and spilled over. A soft pleading sound was born in her throat, and he must have heard it, because she felt him draw her just a little closer at that moment, as if responding to her.

When at last he tore his mouth away, his eyes glittered down into hers like a winter storm. His breath fanned her lips, and the heat from his body seared her from shoulder to knee. Elaine looked at him helplessly. She'd laid herself open to him. She was kneeling in front of him, literally pleading with him to make love to her. She'd never been so completely vulnerable to a man before in her life. Her heart ached, and suddenly she knew exactly why she was doing this. She wouldn't burden him with the knowledge, but in that instant she was completely honest with herself. She loved him. She'd fallen in love with him effortlessly. She knew it was hopeless, really. There were too many things to keep them apart. She doubted very seriously that he was likely to fall in love with her. In that blinding moment of insight, she also knew that that didn't matter. She'd been promised love once, and it had been a lie. She wouldn't ask him to lie to her. She much preferred his honesty. This would be enough for her. She would gladly take his honest passion over anything others might offer.

He slid his hands up her shoulders and cupped her face. He was less than gentle, close to bruising her. "You could end up pregnant," he said desperately.

She smiled. "No. That won't be a problem."

He clenched his jaw, working the muscles. She leaned forward and brushed her lips erotically across his. He inhaled sharply and pulled her into his arms. His resistance had begun to crumble, and he wasn't particularly gentle. His mouth was hard and demanding, his hands touching her with a wolfish hunger. He came to his feet, dragging her up with him, his hands sliding down to her bottom, then pressing her hard against him. His breathing became harsh, and he lifted his head to look into her eyes one last time.

"You're playing with fire now," he told her. His voice was odd...thick and harsh and grating. "Think what you're asking...."

Her eyes were liquid. Her bones softened. The warm desire flowing through her made her lean against him to keep from falling down. She looped her arms around his neck and smiled slightly.

"I don't want to think anymore," she said, barely above a whisper. He had to tilt his head to hear her. She slid her fingers down his chest and unfastened the buttons of his cotton shirt. She smiled as he sucked in his breath in response. "Burn me in your flames," she told him. "Turn me to ashes. I want you to."

"Elaine..." It was a groan of surrender.

He swore softly as he swept her up into his arms. The swearing stopped as he urgently found her mouth with his, kissing her like a dying man who'd suddenly been yanked free of his chains. Wild, passionate, masterful kisses of her mouth, on her lips. He stroked her with his tongue, sucked provocatively at her upper and lower lips, teased her roughly with each quick touch of his mouth. The kisses became more and more demanding as he realized she was meeting him eagerly, kissing him back with the same desperation he felt himself.

The barriers of his resistance crashed down with deafening thoroughness, and he methodically stripped her of her clothing. His fingers made quick work of her silk blouse. As she wriggled her shoulders free and slid her arms out of the long sleeves, he lowered his head and found the soft skin in the hollow of her shoulder with his lips. She gasped softly in pleasure, only to close her eyes against the lovely feeling as his hand caressingly found her breast.

"I've lain here at night thinking of you like this," he murmured huskily. He ran his hands over her bare skin, playing with her taut nipple, looking down at her intently.

She opened her eyes and smiled gently up at him. "Have you?"

He nodded and stripped off his shirt with her help. He was handsomely muscled. Compact, with just a light smattering of dark gold hair grazing his chest. His eyes darkened as he watched her look at him.

"You're beautiful," he told her, bending to kiss her cheek with near reverence.

She found his hand at her breast and covered it with her own. She wanted to tell him that he was the handsomest man she had ever known, but she felt it would sound a little silly, coming so soon after his own compliment, so she told him with her eyes instead.

He groaned softly and yanked her belt loose, then pulled at her camel-colored wool slacks. "If you keep looking at me like that, this is going to be over in no time at all," he warned her.

She laughed softly and watched him shed his own jeans and drop them onto the growing pile of clothes on the floor next to the bed.

"Then I'll just have to stick around for a while," she teased.

His eyes darkened, and he quickly divested them both of their underwear, lingering to stroke her thighs and admire her for a moment. Everywhere he looked at her, Elaine felt her skin tingle and glow. She wanted to bask in his admiration forever. She hungered to see that look on his face. She reached out to him, welcoming him.

The fire glowed on their naked flesh as he laid her down on the bed. He was leaning over her like a golden god from some bygone age of conquest. His face was lean and intent, the muscles in his shoulders and arms bunched as he held himself over her.

"Where do you want to be touched first?" he asked softly. He almost smiled at her. "Why don't you tell me as I go?"

He was talking to her soothingly now, as if quieting her. Easing her into the love play. Elaine relaxed.

"That's it, sweetheart," he murmured, coaxing the rest of the tension from her with his voice and his hands. "Easy does it."

He found all the places she wanted him to touch without her saying a word. Or perhaps anyplace he touched her would have been the right spot, she thought in a warm haze of desire. Wherever his hands were, she began to burn. Wherever his mouth touched her, she started to ignite. Wherever his body touched hers, her skin turned to flame. And all the while she ached for more. She moaned for more. She begged for more.

He kissed her mouth, a long, languorous kiss that drew out her deepest longing for him. With one hand he discovered the sleek, eager flesh of her breast and thighs. Fondling her, he slid his fingers over her stiffening nipples and the swollen, slippery folds lower down. He embraced her with his other arm, rolling her onto her side until she was facing him, sliding his knee between her thighs and pulling her close.

He was hard against her, pulsing and rigid. He pulled her against him until those soft folds nestled against the part of him that could ease the awful ache twisting inside her. He rocked against her and withdrew a little, grasping her buttocks with his hand, pulling her against him as she moaned. The rasping of his tortured breathing excited her even more. She knew exactly how hard it was for him to prolong this. He'd been ready for this for a long time.

Where their skin touched, they were becoming slick with sweat. Where his male body touched her, the slickness was of another kind. Elaine ran her hands hungrily over his back and buried her face in his neck. He was as hot as fire. She wished she could melt into him, become one bright flame with him. She wished she could say that she loved him.

He pulled her under him and rolled on top of her, cupping her face in his hands as she cradled his hips between her soft thighs. His eyes were dark with desire, yet when he spoke there was a hoarseness that held the hint of more than just a man's desperate physical wanting.

"You're the most beautiful woman I've ever known," he said, gritting his teeth against his own desire. He kissed her mouth so tenderly that tears came to Elaine's eyes. "In all my life, I've never wanted anyone the way I've wanted you, Elaine Faust."

He gently kissed the tears that clung to her lashes. Then he kissed her lips, and she could taste her own tears on his mouth. He pushed his hips forward slightly, bringing himself just into her body. His body shook with the effort it cost him to hold himself back, and Elaine moaned in surrender. He slid his fingers into her hair, holding her head, his fingers gripping her scalp tensely for a moment as he strove to control his own need. Then he pushed into her, filling her, and he wrapped his arms around her shoulders and under her, burying his face in her hair with a primitive groan of satisfaction.

He swore softly as Elaine slid her hands down his back, raking her nails gently across his flesh in her own eagerness for him to be completely at one with her. She lifted her hips against him and held him fast when he moaned raggedly in response.

"I wish this could last forever," he murmured, his breathing forced and rasping against her throat.

Then, as if he couldn't quite help himself, his hips flexed, and he thrust farther into her. Slowly at first. Rhythmically. Deeper and deeper. Groaning, grinding his hips into her over and over again. Finding her breast with his hand, then her mouth with his, as desperation overtook them and they were slamming violently against each other, writhing, their breaths coming in soft, sharp, panting cries, twisting in each other's arms until they were at the frantic edge.

She felt the rising crash of pleasure within her just as his body arched against her. She cried out, and he covered her mouth, swallowing the sound in a kiss that was as cataclysmic as the ecstasy that was racking the rest of her body. She felt him impale her with three quick, sharp thrusts. Then, pressed hard and deep inside her, he shuddered violently, emptying months of pent up longing into her with a long, mournful cry he half swallowed at the end.

He lay collapsed on top of her, breathing roughly, still holding her as if he would never let her go, still buried inside her damp body.

Elaine held him close and closed her eyes, remembering with pleasure every glowing feeling he'd created in her. She engraved them all on her heart for safekeeping, knowing such memories would be few. Maybe the fact that she expected so little from him made each memory that much dearer. And he had given her such a very special gift: the shattering joy of having been devoured in the flames of ecstasy. She silently treasured his honest hunger for her. Unvarnished by lies and deceit, it was all the more beautiful in her eyes.

"Thank you," she whispered, murmuring the words against the damp hair curling over his temple. She kissed his hard cheek—softly, though, not wanting to disturb him. When he would have moved, she held him. "No. Don't move. Please. Not yet. Stay with me like this. A little while..."

He slid his arms more comfortably around her back and held her tenderly. The peace that settled between them was so clean and profound that he sighed. As his body relaxed in the aftermath of their lovemaking, his conscience struggled to make itself heard once again. It told him that this had been as terrible an idea as he'd known it would be, that he ought to be horsewhipped and hung over a slow fire for what he'd done. Every other cell in his body rumbled that he should trade his mind for a newer model. Beau knew he wasn't in any condition to debate the issue at the moment. Besides, he'd more or less concluded that he must be out of his mind anyway. With Elaine falling asleep in his arms, he found it exceedingly difficult to care, one way or the other, about the state of his mind.

However, he knew that eventually he would have to face their new set of circumstances. What the hell was he going to do with her? He'd gone out of his way to make no promises, but making love to her had changed everything for him anyway, as he'd known it would. He felt...connected to her. The protectiveness he'd felt toward her was going to become worse. And while making love had been quite satisfyingly draining, he knew very well that the feeling wouldn't last. He was beginning to feel a familiar coiling in his loins just lying with her now, and the sweat had barely dried on his skin.

Her body was soft and relaxed, and from the sound of her breathing he sensed she was asleep, or well on the way there.

He eased his weight over a little, keeping her close to him when she mumbled in protest. He kissed her lips and closed his eyes comfortably.

"To hell with being noble," he muttered slumberously. Elaine made an incoherent sound in her sleep and he caressed her back tenderly. "You do know how to put me out of my misery," he whispered to her.

There was a faint grin on his face as he dozed off. It was the first time he'd smiled as he fell asleep in a long, long time.

Sometime in the night, Elaine began to feel cold on one side. Aware of a comforting warmth on the other, she snuggled against the heat, wrapping her arms around its solid, welcoming shape. She was vaguely aware of being lazily caressed. Slowly the memories came filtering back. Through half-closed eyes she became conscious of Beau, lying facing her, stroking her in the slow, steady, undemanding way of a lover willing to make love or not, as his partner desires. She leaned forward and found his mouth with hers, and the sweet pleasure she tasted there made her want to cry.

This time it was even sweeter than before. The first rough edge of need had been satisfied, and now a deeper, gentler longing was fulfilled. Even half-asleep, Elaine was aware of the velvety texture of his warm skin against her calf, thigh, stomach and arm. He kept her on her side and drew her thigh over his hip, letting her pick the moment he entered her, urging her on with his magical hands, his husky words, his chuckles and groans of pleasure as they teased each other. When the leisurely pace ceased to satisfy them, he pulled her hips urgently, and she tightened her arms around his shoulders until she thought surely they'd break. She was kissing him frantically at the end, and when they climaxed, it was together, shaking and groaning as one.

Elaine squeezed her eyes tight to keep back the tears that suddenly welled up. She buried her face in his sweaty shoulder, hoping he wouldn't notice that some of the dampness came from a sudden and unexpected sadness inside her. She thought for a moment he must have felt it, because his hand stilled on its gentle path down her back. He adjusted her, cradling her against his body, and kissed her softly on the mouth.

"Do you want to leave?" he asked softly.

She clung to him and shook her head. "If you don't mind," she murmured huskily, "I'd like to stay a little while longer."

He went back to slowly stroking her back and sighed. "Why should I mind? Stay as long as you like, sweetheart."

And the word *sweetheart*, said in the tender way he had uttered it, went with her as she dozed off again.

Beau pulled the old quilt over them and held her. Over her bare shoulder, he could see the dying embers of the fire. Her dark hair spilled over her, hiding her face from him.

Tomorrow he would have to face the consequences. Tonight, he wasn't going to think about them anymore.

He tucked the quilt carefully around her back and closed his eyes. His last coherent thought was of Elaine and how well she fit in his arms, even in his narrow bed.

He felt her stir, carefully sliding out from under his arms, as if trying not to wake him. He knew it was still dark. Even with his eyes shut, he always could tell. He heard her rustle through the pile of clothes near his side of the bed, picking up her things and putting them on, one at a time.

He could have turned over or sat up, but he didn't. From the nervous snapping of elastic and fasteners, he sensed she would prefer these few moments of privacy to dress and gather herself together.

It wasn't hard to know when she was finished, either. She stood there next to the bed, silent and unmoving. The poor kid didn't know what to do, he realized. No doubt she'd never done anything like this before. Never come to a man and asked him to take her to bed. But in the heat of the night, he'd somehow forgotten that. To him, they'd passed that stage.

He rolled over onto his back and looked up at her then, reaching out unerringly to take her hand in his. "What do you want me to say?" he asked her softly, holding her hand as comfortably as he could.

She smiled down at him, but it was an awkward smile, not the natural one he was used to seeing, not the searing one he'd seen during the night. She swallowed, and the effort she was making to be casual about saying goodbye made him ache. He rubbed his thumb slowly across her palm, trying to help her relax.

"I don't know what I want you to say," she admitted honestly. She sat down on the bed next to him as he shifted over and patted the space invitingly. "I don't want you to say anything, I guess."

"Regrets?" he asked. His eyes were steady, but he let her know he cared enough to worry about her feelings on that score.

She bent down and kissed him lightly on the lips, pulling away before he could hold her there. "No. No regrets." She laughed a little and smiled at him teasingly. "I feel much better. Don't you?"

He laughed and grabbed her shoulders, drawing her down for a firm, hard kiss in spite of her effort to avoid it. He gazed into her eyes as their lips parted, saying, "I have *never* felt this good."

Elaine pulled away from him and rose to her feet. "I'm glad to hear that," she said softly.

He got up and pulled on his jeans while she retrieved her coat from the rack in the corner. He met her at the door, but he made no effort to open it for her.

Elaine looked at the floor. "This was for us," she said quietly. "I want you to decide whether to stay or go based on what makes sense for you professionally and personally. Don't think of this as... blackmail to stay...."

"I don't."

She found the door handle and smiled at him, remembering the intimacy between them, and the sweetness of those memories softened her eyes and lit her face. "Good night. See you tomorrow."

She left quickly then, not wanting to drag out the goodbyes, not wanting him to say things he wouldn't mean, not wanting to blurt out her own feelings and embarrass them both. She looked straight ahead, too, trying hard not to even want to look back at him. It helped to walk fast, she found, and within a matter of moments she was practically running toward home.

Beau stood in the open doorway, watching her until the night swallowed her. There was a slow dull ache in his chest that hadn't been there before. He clenched his fist and rested it on the doorjamb. He wanted to run after her and drag her back and tell her he wasn't going to let her leave.

He wanted her with him. Even worse than ever.

Chapter 11

When Elaine came down to breakfast the following morning, Richard was already there. He looked up from his newspaper and studied her as she joined him.

"You look more relaxed than you did yesterday," he observed as she buttered an English muffin.

She didn't look at him, paying careful attention to stirring her cream into her coffee instead. "Good morning to you, too," she said lightly. She glanced at him over the cup as she took a fortifying swallow.

Richard laid the paper down and gave her his full attention. "Did you follow Beau last night?" he asked casually.

Elaine, not fooled by her brother's seeming disinterest, took a bite of her muffin and took her time in answering. There was no point in evading him if he was interested enough to be so blunt. He would find out some other way if she refused to tell him. He always did.

"Yes," she replied, meeting his eyes steadily with her own. In spite of her effort to remain cool, she felt a betraying gossamer wash of color warm her cheeks.

"And what was the upshot of your meeting?" he asked softly.

There was a tenderness in his voice that bespoke his genuinely deep love for his younger sister. There was also a slight hardness in the way he formed each word that let her know he wasn't going to tolerate any pain being inflicted on her by Beau. One word from her and the man would be history, as far as Richard was concerned. And that was if he was lucky.

She had finished her muffin and was sipping her coffee as Ambrose brought in a tray of fresh fruit. She declined them, and he silently began to clear away Richard's dishes. Richard was waiting for an answer, letting her choose whether to respond while Ambrose could overhear. Elaine didn't see any point in keeping secrets from Ambrose. He always knew what was going on, anyway. He might as well hear her side of it, she thought. At least she might keep him from misunderstanding the situation between Beau and herself.

"I don't know," she admitted with a sigh. She shrugged and gave her brother a level look. "This is personal, Richard. Just between Beau and me. Don't try to get into it. Please?"

He sighed. "I seem to have heard something like this before," he pointed out.

Elaine shook her head. She knew he was thinking of Cam. Richard had never liked him and had told her so. She'd gone ahead and married the man anyway, blinded by Cam's skilled charm.

"Cam was a chameleon," she told him. "You were right about him, and if he'd been less successful in camouflaging himself from me, I would have seen him as clearly as you did." She felt the old revulsion and sense of defeat begin to blossom inside her. With an effort, she fought against them. "Beau is the same person to all of us. He never makes promises. He's gone out of his way to avoid doing anything that would even appear like chasing me."

Richard rested his elbows on the tablecloth and folded his hands into a steeple, fingertips touching. He was frowning now, unconvinced by her. "Sometimes the most successful way to chase a woman is to let her pursue you," he observed.

Elaine considered that. Then she shook her head, rejecting it. "I don't think that's what he's been doing." She grinned at her brother and shifted the subject a little. "Is that one of your secrets with the ladies?" she asked teasingly. "Let them chase you until you've caught them?"

He lifted a dark eyebrow and gave her a censuring look. "We aren't discussing my past peccadilloes," he pointed out. "We're talking about your not making the same mistake twice."

Ambrose quietly set the tray of fruit on the sideboard and left the room. Elaine sighed and laid down her linen napkin, rising to leave.

"I'm certainly clever enough not to make that mistake again," she assured him. She placed her hand affectionately on her brother's shoulder as she prepared to leave. "This isn't the same thing. I'm a big girl now, Richard. If it's a mistake, I'll be able to survive it. If nothing else, I've become a lot stronger in the past year. You'll never see me crushed like that again. Besides, this isn't about marriage, so quit being so melodramatic!"

"All right." He smiled slightly. "Let me know if the situation changes and you want help." The smile became a wry grin. "I'll try to remember not to kill him."

Elaine laughed. "It's more likely *me* you'll want to kill," she exclaimed. "I'm afraid I've plagued the man mercilessly."

Richard grimaced and nodded painfully. "I can believe that. I know just how much of a nuisance you can be. Maybe I should be offering *him* my sympathy instead of *you*."

She pulled his hair gently and laughed. "Don't you dare!" But she knew from the easy way that Richard was relenting that he liked Beau, and that warmed her heart. She didn't want to come between them.

As if thinking along similar lines, Richard added, "I have great confidence in the job he does for us. I trust Bradley's judgment about his honesty and trustworthiness. I trust my own instincts about him as a man. And I had a fairly thorough background check done that satisfied me completely—at the time." Richard's brows drew into a straight, serious line. "However, I wasn't investigating him as a man who might become involved with my sister. I was investigating him as a potential stable manager with sizable responsibilities to shoulder here at Foxgrove. I can't promise you that I won't take another look at him, since the circumstances seem to be changing."

Elaine was appalled. "Don't do that, Richard. It's... insulting."

He rose, and they walked out of the dining room together. "Insulting to whom?" he challenged.

"To Beau!" she exclaimed.

"Tough. Besides, one of the skills I've cultivated in the past five years has been subtle investigation. I promise you, he won't know anyone is asking."

Elaine turned on Richard in genuine alarm. "He'll find out. Somehow it will get back to him. Things like that eventually do. And when he hears about it, how do you think he's going to feel? And what do you think he's going to think of me?" She shook her head. "I want you to promise me you won't do it, Richard."

Richard had never liked being managed by other people, and he automatically shook his head. "I won't promise you anything. Except this... that I love you, and I'll do everything I can to ensure that nothing I do results in your being hurt, even indirectly."

Elaine put on her riding jacket and grabbed her hard hat from its hook by the door. She gave her brother a last, pleading look. "Please don't do it, Richard. Just... leave this to me."

Fearing he would be too stubborn to relent, she chose not to wait for a reply. Richard made no effort to offer any.

Eddie grinned at her cheerfully as Elaine carried tack into one of the stalls.

"Everybody's out early today," he said.

She looked at him with interest. "Oh? Who do you mean, Eddie?"

"Mrs. Faust rode Sinbad over to her old house. She said she wanted to see if everything was going along okay."

Elaine had expected Meg to do that. After all, it was her property, and the horses there were dear to her.

Eddie was hurrying on with his news, however, saying, "And Beau is already taking his second horse over the steeplechase course."

Elaine paused in fastening one of the bridle straps. "He must have gotten an early start," she reflected. Since she knew he couldn't have gotten much more sleep than she had, she was a little surprised.

"Yes, ma'am. He was here at six, when I start. He's going to take the other three out, one after the other, he said." He frowned. "I'd better get the next one saddled. He ought to be back soon."

Elaine followed him to the steeplechaser's stall. "Eddie," she said. "Give me the horse he wanted next. I'll take her out to him."

Eddie was surprise, but it never occurred to him to question her decision. After all, she was the owner. And he wouldn't have done anything to make her angry at him, anyway. He liked to see her smile. He saddled and bridled the horse and handed her the reins.

Fifteen minutes later, Elaine was sitting on the horse, looking at the steeplechase course, watching the distant rider urge his galloping horse over a five-and-a-half-foot brush jump.

For the first time, she felt a pang of nervousness. She knew the sooner she faced him, the sooner it was likely to go away. After all, it was the morning after. She would have to face him in the light of day and learn to be nonchalant about their recent intimacy. Remembering the hot, tender kisses, the languorously sweet caresses, made her skin glow anew. She had no regrets. She was glad that she'd gone to him, that she'd lain in his arms, that she'd burned in his sweet fire.

She remembered the rough tenderness in his voice when he'd held her hand and asked what she wanted him to say, and she smiled. She wanted to see him again. She was beginning to ache with the need just to be near him. To hear his voice...see his wary eyes and his dubious smile. Lightly she touched her heels to the big horse's flanks, cantering in the direction that would bring her to Beau as he finished the course.

She broke around a dense cluster of oaks just as he was approaching the last fence on the course. It was six feet tall, and he was heading for it at a slight angle. Elaine drew her mount to a halt and watched, becoming worried as she realized that all was not well.

Beau's horse was shaking his head, resisting, and Beau was tightening his control, demanding that the animal take the jump exactly as he wished. For a moment Elaine thought the horse might shy away at the last minute. At the speed he was galloping, it would be a miracle if Beau wasn't thrown. Without realizing it, she stopped breathing, silently willing the horse to take the jump.

She saw Beau tighten his hold on the animal and urge him forward to the looming chunk of solid wood. The horse snorted. Beau sank his spurs sharply into the horse's flanks and rose over his withers. The horse took the jump, barely striking the top with his left hind hoof. Beau patted him enthusiastically on the neck as they landed safely on the other side, continuing his praise while standing in the stirrups as the horse galloped over the broad dirt stripe that marked the end of the practice course. The horse swished his tail and tossed his head exuberantly, looking as happy as his rider about the whole thing.

Elaine, breathing a profound sigh of relief, rode out to join Beau. She'd seen plenty of riders take falls over the years, but never had she been quite so worried. For a moment her heart had been in her throat. With an effort, she threw off the lingering residue of alarm. Nothing was going to happen. She was being silly.

"Good morning!" she called out cheerfully.

Beau whipped around in his saddle and pulled the big horse up to a slow canter, circling back to head in Elaine's direction.

"Good morning," he called back, looking a little surprised to see her. As they drew close and halted their horses, his eyes flicked over her quickly. Satisfied at what he saw, he permitted himself a small smile.

The horses stood, blowing softly and slapping their tails.

"I thought he was going to refuse for a moment," Elaine said conversationally, indicating the big bay that Beau held so quietly.

Beau grinned wryly and nodded. "You're right. He sure didn't want to take it. The last time he took it at an angle, he banged up his leg. He'd lost his confidence." Beau patted the big bay's dark brown shoulder affectionately. "But he did it in the end. He's got a lot of heart."

"I suppose that's what counts," she murmured, thinking how tempting it often was for people to shy away from things that could injure them. Like herself, for instance. She was suddenly strongly tempted to shy away from Beau. She could leave him his horse and ride back to the dressage ring immediately. But Beau was so strong and so thoroughly delectable, sitting on the big horse, that she found it hard to act on her wayward thoughts. His lean, muscular legs gripped the stallion like steel bands. His strong well-shaped hands held the reins with a masterful delicacy that made her remember how good they could feel sliding tenderly across her eager skin.

Elaine swallowed and lifted her chin, telling herself to get beyond this. She'd slept with him. They knew each other in the most carnal sense of the word. In her heart, in her soul, she felt a secret joy at that and treasured the memory. But she knew everything was going to be complicated between them for a while, while they decided what they were going to do about their intense physical attraction for each other. And while he decided whether he was staying or leaving.

Her gaze slid away from his, and she looked over the steeplechase course with renewed interest. For the moment it provided a respite from facing his curiosity about her unexpected presence here. A small sliver of anger pierced her as she admitted that she wished he could show some feeling for her. Like he had last night. His physical passion was something, at least. Anything was better than this polite, innocuous camaraderie.

"Eddie was saddling this horse," she explained, a little surprised at how easily the words came once she got started. "I thought I'd bring him out to you and see how you were doing before I got started down in the dressage ring." She slanted him a hesitant look. "I hope you don't mind," she added cautiously.

"Not at all," he responded. He rested his hands on the pommel. "Would you like a tour of the steeplechase course while you're here?" he asked courteously. "We've changed a few things...."

The smile that rose on her face nearly took his breath away. He guessed that part of her apparent happiness was really profound relief at his small token of peace. He'd certainly offered her little enough of that in the past few weeks, he recalled with a slight pang of guilt. It had been for her own good, of course, but after their torrid night together he couldn't see much point in trying to keep her at arm's length all the time. Even in conversation.

"Come on," he told her, as the ghost of a grin haunted his lips. He headed his horse toward the beginning of the course, a half mile across the valley. "I'll show you some of it. What we don't walk around, I'll point out for you from a distance."

Elaine was delighted. For once Beau was treating her almost like a friend. Better still, she wasn't going to have to rack her brain for innocent pleasantries in order to maintain some skeleton of a conversation between them. And he wasn't going to restrict himself to "yes," "no" and the shortest answers known to man. Even if the course had been thoroughly abysmal, she would have declared it a marvel of modern equestrian engineering, so happily relieved was she that he'd decided to show it to her like this.

However, by the time Beau had pointed out the upgrades he'd engineered and the overall redesign he'd coordinated, it dawned on Elaine just how tremendous an effort he'd put into Foxgrove. She'd been immediately aware of the exemplary maintenance he demanded at the stables, of course. She had been unprepared, however, for the exceptionally skilled regrading of the land, the extensive rebuilding of so many cross-country jumps and the obvious sophistication of the course layout.

When at last he fell silent, she turned to look at him in amazed admiration. "I'm no expert," she said humbly.

"But I've seen enough courses to know that this is really outstanding."

He grinned at her, and the corners of his eyes crinkled in genuine, almost boyish, appreciation. "Thank you," he said.

She shook her head and looked over the course again from their vantage point on the high ground where he'd brought her at the end. "No. Thank *you*," she protested. "No wonder Richard's horses do so well. No wonder *you* do so well." She slanted a glance at him. "I could almost be tempted to try it myself," she added hopefully.

He laughed and dismounted, coming around to exchange horses with her. Elaine followed his cue and dismounted, as well. He didn't give her his reins right away, nor did he make any effort to take hers. Instead, he stood in front of her, looking more relaxed than she ever remembered seeing him. It made her heart ache with tenderness, and some of her emotion was shining in her eyes, in spite of her automatic effort to restrain it.

"You shouldn't give me all the credit," he drawled in amusement. "You and your brother footed the bill, and quite a few men worked all last fall and winter getting the jumps up," he pointed out. "And as for the horses... well, they were in top condition and had been well schooled when I took them on."

She stiffened her shoulders and told herself to keep their encounter light and pleasant. Since she was beginning to suffer a nearly uncontrollable urge to throw her arms around his neck and kiss him, she knew it was high time she left.

As she held the reins out to him, he fell silent. When her eyes met his, she saw the desire simmering in him. It made the ache in her heart all the harder to bear. His eyes softened, and she knew he'd seen her feelings. When he drew her into his arms, she made no effort to play coy. She moaned softly, closed her eyes and lifted her lips to his, feeling as if she were coming home.

The reins were dangling from her right hand, but her left hand was free to slide behind his neck and finger the hair just above his coat collar. His mouth was warm and persuasive, searching gently at first, then more insistently. There were mounds of cloth between them, his thick jacket and hers being the worst offenders, but she felt the solid strength of his body through it all and clung to him.

After a long, highly satisfying kiss, he slid his free hand more deeply into her dark silky hair and, with obvious reluctance, lifted his lips.

His storm-darkened eyes regarded her, and she shivered as if something cool had touched her spine. For a moment she wondered if she was misjudging him, thinking he was at heart trustworthy and kind. There was a wildness in him, an unwillingness to be ruled by anyone, that she glimpsed every once in a while. It was there now.

He touched her cheek softly with one finger, gently tracing a line to her lips and lingering on them tenderly.

"I can't go back to the way it was before last night," he said honestly. He raised his eyes from her lips, and now there was nothing but the careful shielding he wanted her to see. The wildness was out of sight again. He sighed and studied her. "Have you ever done anything like this before?" he asked quietly.

Elaine blinked in surprise. "What do you mean?"

"Have you ever had an affair you were hiding from people?" he explained.

She dropped her eyes and looked away from him. "No," she told him. "Does that bother you?"

He sighed. "Yes. It bothers the hell out of me," he said grimly.

She heard the self-loathing in his voice and reached up to caress his cheek. Their eyes met and held, and the magic swirled between them, wrapping them in its warm embrace, until Elaine wanted to cry out from the sweetness of the feeling.

"I chose this," she reminded him gently, offering him a tender smile. "It doesn't bother me," she told him. "I'm glad."

That wasn't quite true, and she knew it, but she thought it would help him to hear her say that. It was true that she didn't mind having a secret, intimate relationship with him. As long as he welcomed her, she would go to him only too happily. On the other hand, when he eventually had enough of her, as she fully expected that he would, she knew it was going to hurt terribly to have to let him go. She also knew without a shred of doubt that she loved him enough to pay that painful price.

In the meantime, she wanted to shield him from that knowledge. He might not love her, but he had scruples about their relationship. He'd gone out of his way to point out the danger he represented to her. He'd done everything possible to try to keep away from her, to warn her off. He'd worried that she would suffer. She knew he hadn't wanted that. He was already carrying enough guilt about their relationship for twenty men, she thought. She was willing to do anything to protect him from carrying any more. She smoothed the frown from his brow and kissed him sweetly on the mouth.

"Besides, this isn't an affair, remember?" she teased him affectionately. She wondered why his expression darkened ominously, but she kept on with what she was saying anyway. "We're just two people who are immensely attracted to one another. Neither of us is making any promises...."

She'd thought that would please him, but he didn't look pleased at all. He looked as if he'd swallowed a mass of fish hooks. Her brow furrowed, and she looked at him in confusion. "Isn't that right?" she asked tentatively.

He stepped away from her and straightened his hard hat, which he'd pushed out of the way earlier in order to kiss her. "You sound like you're quoting me," he admitted.

He sounded almost bitter, she thought in surprise. "You mean that's the line you usually gave your..." She hesitated, wondering how to refer to them. Girlfriends? That didn't sound strong enough. Lovers? That implied emotion to her. At last she settled halfheartedly on a word that might realistically capture what she was trying to convey. "Bedmates?"

His head snapped back, and he smothered a flare of anger. "Something like that," he muttered tightly. He handed her the reins to his horse and took her horse from her. He offered her a leg up, then mounted his horse with a military snap. "I'd better get back to work," he said grimly. He looked at her, and this time there was a mist of anger and frustration rising behind his unblinking gaze. "Your brother isn't paying me to make love to you," he said bluntly. He seemed almost amused at the irony in that. "That will have to be done on my own time, sweetheart."

He nodded and gave her a quick, cool grin. Then, with a light touch of his heels, he sent the hunter mare instantly into a canter.

Elaine watched for a moment, then forced herself to get back to her own work. She wondered what he'd been feeling just then, though. He hadn't appreciated being told that he'd promised her as little as all the other women he'd bedded in his life. On the other hand, he'd done nothing to deny it, either. A part of her wished that he *had* denied it. She would have enjoyed hearing him say that she was special to him. When he'd told her that he'd never wanted a woman the way he'd wanted her, her heart could have burst from the pleasure of hearing it. On the other hand, she'd heard how special she was over and over from Cam during his avid courtship. In the end, it had turned out to be the biggest bunch of lies imaginable. The part of her that remembered those lies never wanted to be told such things again. Much as she hated to admit it, she assumed that Beau had used lines like that to maneuver women into his bed. She knew she didn't want to be just another conquest. In that sense, it saved her pride a little to be the one who had come to him. While it laid her open to the possibility of humiliating rejection, it also meant that she wasn't being manipulated as she had been by Cam. As others might have been by Beau.

It was painful thinking of him in bed with other women, and she pushed the horse into a gallop in her need to drive the disturbing vision out of her mind. When she got back, she threw herself into her work with a will.

When Beau eventually joined her to help with one of the dressage horses just after lunch, they were too busy to pick up the threads of their earlier discussion, even if neither of them wanted to, which neither one did.

It wasn't until dinner that Elaine faced the fact that she had to decide what she would do next about Beau. She knew that he wasn't going to come calling on her at the house, nor ask her out for a date. He hadn't asked her to come see him later, either, although he probably could have come up with a pretext if he'd wanted to.

She didn't know whether she had the courage to go to him again without some encouragement. On the other hand, she doubted that he would reject her if she did go. That kiss he'd given her on the steeplechase course had been far from chaste. She knew he still wanted her. All through dinner, she argued with herself about it in silence. To go to him...or not to go to him... Should she wait? A day? Several days? Until he did something to encourage her?

Richard noticed her preoccupation, and patiently repeated questions and waited long periods for her to shake off her blank expression and form replies. Eventually, however, he abandoned trying to draw her out and indirectly discover what was on her mind. She guessed that he suspected something fairly intense was going on, though. And from the knowing looks Richard and Meg exchanged when Beau's name came up in casual conversation, she resigned herself to the likelihood that Meg was aware, as well.

Elaine tossed down her napkin, having pushed her unusually tasteless food around her plate for as long as she could possibly bear. She excused herself and managed to say something vague about errands to do and not wanting them to stay up waiting for her to return. Richard and Meg murmured goodbye and watched her in silence as she left.

She drove into town and wandered aimlessly for nearly four leaden hours. When she finally returned to the estate, it had been dark for a long time, and the place looked utterly deserted, to her great relief. She parked her car in the garage, knowing that the time had come for her to decide whether to throw herself at Beau again or not. She looked into the darkness in the direction that would take her to Beau's cabin, and his ironic words spoken on the steeplechase course that morning beckoned her. *Your brother isn't paying me to make love to you. That will have to be done on my own time, sweetheart.*

She wrapped the memory of his words around her heart and took a deep breath. She was so lonely for him that she ached all over. She just wanted his arms around her. Maybe she could convince him to sit by the fire and hold her for a while. Maybe he wouldn't mind that....

She walked toward Beau's cabin, trembling a little. It wasn't all that much easier to do the second time, she found, quelling a slightly hysterical giggle. She had a little more sympathy for all the boys who'd asked her on dates over the years.

Beau heard her footsteps as he stood in front of his blazing fireplace. He'd been staring into the dancing flames for the better part of an hour, wondering whether or not Elaine would decide to come to his rustic home again. He would have understood if she'd chosen not to. He was still amazed that she'd had the courage to come the first time. Today he had certainly made no effort to indicate she would be particularly welcome, other than that admission at the steeplechase course. He could have bitten his tongue later when he realized how she could use that if she needed encouragement. He'd been telling himself all day not to encourage her, even though he wanted to make sure she felt cared about at the same time. He didn't want to reject her, even if he had the strength to—which he certainly didn't seem to. He grimaced at his own weakness for her.

The moment he heard her footsteps, though, he knew he was going to do everything he could to see that they forgot what lay between them in the daylight. If she had the courage to come to him, he ought to be able to dredge up the strength to care for her at night.

He opened the door just as her knuckles were hovering over the wood. She stood there, her hand frozen in the act of knocking, her big blue eyes wide and a little hesitant as she stared at him. He doubted whether she had known herself if she'd have the nerve to come to him again. Something twisted painfully in the region of his heart, and he regretted for the millionth time that he couldn't tell her how he truly felt about this. And about her. She was so tenderhearted, she would no doubt stick to him like glue, and she deserved more than that out of life. He was embroiled in a titan, nasty struggle. The odds were that it would take years, if ever, for him to win. He didn't want her to go through that. And he couldn't give it up. His own self-respect was on the line. Without that, he would truly have nothing.

Elaine opened her mouth, about to say something bright and amusing about being on his doorstep again, anything to ease her aching ambivalence at having to take the initiative in their relationship—if it could be called a relationship, he thought grimly. He lifted his finger to her lips, forestalling her jest. Then he pulled her gently inside and closed the door behind her.

"You don't have to say a thing," he murmured, lowering his mouth to hers to kiss her, as he'd wanted to all day.

The kiss was so sweetly demanding, so full of his own need to feel her mouth intimately connected to his, that tears filled Elaine's eyes.

He raised his head and saw the glittering diamonds on her long, silky lashes, and a grim, bittersweet smile touched his lips. He could have told her that it hurt him, too, having her be the one to choose whether they saw each other or not... the fact that this was supposed to be a sexual liaison with no strings, while he felt strings all around him, clear through him. Ironically enough, for the first time in his life, he actually didn't mind feeling the damn things, either. He wanted to feel them binding him to her. He would have welcomed her feeling the same, if things had been different. If he'd been free. But he couldn't let her feel them. He had to let her think that he didn't love her. He didn't have the strength to keep away from her physically, but maybe he could marshal enough resolve to make her believe that was all the attraction consisted of. It was the only remaining way he could think of to protect her a little from being hurt by him.

He kissed her tears and eased off her coat, dropping it carelessly onto a chair.

She tilted her head to one side and put on a brave smile, trying to be lighthearted about being here. "You're very habit-forming," she said jokingly, her smile a little too wobbly to be thoroughly convincing. "I hope you... don't mind...."

He smiled against her hair, threading his fingers through the luxuriant silk. "No," he told her. "I don't mind. I'm ... flattered.... Honored."

He was barefoot and bare chested, wearing jeans with the top snap undone. Golden brown hair curled in a faint line down his stomach and across his chest. She rested her cheek against his shoulder and closed her eyes, savoring a closeness that went beyond words. She knew he was glad she had come, and all her fears dissolved.

He cupped her face in his hands and tilted it up for his kiss. Warmth, like hot wine, swirled through her, spiraling downward and outward, and she relaxed against him.

"Come to bed," he murmured against her mouth, seducing her slowly with his drugging kisses, with the warm kneading of his hands, the intoxicating feel of his strong, muscular body against hers.

Her eyes were half-closed, but she felt a faint obligation to let him off the hook, if he wanted it. "If you don't want to," she murmured hesitantly, "we don't have to...."

He laughed, genuinely laughed. "Believe me, sweetheart, I want to...." He devoured her mouth with a ravenous kiss, deftly removing half her clothing and sliding his hands hungrily over her. "I want you like hell."

When they were both completely naked, he lifted her in his arms and carried her to his bed, lowering her and following her down without breaking the contact of their bodies. He stroked her satiny skin, raising eager goose bumps everywhere his lean fingers touched. He found her breasts, stroking the sensitive skin first with his fingertips, later with his lips and tongue, teasing her until they were both shaking and the sheen of desire glistened on their taut bodies.

He ran his hand possessively over her waist and hips, her abdomen and thighs, sliding between her legs to caress her intimately. When she groaned for him then, he rolled on top of her and entered her in one hard thrust, muttering something incoherent against her eager mouth. She was starving for him, though, and they kissed as passionately as they had the night before, while he began to move slowly, deeply within her, and whatever he'd said was lost in their groans of pleasure.

She slid her thighs up around his hips, and he pulled her calves up over his buttocks. He drove himself into her, gasping against her mouth, kissing her wildly as the small irrevocable convulsions overtook her, deep inside. Her fingers bit into the muscles of his back, slippery against the sweat, and she was racked by the deepest spasms of pleasure she had ever known in her life. She lifted her hips up and cried out as he shuddered violently against her, consumed by the vortex of his own prolonged climax.

"I love you," she cried out at his last climactic thrusts. But the words were drowned in his own animal cries of completion, swallowed by his last desperate, plunging kisses and their mouths were so passionately fused that she hadn't the will to say the words again.

Gradually he relaxed against her, burying his face in her neck, murmuring incoherent love words while she held him tightly in her arms. She wished with all her heart that they could shut out the world and stay in this room alone together. Perhaps then she could tell him that she loved him. Perhaps then he wouldn't mind too much if she did.

She stroked his bare back and closed out everything but the comforting feeling of his hot body sprawled intimately on top of hers. Soon enough she would have to go back. But the night was her escape. Tonight, he was hers.

Chapter 12

Three weeks later Richard Faust was going through his mail when the name and address on one of the letters caught his attention. The long business-size white envelope was addressed to Mr. Beauregard Lamond. That in and of itself was not particularly noteworthy. The mail occasionally got mixed up at Foxgrove, as anywhere else. What drew his dark brows into a frown was the return address in the upper left-hand corner. Richard recognized the name. It was that of a private investigator. A rather well-known one. One that Richard himself had dealt with briefly and quite satisfactorily during his meticulous pursuit of the nasty truth about his late father's death.

He walked out of his study and went directly downstairs to personally deliver the misdirected communiqué. He was curious as to why Beau was dealing with Midford Blane. Richard was well aware that Elaine had been spending a great deal of time with Beau in the past few weeks. She'd firmly drawn him into the family's Thanksgiving celebrations; she spent endless hours with him, working with the horses, and apparently she found a great deal to discuss with him after hours, if the brief glimpse that Richard had had of her returning home from Beau's cabin in the dead of night was any indication.

Meg had encouraged Richard to take a wait-and-see attitude, and he'd felt additionally hampered because of his promise to Elaine not to interfere in any way that would hurt her. This, on the other hand, was an opportunity too blatant for him to overlook.

When he found Beau alone at the computer in the stable office five minutes later, Richard placed the letter on the desk in front of him and said smoothly, "I see we have a mutual acquaintance...."

Beau looked at the letter and, after a moment, turned off the computer. He swiveled the chair halfway around and stared thoughtfully at Richard, who was obviously waiting for a reply. "Apparently, we do," he agreed.

Richard had closed the door after him, and now he lounged against the wall nearest Beau. "Does this have anything to do with Foxgrove?" he asked bluntly.

"No," Beau replied. "This is personal."

"I see," Richard said. He straightened and wandered around to the front of the desk, as if choosing his next words carefully. When he turned, his expression was decidedly less casual than it had been. "Does it have anything—*anything whatsoever*—to do with my sister?"

Beau had guessed from the way Richard was acting that he would ask something like that. Even though he wasn't exactly surprised, it was still difficult to hear the concern voiced aloud. Beau's jaw hardened, and his lips tightened into a thin straight line. He met and returned Richard's hard look. "No," he said grimly. "It has nothing to do with her."

Richard stared at Beau for a long, hard moment. Finally he looked away, frowning. "I know what's going on between you," he said slowly. He shrugged. "Enough, anyway." He sighed. "She's very dear to me. You know that. I promised her that I wouldn't make an ass of myself and embarrass her by looking into...your life." He exhaled and rubbed the back of his neck. When he looked at Beau this time, it was purely as man to man. "If asking for my help will save her any pain, any pain whatsoever, I want you to ask."

Beau stood and faced Richard, angry at having to listen to this and at the same time sympathetic with Richard's need to say it. For Elaine's sake, he bit back the first words that came to mind. When he felt he had a grip on himself again, he replied, "If she were mine, I'd probably be saying the same things you are." His voice grew hard. "And it's only out of consideration for her that I'm not flat out telling you something rude."

Richard was an astute listener, and he heard the frustration under Beau's anger. "It sounds like you just told me off, anyway," Richard pointed out.

Beau nodded in agreement.

Richard, however, was instinctively pleased with the way Beau was dealing with him. The other man was angry at being in the position he was, and also clearly determined to solve his problem on his own. Richard respected the grit it took for Beau to face both situations. Elaine was beautiful and an heiress. It would be easy for a lesser man to take advantage of that fact to solve any difficulties he might have. Richard decided that his initial impression of Beau had been well-founded, and that Meg and Elaine were probably right about the man, too. Under the circumstances, he imagined Beau was being harder on himself than any of them would be. That struck him as mildly amusing, since he was well aware of Beau's rampant success with the opposite sex in the past.

Elaine would be safe with Beau, although Richard seriously doubted that Beau would think so. He held out his hand, restraining a completely betraying grin of amusement. Beau didn't look as if he would be in the mood to hear Richard's opinion about how safe Elaine was.

"My apologies," Richard said formally.

Beau shook his hand, still looking grim.

"Forget I said anything," Richard added. He paused at the door and raised his eyes to heaven pleadingly. "And please don't mention this to Elaine unless you want to see me flayed alive."

Beau laughed. He could imagine her doing just that. "Consider it forgotten."

A moment after Richard had left, Elaine walked into the stable office, slapping her crop casually against her thigh. She was wearing light gray jodhpurs, boots and a dark turtleneck sweater. Her cheeks were pink from the cold, her dark hair tousled from the wind.

Beau, who'd been in the middle of opening the letter from Midford Blane, stopped. It still took his breath away a little, seeing her when she walked into a room. It didn't matter what she was wearing. Or not wearing. It still hit him in the stomach like a soft blow. He exhaled and gave her a mildly quizzical look, wondering what she had up her sleeve this time.

Elaine grinned charmingly and perched herself on the corner of his desk, swinging her leg in a casual fashion. "Don't stop on my account," she told him blithely. "I just finished my last horse of the afternoon and I'm going to sit here and make a nuisance of myself. I can be a much better nuisance if you're doing something...."

He smothered a laugh, trying not to encourage her. "All right," he agreed with a shrug.

He would have preferred to read Blane's letter in private, but that obviously wasn't going to be possible for a while, and he had no intention of waiting. While Elaine cheerfully fiddled with stray papers and odd items, straightening his desk while she whistled in boredom, he read the letter from the private detective he'd been paying for three long, expensive years. He couldn't believe he'd read it correctly the first time, so he read it again. Then he grinned the slow, feral grin of a predator who has his quarry within reach at last.

Elaine stopped fiddling with a red crystal paperweight as she noticed the expression on Beau's face. "What is it?" she asked cautiously. In spite of their total lack of physical barriers at night, Beau had never lowered the other barriers between them. She still didn't know where he went sometimes, where the checks were going that regularly drained his bank account, or what he was doing that involved law firms in Washington and Richmond. She glanced at the envelope and wondered what a private investigator had to do with

Beau. "It looks like very good news," she observed when he simply stared into space and didn't reply at first.

He stood up and slipped the letter into his shirt pocket. "Yep," he said. "This is very good news."

He leaned forward and kissed her on the mouth. Elaine was so startled that she nearly fell off the desk in surprise. She clutched his shoulders to regain her balance and raised questioning eyes to his.

"This is the first time you've ever kissed me outside of your cabin," she exclaimed in breathless amazement. Her eyes softened. "Since that time at the steeplechase course, anyway... the morning after that first time I came to you."

He disengaged her hands from his shoulders and slowly pulled himself away. "The good news overwhelmed my good sense," he said quietly.

"I don't suppose you're going to share it with me?" she prodded with gentle cheerfulness.

He nodded. "I don't suppose I am." He was getting his winter jacket off the hook and searching for his keys. "I've got an errand to take care of. I probably won't be back until late...." He hesitated at the door and turned to find Elaine studying him. His eyes softened in spite of his best effort to remain unfeeling. "I'll see you tomorrow. Be sure and lock up when you're through here."

Elaine watched him leave and paced back and forth, growing angrier by the minute. The man could write an original text on stubbornness! He had wanted to hold her in his arms. She had seen it in his eyes. But had he? *No!* He'd pulled away and reminded her to lock up. He was struggling with a problem that involved his jailed father, a major law firm, a private investigator even *she* had heard of, but did he tell her anything about it? *No!* Not even when they were alone in bed together. Not even when he was sighing her name in agonized relief. Not even when he was kissing her with such reverence that she felt as if she were shattering in his hands. The man was going off to take care of obviously urgent personal business, and he'd made a point of shutting her out. Unless she was mistaken, he'd even told her in a roundabout way not to come to him tonight. She reheard his firm farewell. *I probably won't be back until late. I'll see you tomorrow.*

She wanted to cry in frustration. She had to content herself with slapping her boots with her crop and rolling her eyes heavenward, silently pleading for strength from above.

And after all the disasters in her life that he knew all about! She could have strangled him. Especially since she was *certain* he thought this was for her own good.

"Beau Lamond, I don't know why you're going out of your way to keep this a big dark secret, but I'm going to find out. And so help me, I wouldn't humiliate myself this way for anyone else on this planet." She immediately had to amend that. "Except maybe Richard and Meg, of course." She sighed. "Or maybe Ambrose and Mrs. Adams." Or a few other close friends, she silently admitted. "So I care about the people I love," she grumbled at the empty room. "We'll deal with that character fault later."

Elaine had no idea where Beau was going, and she wouldn't have followed him, in any event. That would have been too intrusive even for her. But she knew of two sources of information in the area, and she decided to see what she could glean from them both: Bradley File and Margaret Innery.

Bradley was easy to approach. He was mildly surprised at her sudden appearance, unannounced, in the late afternoon, but he recovered easily enough and sat and talked with her over coffee.

"So Beau has been supporting his parents since they lost everything?" Elaine asked in surprise.

"Basically. His mother is living with her sister's family about twenty miles from here. His father..."

"Is in jail," Elaine said sympathetically. "I know."

Bradley shrugged. "Beau has always felt responsible for it."

She bit her lip. "Because of Babs Carlton..." she murmured.

His shaggy old brows rose precipitously. "You sound jealous, my dear," he said with a chuckle. "And angry, like a mother cat protecting her only kitten."

Elaine blushed and tried to laugh off his comment. "Jealous? Of Babs? I'd have to be out of my mind. She's...dreadful...."

He chuckled. "I've heard it described as temporary insanity, I guess." He didn't have to explain that the "it" he had in mind was love. "And 'dreadful' is nowhere strong enough a word to describe that woman!" He shook his head. "I still say you sound...very involved," he amended, amused at her embarrassment at being called jealous.

Elaine swallowed. She didn't know what Beau had told Bradley about them, but considering how determined he was to avoid a publicly intimate relationship with her, she doubted it was much. She returned to his other comment. "There's nothing kittenish about Beau," she argued. "And I'm not his mother!"

Bradley was guffawing now, and he slapped his knee. "You know, you two spend more time denying how you feel than any two people I have ever known. Why Beau is as bad as you are. When I tease him a little about his pretty boss, you should see his eyes go that fighting color! And his back gets twice as stiff as yours!"

Elaine was fascinated. "You talk to him about...me?"

Bradley wiped a tear of mirth from his eyes. "Oh, yes. When he's throwing darts, it's a surefire way to ruin his game. He's getting sick and tired of it, too."

Elaine bit her lip, then plunged ahead. "Bradley?"

"Yep."

"Would you tell me everything you know about him?"

The older man's jaw dropped in surprise. "Everything? Right now?"

She laughed, and her cheeks colored a little more in embarrassment. "Well, I know he has a checkered past where women are concerned, and I know he's got some kind of problem involving a lawyer and a private detective, and I know you're trying to hire him away from my brother, but...could you fill me in on the details?"

Bradley's surprise mellowed into sympathy. "I take it he won't talk to you about any of it?"

Elaine sighed in frustration. "No. He keeps me at arm's length...."

Bradley looked doubtful of that, and Elaine laughed.

"Not always at arm's length," she amended. "But..." She hated to think about the possibility, but she had to ask. "Is there another woman in his life? Someone he's trying to protect? Or...go back to someday?"

Bradley had never considered that. He rubbed his chin thoughtfully. He didn't want Elaine to hold on to any false hopes. Not after what she'd been through with her husband. And Beau played his cards close to his vest with all of them, so he wasn't sure he knew all the answers. Especially about Beau and women.

"Well he's spent years trying to accommodate the women who kept after him," Bradley admitted wryly, "but he never was the kiss-and-tell type, so I wouldn't necessarily know. I don't think there's another woman," he said. "But to know the answer to that for sure, you'd have to ask Beau."

Elaine nodded. She felt a little sick, though, hearing him describe women chasing Beau. She must seem quite common, then, she thought with a pang of deep regret. She'd always envisioned him doing the chasing. Obviously that wasn't quite the case. She tried to ignore the pain that cut through her heart as she wondered if he saw her as just another woman who wanted him. Humiliation stung her, but she forced it away. She needed to talk to Bradley and learn what she could. There would be time later to feel humiliated.

Bradley organized his rusty thinking on the subject of Beau Lamond. "I'm just annoyed enough with him to tell you what I *do* know," he muttered. "He's developed a disgusting habit of trying to carry all the blame and all the responsibility smack on his own shoulders. If he won't tell you anything, that's his business. But it's a free country, last I heard, and I think it's high time I exercised a little of my constitutional right of free speech."

Elaine clapped encouragingly and laid her soft hand on his gnarled one. "Thanks, Bradley. You won't regret it."

He chuckled and rolled his eyes. "I hope not. Beau can be plenty furious when he wants to be." He looked at her significantly. "And I'm *still* trying to interest him in being my partner."

"Bradley, I'll be your partner myself, if it'll help," she offered with a laugh, relieved to hear that Beau hadn't made any effort to take Bradley up on the offer as yet.

"All I know about Beau Lamond..." He poured more coffee into the two thick china cups and began to reflect. "I first met him when he was just making a big splash on the event circuit, oh, about eighteen years ago, and he was a handsome rake who could tease performances out of his horses that I wouldn't have believed. I knew his parents a little. They were very quiet. Old-fashioned. Pillars of their small community, you could say. They just didn't know how to handle a firebrand like Beau. They tried too hard to get him to fit in a mold...wanted him to be a banker or a doctor or something. But he wanted to raise hell and tear around on a horse at top speed and travel. Did you know he got a degree in engineering?"

Elaine shook her head. "No." She didn't know anything about him, she thought sadly. She ignored the hurt of his rejection. "Engineering? Did he ever work as an engineer?"

"Oh, yes. He was going to be a partner in a firm with an old friend of his down in Charlottesville, but then Enoch Carlton's lawyers had his father charged with embezzlement."

"And his friend didn't want him anymore?" Elaine asked, hurt and outraged for Beau.

"No," Bradley said. "They were like two peas in a pod. His partner relished the challenge. He was a good friend. It was Beau who didn't want to go ahead with it. That's why he eventually came up here. When the trial was over, and his father had lost, the Lamonds had to sell everything to pay what they could toward the lawyer's fees and the damages levied against Mr. Lamond. Beau had to do that. It was like rubbing salt in an open wound, making him supervise the sale of everything his family owned. I never saw him look like he did then. Anyway, his father was sent to a prison about fifty miles from here, and Beau wanted to be near him. He was afraid his father wouldn't survive in jail. And then, it was close to his mother's people, and she could have some support from them. He said it would work for him, too, since he could find out some of the things he needed to know, if he were in this area."

"What things?" Elaine asked.

"I don't know. He never wanted to say. It had something to do with trying to prove that Carlton had framed Mr. Lamond."

There was a funny note in Bradley's voice.

"Don't you believe his father was framed?" Elaine asked in surprise.

Bradley shrugged. "I don't know. Carlton might have uncovered something and made it look worse than it was, but I find it hard to believe it was a complete frame-up." He looked a little embarrassed to admit it. "I hate to say that. I love Beau like a son, to tell you the truth, and I know how hard he's fought against the accusations. He's poured every ounce of his blood and sweat into trying to prove his father's innocence, but...hell...I know a couple of accountants who've seen the company's records. They don't think the accounts could have been manipulated without Mr. Lamond being aware of it for a long, long time. If he didn't shine a light on that fact, he must have been getting something out of it." He shook his head sadly. "Beau nearly tore me apart the one time I tried to tell him that. I know his father always had a clean reputation, but...well, you just don't always know how a person's gonna deal with temptation, I guess."

"Poor Beau," Elaine murmured unhappily. "what an awful situation to be in...."

Bradley shrugged. "Even on the outside chance he's right, I don't think he's got a snowball's chance in hell of proving it. He'd have to get a confession from whoever fixed the accounts. Can you imagine them being stupid enough to do that? Their life wouldn't be worth a plugged nickel. If Carlton didn't have them done in right off the bat, they'd be looking at prison walls for the rest of their lives."

Elaine paled. "Enoch Carlton would...murder them?"

Bradley was philosophical. "He'd have little enough to lose if he did. If I were one of his hired thieves, I'd sure be keeping a close eye on my back all the time."

A wave of nausea passed over Elaine. Bradley patted her hand sympathetically.

"Talking about murder and thieving brings back unpleasant memories for you, doesn't it, honey?" he asked her.

She smiled wanly. "Yes. But that doesn't matter anymore. Don't worry about it, Bradley." She smiled gratefully and rose to her feet to leave. "I appreciate your telling me so much about him. Thank you...."

He chuckled and walked outside with her as she got into her car. "Don't thank me yet," he warned, his old eyes twinkling mischievously. "He doesn't know that *you know* yet.... After he finds out, then see if you still feel like saying thank you. After all, he's gone to a lot of trouble to keep this to himself. I don't think he's going to appreciate your having found it out."

"He'll be furious," she said dryly.

"Yep. That's what he'll be all right," Bradley said with a sage nod of his head.

"Well, he won't be the only one," she muttered darkly. She put the car in gear and shot down the road.

Bradley chortled and rubbed his hands together zestfully. "I wish I could be there to see the argument they're gonna have about this," he told himself wistfully. He sighed, contemplating the impending fireworks. "It'll be a humdinger, all right. It's just a matter of where and when...."

Elaine walked into Margaret Innery's office just as Margaret was reaching for her hat and coat. The realtor turned and beamed at her unexpected visitor.

"Well, well! How are you, Elaine? And to what do I owe this unexpected visit?"

"I was in town and I thought I'd see if I could catch you," Elaine said. "But you look like you're on your way out...."

Margaret laid her broad-brimmed blue hat back on the closet shelf and returned her coat to its hanger. "It's nothing that can't wait a few minutes. A client is coming by shortly, and we're going to see an estate that he's interested in." She walked regally toward her sofa and motioned for Elaine to sit down. "What can I do for you honey?" Her voice was sweetly smooth, but her shrewd eyes pinned Elaine sharply.

Elaine had prepared an excuse for her visit, and she launched into it. "I've been wanting to talk to you about what estates are for sale in the county...."

Margaret's eyes widened. "Really? I'm surprised...."

"With Richard and Meg at Foxgrove, I thought I might like a home of my own...."

Margaret nodded sympathetically. "I can certainly understand, honey. Uh...is there any friction?"

Leave it to Margaret to dig for dirt, Elaine thought in amusement. "Not at all. We're the best of friends. But we're adults. We all need our own space. So, tell me...is there much on the market now?"

Margaret obviously would have preferred to talk more about the three-way relationship that was inspiring Elaine to move, but she reluctantly followed Elaine's lead. "Well...there's the old Sanderson-Whythe estate...."

"Still crumbling?" Elaine asked, choking back a laugh.

"Still crumbling," Margaret acknowledged. "But it crumbles so *elegantly*, my dear."

"Save that for the out-of-towners," Elaine advised her in amusement. "Anything else?"

"Yes. The Porter mansion, the Villainy farm...they've done marvels with that old farmhouse.... And then there's Accomac...."

"Accomac... That borders Mr. Aboudi's place doesn't it?"

"Yes." Margaret looked a little sorry that she'd mentioned it. "I think I've got a buyer for Accomac though."

Elaine lounged comfortably in the overstuffed sofa. "Really? Anyone I know?" she asked conversationally.

Margaret looked faintly amused herself. "Yes. You met her at my party last month, and I hear she went fox hunting with you not long after."

Elaine crossed her boots with the utmost care. "Oh, yes..." She frowned, as if trying hard to recall the woman's name. Not that it actually *was* hard, of course, but she didn't want Margaret to know that. "Castleton? Cattleton?"

"Carlton," Margaret supplied helpfully. "Babs and Enoch Carlton." She glanced at her watch. "It's one of Mr. Carlton's representatives who I'm meeting."

Elaine felt cold. "Really? Have the Carltons made an offer yet?"

"No. Mr. Carlton wants to, but his wife isn't sure. I think she has her eye on Amberley Falls, but I've told her the family won't part with that place until the dowager dies."

"What did she say to that?" Elaine asked, trying to sound only mildly interested.

"She said she'd help the dowager along, if necessary!" Margaret laughed. "She has a nasty sense of humor, don't you think?"

"Yes," Elaine murmured faintly. "Have you gotten to know her since you've been showing her around?"

Margaret wrinkled her nose. "No. She's not terribly open." She smiled wickedly. "Personally, I think she's one of those women who opens up to men...to make them do what she wants...and closes herself off to women, because they would see right through her."

"Hmm. That's interesting." Elaine lowered her eyelashes and studied the toe of her black riding boot. "Have you met her husband?"

Margaret rolled her eyes. "Have I ever! And a more arrogant, domineering, ruthless man I have seldom seen. I can't imagine being married to him. Babs must be made of sterner stuff than I am, because I wouldn't have him, even with all the money he's got. And believe me, his money would buy a lot of vacations away from him!"

Elaine laughed.

Margaret shook her head, and her eyes narrowed. "He keeps other women," she said conspiratorially.

"He does?" Elaine asked, shocked. "You discovered that already?"

Margaret looked quite pleased with herself. "Oh, yes, dear. I have an old friend in Charlottesville, and we had a long conversation about them, because, you see, the Carltons used to live in Charlottesville. Some of the time, that is ... when he wasn't in Washington or New York or Miami or out of the country." Margaret was obviously relishing her juicy tidbits. "Years ago he went through two or three women every quarter—like filing his quarterly tax return. And he didn't stop when he married Babs. Poor Babs hadn't quite been expecting that, apparently, and it really hit her hard. He beat her once, when she complained about it...."

"How do you know that?" Elaine asked in surprise.

Margaret raised her eyebrows delicately. "An old school chum told me. She saw him hit Babs by their pool one afternoon. And then he dragged her into the house and locked her in the bedroom. The next day Babs was wearing dark glasses...." She smiled, serenely triumphant at her expert information gathering.

"Good heavens..." Elaine murmured. "How awful."

Margaret waved off Elaine's sympathy. "Well, yes, of course. We women have to stick together on that. If she'd had any sense, she would have had him arrested. I suppose that's never easy to do, but ... well, she came up with her own revenge instead."

"She did?" Elaine tapped her crop on her boot with exaggerated casualness. "What did she do?"

"She talked a charming hunk of a man into being her lover." Margaret chortled and put her hand over her mouth. "And then she told her husband about it. Can you imagine?"

Elaine could imagine only to well, but she remained silent.

"And do you know who the man was?" Margaret eyed Elaine closely. When Elaine shrugged and said nothing, Margaret told her. "It was Beauregard Lamond. Our own Beau! That was why they looked at one another so oddly that night at my party...."

Elaine blushed in spite of herself. She'd heard it already, but having to listen to Margaret gossip about it made her feel very uncomfortable. It was partly embarrassment, but there was also a strong, protective desire to sharply tell Margaret not to talk about Beau like that. Margaret sailed on, saving her the trouble of holding up her end of the conversation for a moment.

"She had pestered him and pestered him until he could hardly turn around without having to step over her. And she did a magnificent job of convincing him that she was a deeply lonely and wronged women. Can you imagine that? Pestering a man like him into her bed?" Margaret laughed until tears came to her eyes.

But Elaine had never felt less like laughing. Was that how he saw *her*? Pestering him to take her to his bed? The blood drained from her face, and nausea threatened. She got to her feet, heading to the door before Margaret could notice her sudden pallor.

"It was so ironic that Beau's family lost everything to Carlton after that. Don't you agree?" Margaret managed as she overcame her mirth and followed Elaine to the door.

"Very ironic," Elaine agreed shortly.

Margaret called after her, "When do you think you might be interested in moving?"

Elaine gave her a blank look.

"To your own house, honey," Margaret reminded her.

"Oh, that." Elaine pressed her fingertips to her temple. "Soon, I suppose."

"Well you just drop in any time," Margaret told her warmly. "Hurry back, y'hear?"

Elaine smiled wanly and pulled her car away from the curb. She wondered if she hadn't been better off before she'd heard Margaret's gossip about Babs Carlton and Beau. She felt dirty now, as if her being with him had been contaminated by what Margaret had told her.

When she got home, she wouldn't let herself look in the direction of Beau's cabin. She walked resolutely toward the pillared red brick estate house, grimly refusing to think about where Beau was. He'd told her not to come. She'd thrown herself at him enough. Tonight she was going to her own suite and she would stay there.

Tomorrow... She would worry about tomorrow when it came....

She showered and slid between her soft clean sheets. Then she curled into a fetal ball and told herself she wasn't going to cry. She wasn't. She wasn't. She wasn't.

Chapter 13

Beau was at the dressage ring the following morning, watching Meg work with the beautiful black Thoroughbred mare, when Elaine came down to the stable to join them. He was grinning at Meg when he turned to see who was approaching. His grin faded a little as his eyes met Elaine's.

"You're getting a late start today," he said easily. "Have a late night?"

She looked away with an effort. "Not too late. I had a few things to discuss with Richard up at the house this morning."

"I see."

He didn't sound particularly concerned, she thought, sighing inwardly with regret. Probably because he wasn't. Unlike her. She'd been aching to see him all the time she'd been grilling Richard about how people generally fixed books.

"Meg and Irish Mist look like they were made for each other," Elaine said, leaning on the fence alongside Beau.

"Yes. They're well matched." He looked at her curiously. "I believe I said the same thing about you, too."

She laughed ruefully and shook her head with feeling. "No. Irish Mist is Meg's baby. I don't want to interfere."

"Interfere?" He sounded slightly puzzled, and his brow furrowed. "You mean you don't want to ride the horse?"

"Not if Meg is."

"That's ridiculous."

Elaine's eyes flashed, and she turned on him, hurting because of the thoughts that had tormented her all night, and alarmed because he'd touched on a sensitive subject. "It's *not* ridiculous," she snapped. "There are plenty of other horses for me to ride. If you don't mind, I'll stick with them!"

She forced a smile and greeted Meg, who was just riding past them at a canter. Then she turned sharply on her heel and stalked into the stable in search of one of the timber racers to exercise. Jumping in a ring wasn't going to work off her anger and frustration. She needed speed today. She found a big hunter who had won one of the point-to-points last season. He would do just fine.

Beau stared after Elaine in utter surprise. "What the hell is that about?" he muttered to himself. He was moving to follow her when Meg called out to him, and he turned to see what she wanted.

"Could you watch her legs on this one?" Meg asked. "She feels a little insecure to me today. Do you think she could have pulled a muscle?"

Beau glanced at the stable in frustration, then turned his attention to Irish Mist. "I'll watch," he called out. "Which leg?"

"Right hind..."

Five minutes later, Beau and Meg were examining the mare's leg with their hands, taking a careful look at her from hoof to hip. Then they heard hoofbeats and raised their heads just in time to see Elaine ride Count Drac out of the paddock area, heading for the open fields.

"Where are you going?" Beau called out, dropping Irish Mist's leg and striding in Elaine's direction. He looked irritated, and there was a hint of aggression in his stance as he halted at the fence, hands on hips.

"The northeast timber trail," Elaine called out. "See you after lunch." She kicked Count Drac's sides, and the horse leaped forward. His long legs effortlessly gobbled up the ground, sending them beyond shouting range very quickly.

"Damn." Beau clenched his jaw.

Meg looked at him in cautious sympathy. "I can take care of Irish Mist," she offered. "Why don't you go with her?"

But Beau had already decided on that course of action and was halfway to the stable, calling in an uncharacteristically sharp voice for Eddie to bring him some tack on the double.

Meg patted Irish Mist's warm black nose and laughed ruefully. "I hope Elaine's prepared for him by the time he catches up with her. He doesn't look like he's in a very peaceful mood, Mist."

The mare snorted delicately and bobbed her head.

The timber trails wound through the most deserted reaches of Foxgrove. Their narrow dirt tracings looked like ancient footpaths through the heavily treed hills and rolling grasslands. Elaine had rarely ridden the trails alone. Until now she'd generally enjoyed riding through the countryside with a friend or two. But today she was grateful that there was no one with her, permitting her to concentrate all of her energies on burying herself as deeply as possible in the isolated wilderness for a couple of hours.

Count Drac galloped easily through the lower reaches of the trail and showed his steely conditioning by not even breathing hard when they continued at that harrowing pace up one steep bank after another. He jumped the fallen timbers and gurgling streamlets easily, his silky ears pricked forward alertly, while his dark brown eyes shone in excitement. Some of Elaine's eagerness to escape communicated itself to him, and he dug in a little harder with each stride, hurrying them away.

Suddenly a rabbit darted out in front of them, and Count Drac swerved sharply to one side, eyes rolling. His sudden and totally unanticipated change of direction left Elaine half slung over one of his shoulders, but she clung to him like a burr and quickly regained her balance. Experience and common sense made her slow the big racer down to a steady canter, however. He shook his head angrily. He'd enjoyed blasting through the wilds like a whirlwind.

It was then that she heard the relentless beat of hooves behind her. She drew Count Drac down to a walk and twisted in the saddle. Her heart thudded, although she wasn't sure whether it was more out of anxiety or out of love. It was Beau, of course.

He looked grim, she realized, taking in the tight set of his mouth and the flat line of his brows. Instinct told her to back away from him, and she tightened her grip on the reins without being completely aware of what she was doing. Count Drac sidestepped away. Elaine's tension increased as Beau neared them, and the big timber racer's muscles tightened right along with hers as he sensed her growing unease.

"Whoa. Easy, Drac," she murmured as he hopped back two steps, his neck arching, his mouth lathering as he champed on the bit. She ran her hand down his neck, feeling the nervous energy rippling through his body. She knew she was the cause, but she couldn't make herself relax enough to make it any easier for her horse. "Whoa, Drac. Easy..." she crooned, doing what she could to calm him.

Beau had been galloping when she'd first seen him, but he'd gradually slowed to a full-bodied canter. He drew the big Dutch warmblood down to a slow trot when he got close. Normally Count Drac wouldn't have been bothered, but in his state of high excitement, he reacted as if he were being ridden down. He snorted and reared, striking out with his forelegs and jumping away.

Elaine had handled plenty of rearing horses and easily stayed in the saddle, but Beau didn't seem to notice, because he bore down on her and grabbed Count Drac's reins near the bridle, sparing her only one brief angry glance before concentrating on quieting the horses.

"Are you trying to be insulting?" Elaine demanded, glaring at him as he struggled to keep his horse from bumping hers and setting both animals off again.

Beau ignored her irate question until both animals were standing fairly calmly, blowing plumes of steam from their nostrils in a slow, regular fashion. Then he released Elaine's reins and turned his attention to her. "Insulting?" he asked very softly.

"Yes, insulting!" Elaine shot back. "I'm not some little kid who needs someone to hold her horse when he bucks. Did it look like I was going to be *thrown*?" Not waiting for him to answer, she charged on, leaving him with his mouth half-open. "I was having a *very* pleasant ride until you came running us down. *What* was so urgent that it couldn't have waited until I got back?"

She saw the vivid anger in his eyes and quailed a little then. She was seized by another sharp urge to flee, and Count Drac immediately started to prance backward. She tightened her legs and held him still, muttering under her breath in frustration.

"You shouldn't be out here," he said sharply.

She shot him a frigid look. "I beg your pardon?" She had never spoken with such upper-crust politeness before in her life.

Beau's face darkened in anger. "You can beg my pardon until the cows come home," he said succinctly, "but you won't get it unless you turn that horse around and take him in."

Elaine's eyes widened and her mouth fell open in shock. "What?" she exclaimed indignantly.

He looked angry enough to drag her down off the horse. Elaine's mount pranced back and sideways, and Beau swore vividly. "You're too upset to be riding him, especially out here in the middle of nowhere."

Elaine's anger burned a little more righteously, and she laughed at him, gratified when her laughter only served to infuriate him more. Good. She was glad he could feel something, anyway. Her vivid blue eyes narrowed, and she struggled to keep Drac down to a few sporadic mincing steps. "I'm *not* too upset to go riding," she retorted. "I was having no problems with him at all until you galloped down on us like a steamroller."

Beau's horse was sidestepping and jingling his bridle, forcing Beau to tighten his legs and firm the pressure on his own reins. Grimly he listened to Elaine's angry denial, and his eyes flashed thunderously. He knew damn well that he'd been overstating his case, but her denial immediately drove all reasonableness out of him.

"I saw the way Drac shied away from something in the woods back there," he said in a hard voice. "Count Drac has *never* done that before in the year and a half I've ridden him."

"No doubt due to your skill," she said silkily.

"No!" he said through clenched teeth. "Due to my not being a mass of conflicting emotions when I'm riding him. Now head back, or I'm taking you off him and you can walk back!"

Elaine couldn't believe her ears. Her face was nearly comical in its disbelief. "What did you say?" she asked in a strangled whisper.

"You heard me." He stared at her, his own anger and determination shimmering in the rigid set of his shoulders, the stiffness of his seat in the saddle, the fiery warning in his storm-colored eyes.

"Yes," she said softly. She gathered the reins and shot him a venomous look. "I *knew* I didn't want company today," she said, shaking with rage and a swirling mass of emotions too complicated for her to sort through at the moment. "So, if you'll excuse me..."

She tightened the reins and sank her right heel into Drac's side. The horse, who'd been nervously waiting to go anywhere at the least provocation, shot forward as if leaping from the starting line at the Grand National.

At a full gallop, covering the trail at what felt like the speed of sound, Elaine had no awareness of anyone behind her. She forced Beau out of her mind in self-defense, concentrating on urging Drac over the safest footing and letting him have his head. He loved to race, and in his overexcited state, he needed no urging to run flat out. The first jump was a huge slat fence, and he soared over it without breaking stride. An eighth of a mile farther on, he cleared a double jump, then a broad water jump fed by a small stream. The wind whipped at Elaine's jacket and stung her face, bringing tears to her eyes. She blinked rapidly and settled for seeing the world as a blur for a moment. She couldn't do that for long, however, and hastily rubbed her gloved hand across her eyes as the ground dropped away up ahead.

She slowed Drac to a canter, letting him choose his own speed on the downgrade. It was steep, a forty-five-degree slope, and not easy to manage at a walk, let alone at speed. But today Elaine forgot any fear she'd ever had and took the dangerous drop without a second thought. Drac's forelegs hit the ground hard at the bottom, and his hindquarters were bunched up tight beneath him as he struggled to keep from losing his balance. But they made it, and she put him into a hard gallop straight through the forest.

She let him run through the course as fast as he wanted to, hearing nothing but the sound of his hard hooves beating against the earth and the dull roaring of her own anger and despair. Not until she reached the knoll overlooking the last leg of the timber trail did she let him slow down.

"Time to cool down," she told him, patting his shoulder and neck. She trotted him for a couple of miles, then let him slow to a walk. Her ears were aching from the cold, and she tied the reins in a loop to keep them short, then put her gloved hands over her ears to warm them—which was why she didn't hear Beau until he was nearly beside her.

She saw his arm reach out to grab her reins at the same moment his horse drew up beside hers. She looked at him in alarm, and the cold fury on his face only made her realize how realistic her alarm was.

He gave her a hard tight-lipped look and pulled the reins over Count Drac's head, leading her back the rest of the way like a child. Elaine's alarm turned to anger. How dare he humiliate her like this! The moment they reached the stable, she vaulted to the ground. She was following him inside, fully intending to clean up Count Drac and icily ignore Beau, but before she could, he had dismounted and called for two of the stable hands. They appeared immediately, clearly alarmed at the sharp note of command in his usually easygoing voice.

"Take our horses, please," he said succinctly. Then he turned and gripped Elaine's elbow firmly with one hand. "Miss Faust and I have a few things to discuss."

He propelled her in the direction of the now empty dressage ring. She tried to wriggle free of his grasp, with no success. He merely tightened his hold.

"I'm not going anywhere with you," she snapped. "Let me go!"

He laughed, as if that were actually an amusing idea. "Not until we've had a little talk," he said angrily.

They were across the ring, and he pushed her through the fence into the grassy meadow beyond.

"Where are we going?" she demanded, rubbing her elbow, which he'd had to release in order to push her between the fence slats.

He looked at her, and his eyes glittered dangerously. "Where we can have a little privacy," he said through barely clenched teeth.

"I don't need any privacy!" she retorted.

"I thought you had a strong urge to be alone today!" he said sarcastically.

She shot him a scathing look. "If I'm with *you*, I will hardly be *alone*."

He glared at her furiously. "Funny. While I was chasing behind you, trying like hell not to startle your damn horse, I had the feeling you were completely alone. I was merely your camp follower. Beneath noticing." His disgust at that role was unmistakable.

"I didn't ask you to follow me!"

He pushed her firmly in the direction of a footpath winding through a small stand of trees. "But you knew damn well I was there," he muttered angrily. "And you know I didn't want you to ride that trail feeling upset."

"I wasn't upset!" she nearly shouted.

Beau rolled his eyes and clenched one hand. "Of course not," he said sarcastically. "You're always rude and angry. You always turn your back on people and ride off in a huff."

"I wasn't in a huff!" she exclaimed, gathering herself for a vigorous defense. She put a hand up to ward off a low-lying branch and looked around in confusion. "*Where* are we going?" she demanded in a mystified tone.

"Can't you guess?" He pulled her down the fork to the left, and fifty feet ahead of them lay his cabin.

Elaine slowed and dragged him back, like a mule resisting going forward. A stubborn look came over her face. "I don't want to...." she murmured rebelliously.

His jaw tightened, and he gave her a determined yank that pulled her forward so fast she almost fell on her face. She braced her hand on his back, and he steadied her. For a moment heat flowed between them and they stared at each other. She looked into his face, and her anger was joined by fear and distrust. She'd defied her husband once, and he'd humiliated her in a ruthlessly primitive way. In spite of herself, the memories began swamping her, making her feel almost ill.

"I don't want to...." she repeated numbly. Her eyes were wide and glazed with apprehension.

Beau looked at her in exasperation. What the hell did she think he was going to do? Assault her? He pulled her along, tamping down his anger at her for dragging her feet every step of the way. He yanked open the door, pushed her firmly inside and blocked her only means of escape by standing in front of his closed door with his hands crossed in front of his chest. He looked about as movable as the entire estate.

Elaine looked around wildly, as if searching for an escape. She knew she was trapped, and she swallowed hard. The room was cold now. There was no fire. It wasn't warm and inviting as it had been on so many nights. She looked at the bed where they had loved with such tender, violent passion, and a lump formed in her throat. She sat down in one of the chairs at the table, feeling it was the safest place, given her limited choices.

Elaine was still wearing her riding jacket, but she began to shiver and wrapped her arms around her stomach protectively. She heard Beau step away from the door and strike a match to the kindling and logs. The soft crackle and snap of a newly started fire assailed her, and she closed her eyes. She heard the sharp rap of his boots on the bare wood floor as he paced halfway across the room, then back to the fireplace. The tension between them was becoming almost unbearable. Why didn't he say something? What did he want from her?

"I'd like an explanation," he said. He sounded less angry, but far from his usual calm self.

She sighed and removed her hard hat. She laid it on the table in front of her and looked up at him. Sitting at the end of the table as she was, she could look across it and see him standing near the fire. There was a distant look in his eyes that was new to her.

"An explanation?" she repeated blankly. "Of what?"

Irritation overshadowed his distant look. "I told you this morning that you were ridiculous to refuse to ride Irish Mist. You flew into a small fit and tore out of the stables on the toughest timber racer we've got, threatening yourself with a broken neck and me with a shortened life span. I want to know why."

Elaine looked at him in astonishment then, and some of her anger ebbed away, replaced with a tiny pebble of gratitude. He'd been worried about her. That was why he was acting like such a concerned idiot. "You know as well as I do that it's very unlikely I would have broken my neck," she argued, unwilling to let that go unchallenged. But her eyes weren't spitting fire at him anymore.

Beau gave no evidence of being even slightly mollified. He frowned fiercely and gripped the raw stone mantel with one hand, as if to keep from doing something awful. "Why did you react like that?" he growled softly.

"I..." She drew in a breath and tried to steady her resolve. "It's just that I never ride horses that Meg rides in competition. I never have. And I never will."

He waited, and when it was obvious that she didn't intend to say more, he looked heavenward and growled, "Damn it, why not?"

The frustrated anger in his deep male voice brought back painful memories and Elaine flinched. She shrank back in the chair; her face paled, her fingers tightening in her lap.

Beau saw her reaction and scowled even more fiercely. "And why are you so frightened of me now?" he demanded furiously. "What have I ever done to merit your fear? If anything, I've..." He bit off what he was going to say and put both hands on the mantel, turning to look down at the floor. "It's rare for me to lose my temper...." he muttered, sounding almost exhausted. "But you—"

Elaine bowed her head, and a tear slid down her cheek. "Please don't say that it's my fault," she blurted out, interrupting him before she had to bear the additional hurt of actually hearing him say it. "I heard that so often before.... But I don't think I could bear to hear it from you." Emotions were overcoming her.

Beau heard the broken sound in her voice, and the rest of his anger began to drain away. He opened his mouth to deny that he'd been about to say any such thing, but now that her defenses had crumbled, he decided he should listen to whatever she wanted to say.

"Cam really was an excellent name for my ex-husband," she reflected, sinking her hands into her hair and leaning her elbows on the bare table. She stared blindly at the wood as if seeing the past. "Only instead of being short for Cameron, it should have stood for Chameleon. He changed his colors with such *ease*!"

She laughed bitterly. She slanted a glance at Beau and found him watching her. She had no idea what he was thinking.

"How did he change?" he asked in a low hard voice, quite unlike the one she was accustomed to.

She smiled wanly. "He was the model of passionate attention before we were married. Fondly promising all the things a young woman longs to hear. But after..." She closed her eyes and swallowed. "For a few months he tried to maintain a semblance of a happy marriage. I wasn't all that happy, but I thought it was just a matter of having to adjust to marriage. I could never put my finger on what, exactly, was wrong. I mean...he took me out to dinner, the theater, to visit friends.... He sent me flowers.... He listened to me over dinner when I talked about things that I took an interest in...."

Elaine shook her head and opened her eyes. "But there was something missing. I realized it the first night...." She looked at Beau and was surprised at how tightly drawn he looked. She smiled sadly. "Does it bother you to hear about him?"

He expelled a long breath. It bothered him a great deal, but he sensed she'd feel much better if she told him whatever it was, so he didn't admit it. "No," he lied. "It doesn't bother me."

Elaine nodded. "I didn't think it would," she said, sighing. She wished it did. At least that would have meant he cared enough to be a little jealous, which would be a sweet solace. "Even on our wedding night I knew there was something wrong. He was saying all the right things, I suppose, and he went through the motions eagerly enough, but..."

Beau clamped down the rage that was pouring through him at the vision of Cam Bennett making love to Elaine. "But what?" he asked through half-clenched teeth.

She frowned. "It was as if there wasn't any genuine intimacy there. No real tenderness. No warmth. No honest caring. At first I put it down to my own inexperience. After a while, though, it bothered me too much for me just to dismiss it like that. I tried to talk to him about it when we'd been married for seven or eight months and..."

Her eyes clouded, and she found it hard to continue.

Beau's knuckles whitened under the increasing pressure he was applying to the stone mantel. He gritted his teeth and forced the question out of his unwilling mouth. "What happened when you tried to talk to him about it?"

Elaine looked away from him in embarrassment. "He told me that I was too conventional to stimulate him. That I... was a big disappointment to him." She brushed away the tears that glittered on her dark eyelashes.

"And you believed him!" Beau's anger exploded across the room.

Elaine shrank back and nodded miserably. "He spent the next three months pointing out to me in the crudest possible ways exactly how I was failing him. He was so charming about it, too, as though he were being perfectly reasonable and I was out of my mind to even question some of the things he wanted me to do...."

Beau took a steadying breath and wished he could wrap his hands around Cam Bennett's throat. The look of abject humiliation on Elaine's beautiful face made him feel murderous.

"I tried to do what he wanted, but...most of the time I just couldn't. He would remind me of the few things he'd managed to force me to do and..." She covered her eyes with her hands. "He was a master at making me feel degraded and humiliated. But when we weren't alone, he was entirely different. When we were in public, we were like other couples.... I thought I could be happy. I thought I'd be able to get through the..."

"Sex," Beau snapped.

"Yes," she admitted miserably. "Why are you angry again?"

"Never mind. There's more, isn't there?" He didn't want to have to hear this twice, so he thought it would be easier to get it all out at once.

"The last few weeks, before I left him, he was out a lot. And there were bills for things that I hadn't seen...flowers, lingerie, theater tickets. I asked him about them, and he always had an excuse. Finally a friend told me that he'd been seen with another woman when he'd told me he was at work. When I confronted him with that, he flew into a rage. He dragged me by the arm all the way through the house, pushing me and screaming at me, accusing me of being the cause of his problems because I was such an unsatisfactory wife...."

Beau's fury at hearing about Cam's abusive behavior was tinged with anger at being tarred by the same brush. "Is that why you cringed and dragged your feet when I was pulling you in here?" he asked in angry dismay.

Elaine nodded.

He slammed his hands against the stone mantel. "Thanks a hell of a lot," he muttered.

Elaine swallowed. "In my mind...in my heart, I know you wouldn't hurt me," she said softly. "But...you see, that night he..."

Cold dread wrapped itself around Beau's aching heart. "He what?" he whispered. When she didn't answer, he impaled her with a commanding look and repeated his demand. "What did he do?"

"I don't think I can say it," she whispered miserably. Her hands were shaking, and tears brimmed in her eyes. "I almost told Meg once, but I was afraid to have her know.... And I couldn't tell Richard. I was afraid he might actually kill Cam if he ever got his hands on him...."

Beau took off his jacket and crossed the room to Elaine. He pulled her hands away from her face and pulled her to her feet. Without speaking he removed her coat and sat down himself where she had been seated. He drew her down onto his lap and put his arm around her shoulders. Lifting her chin with his hand, he looked into her eyes.

"If you don't want to talk about this anymore, I'll understand," he said quietly. He drew in a ragged breath and told her, "Whatever it was, it wasn't your fault, sweetheart.... Believe me."

The gentle endearment was more than she could bear, and Elaine wrapped her arms around his neck and sobbed. Racked with her own tears, in gulps, she told him about how Cam had beaten her, how he'd sadistically pleasured himself on her in the midst of it, how he'd laughed at her as she'd begged him to stop.

"I was never afraid of a man hurting me before that," she sobbed against his shoulder. "I'm sorry.... For a moment...it just all came back...."

Beau closed his eyes and hugged her, laying his hand behind her head and drawing her close. He wanted to wrap himself around her and protect her from her own painful memories. And he wanted to kill her dead husband with his bare hands.

"I'm so sorry, baby," he muttered in an oddly strained voice. "I'm so sorry...."

He sat there with her, rocking her, soothing her with his voice and his arms, until she was exhausted and empty of tears. She sniffled, and he found a handkerchief in his pocket for her.

She laid her head against his shoulder and splayed her hand against the comforting warmth of his broad, solid chest. "That's why I was...acting a little scared," she finally managed to say. "If I hadn't already been so keyed up, it probably wouldn't have happened."

Beau wasn't so sure, but he hoped she was right. For both their sakes. He no longer particularly cared why she'd ridden off in a huff, but Elaine switched the conversation back to his original question.

"About Meg...I always try to let her have the horses she wants," Elaine explained. "It started when we were kids and I felt sorry for her, because she had such a hard life with her father and not much money. So if she wanted to ride one of our horses in a show, I didn't." She looked at Beau anxiously and laid a pleading hand on his cheek. "Please don't tell her.... I've tried to make sure she never knew. You see, when she was growing up, her horsemanship was her entrée into everything here. People didn't look down on her, because she was so good. I've always loved her. She's my best friend. I couldn't bear it if I did anything to hurt her, even a little bit. I always had so much...."

Beau turned his head slightly and kissed her palm tenderly. Elaine was such an overprotective soft touch. He smiled slightly. "Your secret is safe with me," he assured her solemnly. "But don't you think it's about time you outgrew that habit? After all, Meg's all grown-up now. She's well established. She can take competition in stride." He added, "In this particular case, I think you'd probably be doing her a favor to take Irish Mist off her hands for a while. She has too many horses on her card for the next six months."

Elaine was still troubled. "I *hate* competition. And I don't want to come anywhere close to competing with Meg." Her lashes were still damp as she raised her eyes to his. "In a competition, someone always loses. I don't want either of us to lose."

Beau considered that for a moment. "Does that carry over to the other areas of your life?"

"Avoiding competition?" Elaine wrinkled her brow. "I don't know. I never thought about it."

He closed his eyes and leaned back in the chair, thinking of how noncompetitive it must have been for her to chase him. He was a willing captive when it came to her. The idea that she might care for him primarily because he was safe both amused and infuriated him. He opened his eyes and drew her chin around so that she was forced to look at him.

"Am I a way of avoiding competition?" he asked dryly.

"What on earth are you talking about?" she asked, not following him at all.

He spelled it out for her. "Do you come to me because I'm safe? I'm not surrounded by women, nor likely to be in the near future. Does that make me a noncompetitive commodity?"

She looked so completely nonplussed that he nearly laughed. Then she blushed furiously and looked away. "Actually, I always thought of you as quite the opposite," she admitted. "And you told me yourself about how successful you've always been with women...." Her voice trailed off miserably.

"That was in my checkered past," he objected teasingly. "You know very well that I've been living the life of a monk."

Elaine looked at him, and her eyes glimmered suspiciously. "Well, you've embraced the hair shirt and the bare cell to a certain extent," she conceded. "But I'm not sure about the rest of it...."

He drew her up against his chest and lowered his head inexorably toward hers, hesitating when their lips were barely separated.

"What rest of it?" he demanded softly.

She slid her arms around him more comfortably and smiled up at the tender amusement in his gray-blue eyes. "Isn't there something about avoiding close contact with women?" she asked innocently.

"Is there?" His warm breath fanned her mouth, sending tendrils of heat down across her skin.

"I think there is...."

"How close can I get without violating the rules?"

"I think you've already broken them."

His mouth covered hers, and their interest in further conversation began to wane considerably.

"It's *afternoon*," Elaine reminded him shyly as he lifted his lips to look down at her, his eyes glittering with desire.

"Tell me," he murmured huskily. "How did you ever find the nerve to come here that first night?"

She blushed, and her dark lashes lowered. Beau's fingers on her chin forced her to meet his compelling gaze.

"I couldn't help myself," she admitted softly. "I was afraid to come to you, but I was more afraid not to. I... needed you... and I thought you needed me...." And I loved you, she added silently, aching to say it aloud, but afraid it would drive him away.

He kissed her searchingly, opening his mouth over hers and sliding his tongue over all the silken surfaces, deepening the kiss gradually until he groaned, breaking off with a stifled gasp.

"Have I ever showed you my shower?" he asked unsteadily, loosening her clothing and finding her bare warm skin with his hand.

Elaine half closed her eyes in pleasure. "No," she moaned. "But don't you have to go back...?"

"I'm giving myself the afternoon off," he told her. He looked into her eyes and murmured, "I missed you last night...."

Elaine captured his face with her hands and kissed him with all the frustrated longing that had lain in her heart since he'd told her not to come to him. "And I missed you," she whispered unsteadily. "Maybe that was part of my being upset today, too."

Beau washed her body under the warm, cleansing water, then dried her and carried her to his bed, as he had once before. But this time she felt burned in the crucible of his desire for her. Beneath his hands, his lips, she felt radiantly clean. The most beautiful and desirable woman in the world. If only he was willing to love her... be hers in front of everyone.

She didn't want to reach for more than he could give, though, so she curled against him and fell asleep in his arms. She knew she had to let this be enough. It would be greedy of her to want more.

Chapter 14

"It looks like snow," Elaine observed wistfully. She was standing in the main living room just off the foyer, looking through the large panes of nineteenth-century glass at the bleak gray sky blanketing them.

Meg was putting a small red-and-gold ball on the Christmas tree, and she mumbled, "Uh-huh," like someone who hadn't the faintest notion of what had been said to her. She stood back and put her hands on her hips, proudly admiring their decorating skill.

"I hope it holds off until after Christmas," Elaine murmured.

Meg turned and blinked. "What's the matter with you, Elaine!" she asked in amazement. "Everybody loves a white Christmas! Don't you remember how we used to pray for it starting the day after Thanksgiving?"

A fond smile curved Elaine's lips, and she moved away from the window. "Yes," she said. "And you'd pester me to find out what Richard would like for a present."

Meg laughed and sank down on one of the three overstuffed sofas in the room. "Do you remember the year you told that boy you were dating that it was against your religious convictions to celebrate Christmas with an exchange of gifts?'' she asked. Nostalgia softened her laughing eyes, and she leaned her elbow along the back of the sofa, remembering.

Elaine grinned. "I had it on the highest authority that he was going to embarrass us both by presenting me with his fraternity pin. I liked him very much. He was sweet and lots of fun, but it had never crossed my mind that it would last."

Meg nodded, still grinning. "Who told you?"

Elaine rolled her eyes. "His mother!"

"Oh, no!" Meg howled.

"Oh, yes." Elaine shook her head ruefully. "And believe me, I hugged and kissed the woman for telling me. It would have been so awkward to refuse him."

"You were always a softie, Elaine," Meg murmured affectionately.

"She still is," said Richard from the doorway. Beau stood beside him, frowning slightly, his eyes fixed on Elaine.

Meg bounded off of the sofa and joined her husband, giving him an affectionate kiss on the cheek and slipping her arm through his. "All finished working?"

"Yes." Richard looked down at his auburn-haired wife as if he were slightly injured by her greeting. "Is that the best you can do for a kiss?"

Meg giggled and led him into the room. "No," she conceded. "But you'll have to find the mistletoe to get something better."

Richard shot an amused glance at Beau, who was still standing in the doorway. "Will you excuse me? I have a small search to make...."

Meg's laughter spilled into the air as she and Richard wandered around the tree and into the hall in search of the elusive little plant.

Elaine walked over to the tree and straightened a small toy soldier that was listing precariously on a slender bough. "When are you leaving?" she asked.

"As soon as I get my coat on," Beau replied. He made no move to get it, however, and just stood there looking at her.

"It hasn't started snowing yet," she said lightly, although it required an effort to sound cheerful about it.

"You ought to get to your aunt's before the bad weather hits."

"Yeah. I guess I will."

Elaine turned on him and forced a blazing smile. "I, uh, hope you have a good visit."

He remained silent.

She nervously straightened the huge poinsettias on the table nearest her. Then she started moving the greens that framed the doorway, a centimeter here, a centimeter there. She looked at him, and this time she couldn't dredge up a smile to save her life.

"I have a present for you...." she said with a sigh. "Would you like to take it with you, or would you rather wait until you came back?" That would be after Christmas. He had told her he'd be gone for three days. Maybe four.

She had no idea whether he would be angry at her for getting him something. He obviously wasn't spending anything on luxuries like Christmas gifts this year. And she didn't expect him to give her anything. That didn't bother her in the least, since what she most wanted from him was something that money couldn't buy and he was unlikely to offer her: his love.

She let her attention wander back to the gaily decorated blue spruce in the middle of the large room. She was bracing herself to hear him say that he didn't want to accept a present if he wasn't giving one when the telephone rang. She hastily crossed to the phone and eagerly answered it, grateful for a few more moments before he could tell her that he didn't want her gift.

"Hello," she said. "Foxgrove. May I help you?" Then she stared at the phone in surprise and slowly held it out to Beau. "It's for you. A Mr. Fogarty's secretary of Fogarty, Lineham, Strindberg and Beecham."

He took the phone from her, and Elaine sat down with a plunk, wondering what news would be important enough to merit a call from his lawyer's office after five o'clock on Christmas Eve.

"Lamond," he said tightly. He listened intently, and for a moment he looked as if he weren't comprehending what was being said. Then he cleared his throat and took a deep breath. "Thank you," he said simply. A faint smile softened his grim-set mouth. "Merry Christmas to you, too. And tell Fogarty—" Beau swallowed and closed his eyes "—tell Fogarty I'll never forget this." He hung up the phone and laid his hands on either side of it, bowing his head.

Elaine was afraid to ask and afraid not to. "Beau?" she ventured softly. "Is everything okay?"

He gathered himself and slowly straightened. When he turned to look at her, he seemed almost ravaged with emotion. "Fogarty got the judge to permit my father to spend Christmas with my mother and the rest of the family." Beau closed his eyes and took a deep breath. "He's free. And because of his age, the deteriorating effect of imprisonment on his health, and the unlikelihood that he'd be a danger to anyone, he's going to serve the rest of his sentence by donating his talents in a community service project supervised by Probation and Parole."

Elaine was putting her arms around him and hugging him fiercely by the time he finished explaining. "I'm so glad!" she exclaimed. "For all of you."

His arms came around her, and he crushed her to him, burying his face in her hair. "He couldn't have lasted another year in there," he said, his voice sounding odd.

Elaine hugged him even tighter. "Don't think about it anymore," she urged. "I'm so happy for you," she murmured brokenly. She felt her own tears and buried her face in his shoulder.

He lifted her chin and gazed into her shimmering eyes, and through the blur she saw his golden smile. He kissed her with slow, aching tenderness. It was a heartrending kiss of great sweetness, of soul-deep honesty. When he reluctantly lifted his lips, he was barely able to smile.

"What are you doing tonight?" he asked her solemnly, his voice husky with emotion.

Elaine lowered her eyes to hide her sadness. "Having dinner with Richard and Meg, Ambrose and Mrs. Adams, and anyone on the staff who's decided to join us for Christmas Eve dinner. Then... sing carols." She managed a small laugh at that. "You should hear the Foxgrove chorus! Every year we become more tone-deaf than the last. But it's a tradition."

She laid her face against his chest, feeling the warm strength of his solid muscle through the cotton fabric of his shirt. And the scent of him, the intoxicating aphrodisiac of his scent... She made a small sound of contentment and closed her eyes, savoring their remaining moments together with every one of her senses.

"Would you be interested in breaking with tradition this once?"

Elaine held her breath and opened her eyes a little. "How?" she asked softly.

"By coming with me and spending Christmas with my family."

Her head snapped back, and she stared at him in complete and utter shock. She swallowed and managed to find her tongue. "I would love to."

He relaxed a little, and a smile dawned on his face.

"Did you think I might say no?" she asked gently, her eyes soft and tender with her love for him. She'd felt the tension leave him.

His grin was charmingly boyish. "At the best, it was a fifty-fifty chance," he pointed out. "And I figured there were more people pulling on you to stay here than there were pulling for you to come with me."

She smiled at him and said very softly, "But one of you is worth quite a lot of all the others."

His eyes darkened, and his smile faded. When he kissed her this time, it was as if their hearts and souls touched.

"Can you give me five minutes to pack a few things?" she asked unsteadily when at last they broke off the kiss. She was shaking, and her knees had turned to jelly.

"Take ten," he offered generously, giving her an uneven grin as she whirled and dashed toward the stairwell. He turned to stare out the window and contemplate the sudden and dramatic good news that Fogarty's secretary had delivered. The moment he'd known his father was going to be released, a tremendous weight had lifted from him.

A white snowflake floated down in front of the pane. Then another, a few yards away. Then another.

Elaine came downstairs a short time later, carrying a small, hastily packed suitcase. As Beau came to take it from her, she fingered the small, neatly wrapped present she'd left on the table by the telephone.

"Would you rather I give you this when we get back?" she asked tentatively, hoping again that he wouldn't reject her gift.

He nodded. She was glad he didn't seem angry about it. He was too relieved about his father, she decided.

"I think we're going to have a white Christmas after all," he said wryly as he walked toward the car with Elaine.

She grinned at him. Now that she was going with him, it could turn into a blizzard as far as she was concerned. She slid her arm through his and squeezed him affectionately. "If we get stranded, I'll help you shovel," she offered magnanimously.

Beau laughed. "I don't think that will be a problem. It's not coming down that hard, and it doesn't take that long to get to my aunt's house." He glanced at her curiously. "What did your brother say when you told him you were coming with me?"

Elaine giggled. "He said it was about time you took me somewhere and thank God I was going to be out from under his feet for a while. The ungrateful wretch! Of course I caught him under the mistletoe with Meg, and it took him several 'ahems' to hear I was there and another thirty seconds to unwind his body from around hers, so that could have something to do with how cheerfully he said goodbye."

"I suppose it could," Beau agreed, half-choking on his laughter. Poor Richard. The man had his complete sympathy.

After they'd put everything in the Mercedes and opened the garage, Elaine asked cautiously, "Are we going to pick up your father?"

Beau shook his head. "No. My uncle's already gone to the prison to do that. Fogarty called him first. He's closer, and my father wanted my uncle to pick him up. By now they could be back at my aunt's."

Elaine was somewhat relieved to hear that. She guessed that his father would prefer not to have a total stranger witness his release, not to mention his reunion with his wife. It would give him at least a little time to be wrapped in the bosom of his family before she and Beau joined them.

"Will they mind my being there?" she asked tentatively.

He shook his head, resisting the urge to pull her closer to his side as they drove through the snowy darkness. "No." He could have told her that he was the one they would be less than thrilled to see. But she might as well see that for herself, he thought.

He was also thinking that this visit might make clear to Elaine that she wouldn't want to be a part of his life. She kept seeing him through those rose-colored glasses of hers. Much as he didn't want her to see what his family life was truly like, he forced himself to expose her to it. She would be grateful that he had. His jaw clenched, and his hands tightened on the steering wheel. It was his gift to her. The truth was all he had to give her. Other than himself. And she already had that.

Beau's aunt and uncle lived in a semirural area dotted with expensive houses. A respectably modest acreage surrounded each home, and here and there a horse pasture could be seen. Beau pulled the Mercedes sedan into a long, winding driveway and up to a large two-story house of pale salmon-colored brick. The Georgian-style architecture was typical of moneyed Virginia.

As they left the car, a woman came out of the house to greet them. She was smiling, although not as warmly as Elaine would have expected, considering the holiday atmosphere and the fact that a member of the family had just been given his freedom. She glanced at Beau, whose smile hardly looked any cheerier. The woman, dressed in a red-and-green plaid wool dress and Christmas-colored red necklace and shoes, opened her arms and gave Beau a fastidious hug. She closed her eyes and offered him her slightly puffy, powdered cheek. Dutifully he kissed it.

"Merry Christmas, Beau," the woman said graciously. She turned to Elaine. "And you must be Elaine."

Elaine offered her hand, and the woman warmly squeezed it. Her eyes had a kinder, warmer light than Elaine had expected.

Beau introduced the woman, saying, "This is my Aunt Kitty. Katharine Deverell to everyone else."

Kitty Deverell slipped her arm through Elaine's with the easy affection of a Southerner. "We're happy to have you join us, dear," Kitty said, drawing Elaine toward the house while Beau followed with the luggage. She turned her head and told him, "Beau, take those bags to the guest rooms down the hallway to the left. You know the ones I mean... the gray room and the peach."

As they went inside, a tall thin man with slightly graying hair held the door. He wore a three-piece suit, polished black shoes and a red carnation boutonniere. Kitty paused inside the large foyer to introduce him. "This is my husband, George. George, this is Beau's... friend... Elaine Faust."

George looked grave as he shook hands with her. "A pleasure meeting you," he said politely. He hesitated, cleared his throat and then asked rather diffidently, "I believe your brother is Richard Faust?"

"Yes. That's right," Elaine said, smiling.

George nodded. "I work with an international trade group, and we know of your brother's reputation, of course."

Kitty was gently but firmly drawing Elaine toward the main living room, however. She told her husband. "George, why don't you make sure Beau finds the rooms and then joins us for a drink?"

"Of course, dear," he said congenially.

Elaine did not have long to wonder when she would meet Beau's parents. They were sitting in the main living room, side by side. Kitty performed the introductions.

"Elaine, this is my sister, Beau's mother... Eloisa Lamond."

Elaine bent down slightly, since Mrs. Lamond made no attempt to rise, and offered her hand. Eloisa Lamond took Elaine's hand in her cool slender one, shaking hands with the warm civility of one well accustomed to social occasions.

"Hello, Elaine," Beau's mother said calmly. "We're so glad you could join us." The words seemed more perfunctory than heartfelt.

Elaine smiled warmly anyway and then tactfully withdrew her hand from Eloisa's unenthused clasp. "I'm honored to be here. Thank you for letting me come," she replied easily. She noticed that Beau was joining them, and her smile softened, subtly changing from the graciously polite one expected of a well-mannered guest to a more private, much warmer one intended just for him.

Beau's eyes held hers for a long, aching moment; then he shifted his attention to his parents. His action drew Elaine's gaze back to the man seated next to Eloisa Lamond. He was white-haired and gaunt, his skin pale and his expression embittered. And he was staring at Beau as if they were distant acquaintances, Elaine realized. He obviously had to be Beau's father, and he owed the fact that he was sitting there to his son, but there was no emotional welcome, not even a paternal smile, coming from him.

Beau didn't appear surprised, and Elaine held out her hand to Beau's father as the introductions were again made. As the man's smooth, neatly manicured hand touched hers, she was struck by the hardness of his handshake. And the brevity of it. As if he didn't wish to shake her hand at all. Elaine swallowed her surprise and dismay and tried to be gracious for Beau's sake.

"Good evening, Mr. Lamond," she said in the beautifully modulated voice that always soothed beasts and out-of-sorts men. "It's a pleasure to meet you." She was tempted to add, *Especially now, and congratulations on your release*. But she wasn't quite sure what kind of a reception that comment might receive. No one was mentioning the release. And no one was embracing Beau for sacrificing everything he'd earned for the past two years to pay for the legal services necessary to win it. They weren't even teary eyed with joy. She glanced at Beau, a slight question in her eyes. He merely gave her a cynical smile and leaned his shoulder against the doorjamb, as if watching a black comedy unfold.

Elaine looked at his relatives, who were beginning to talk about small items of mutual interest. Then they passed her a plate of Christmas cookies and urged her take a seat amongst them. They were just going to go on as if nothing had happened, she thought in amazement.

Eloisa and Carter Lamond seemed somewhat mystified about what to discuss with Elaine, so George Deverell stepped cautiously into the breach to ask Elaine polite questions about Richard's international business interests. Every once in a while she looked over at Beau mutely asking him what this was all about, but he merely stood there, being ignored most of the time by his relatives, except for the occasional rhetorical question tossed his way by his aunt or uncle.

Kitty stood up suddenly and declared brightly, "Well, why don't we all go sit down to dinner now? I'm hungry enough to eat a horse!"

Everyone followed Kitty into the formal dining room and sat down to a traditional dinner of roast beef, baked potatoes, molded vegetable salads and mincemeat pie. And only the most perfunctory conversation was directed toward Beau.

Over coffee and dessert, Eloisa Lamond finally turned to her son with the clear intention of addressing something of importance to him. "Beauregard," she said in a clear soft voice. "I want to thank you for all you have done to bring your father home to us for Christmas."

Beau gave his mother a slight smile. "Since it was largely because of me that he went to prison in the first place, I'm not sure you have much to thank me for, Mother," he said sardonically.

"No, dear, don't think that...." his mother murmured in distress.

The elder Lamond looked decidedly pained. "This is very distasteful dinner conversation, Eloisa," he complained. "We have lost almost every material thing we ever had, but surely we can hold on to our dignity and our pride."

"I'm sorry, Carter," Eloisa apologized anxiously.

Carter Lamond glanced from his wife to Elaine. "I hope we haven't spoiled your Christmas Eve with our family problems, Miss Faust," he offered somewhat sadly. "I'm sure you did not come here to listen to this." He lowered his eyes, and his pale cheeks ruddied.

Elaine managed a reassuring smile. "Of course not, Mr. Lamond. I meant what I said earlier about being honored to join you." She glanced at Beau, who was looking as unyielding as one of the faces on Mount Rushmore. She reached out to touch his hand affectionately with hers. "My family and I owe Beau a great deal. He has been there for us when we desperately needed him. We think of him as part of our family." She grinned unrepentantly at his threatening expression. "He's a hard man to adopt, though," she conceded.

Kitty and George were looking mildly stricken at the way the conversation was skirting the family's dirty laundry.

"Would anyone care for a brandy?" Kitty asked hopefully, remembering her role as hostess and rising to go to the liquor cabinet.

Carter Lamond methodically folded his napkin and laid it down by his plate. He rose and communicated with a gentle motion of his hand that he wished for Eloisa to come with him. Instantly she got up from the table, murmuring, "excuse me," and dropping her crumpled napkin onto her chair.

"I'm sorry to have dampened our festivities," Mr. Lamond said stiffly once she was by his side. "I'm afraid I've had many months in which to forget the manners that I once learned as a boy." He offered his wife his elbow, and she slipped her arm through his. He smiled down at her tenderly. "But I shall try to relearn them."

Kitty Deverell handed out brandy snifters to everyone who would accept one, pouring the sweet liquor into each in turn.

"I'm sure we're *all* deeply happy that you're with us, Carter, and that we can all be together, especially now, at Christmas..." Kitty babbled, hoping to smooth over the strain.

No one was smiling. No one was even looking at Kitty. Her wobbling smile faded, and she looked helplessly from one guest to another.

"Good night," the elder Lamond said, nodding to everyone in turn. "I think I will retire, if you will excuse me...."

Beau and George had risen to their feet as the Lamonds prepared to leave the room. Beau's mother gave them each a look of poignant apology as she accompanied her husband out of the room.

"Well," Kitty said limply, "I think George and I had better clear the table and do a little cleaning up." She swallowed half her brandy and looked helplessly at her husband. "Don't you think so, dear?"

George responded by picking up his own plate and taking it into the huge adjoining kitchen. Kitty chased Elaine away from the table as she began to help.

"No, dear! You're a guest. I don't let my guests wash the dishes!" she said with an embarrassed laugh. "Beau, why don't you take Elaine and show her our Christmas tree? It's in the den...in the east wing."

Beau inclined his head and reached for Elaine's elbow. "Sounds like a fine idea, Aunt Kitty," he said dryly. He reached for the decanter of brandy as he passed it. "Mind if I take the brandy with us?"

"Not at all," Kitty said, sounding tremendously relieved that they were heeding her suggestion.

"Are you sorry you brought me along?" Elaine whispered as they entered a comfortably decorated room with a Christmas tree in the center of it.

Beau sat down in an easy chair and put the decanter on the small end table next to him. He looked a little amused that she had asked that particular question. "Sweetheart," he drawled, "bringing you along is my Christmas gift to myself." He took a swallow of brandy. "I wanted you to see how well I'm thought of by those who know me best," he added.

The soft sarcasm in his voice was painful for her to listen to, and she sat on the side of his chair, wanting to be near him. "Do they really know you best?" she challenged gently. She laid a tender hand on his arm. "Or do they find you a convenient scapegoat for all their disappointments?"

He finished his brandy and poured himself a fresh drink. "They know me, all right," he said. He held his glass up and looked at it thoughtfully, then carefully placed it on the table next to the decanter.

He looked up at her, and his eyes were dark with emotion as he pulled her down onto his lap, bringing her shoulders back across his arm.

"Well, I think I know you, too," Elaine murmured. "And I think you're too hard on yourself. It wasn't your fault that he went to jail."

He stiffened a little. "If I hadn't gotten involved with Babs, they would still have their home, their stable and horses, their business, their life," he said tightly.

Elaine laid her hand against his cheek. "How do you know that?" she asked softly.

He closed his eyes and leaned back. "Because if I hadn't drawn Carlton's attention, he never would have taken a close look at the books and noticed the... oversights...."

Elaine stiffened, then grabbed his forearms and shook him slightly. "Do you mean to tell me that you've known all along your father had done something wrong!" she exclaimed.

"Not all along," he admitted, his mouth twisting slightly in amusement at her outrage. He let his hand wander down across her hip and thigh. "But before the trial, Fogarty and Blane had seen enough. They... spelled it out for me quite plainly," he said grimly. He opened his eyes long enough to locate his brandy and lift it to his lips for a healthy swallow. "But my father had only made a rather small mistake, and he was trying quite hard to rectify it. His only fault was in being too egotistical to admit that he'd made an accounting error that had cost Enoch Carlton several hundred thousand dollars in lost revenues over five years. If he'd just admitted it... it wouldn't have looked like theft. It would have looked like what it was... a careless, sloppy, needless mistake. His business reputation might have suffered for a while, but he could have weathered it."

Elaine buried her face against Beau's chest and groaned. "Oh, how awful," she said.

"Yeah. Awful." Beau drained the rest of his drink and put it down. "And then I added the fatal blow. I drew Enoch Carlton's fire. And when the fire was directed at his little mess, they had all the raw material they could have wished for. A small conversion here and there in the electronic accounting records and in the books, and instead of my father being found guilty of incompetence, he was found guilty in a court of law of embezzlement."

Beau's expression hardened, and he fell silent.

Elaine lifted her face and looked at his stoic expression. "Does your mother know?" she asked softly.

He shook his head. "No. I don't think so."

He slid his fingers through her silky hair, and his eyes wandered over her face as if seeing something of great and moving beauty. "My father loves her very much," he said, barely speaking above a whisper. "Keeping her from knowing the truth is all he has left to cling to. If she knew..." Beau shook his head. "I thought for a while that he might try to kill himself. As it is, she believes he was framed. Period."

Elaine hugged him sympathetically; then, frowning, she drew back to look at him. "But what are you paying Midford Blane to find out?" she asked.

"The identity of the person or persons who made the books look worse than they really were," he said grimly.

"Is Blane having any luck?" She held her breath.

"Some."

But that was all he would say, and when she opened her mouth to ask another question, he covered her lips with his and kissed her until they were both nearly senseless. He finally tore his mouth away, struggling to resist the burning desire to strip her naked and mate his hard body to her softness and forget all the bitterness he'd known.

Elaine slid her arms around his shoulders and achingly whispered in his ear, "Right now, I'd give anything to be in your cabin."

He groaned and slid a hand under her cashmere sweater to caress the soft silky skin of her abdomen and breasts. "I know what you mean," he said wryly. He rocked her gently in his arms. "But it's better this way. You need to know how things really are for me." It will be easier for you to move on, he added silently.

She covered his mouth with hers and felt the fire sizzle through him, just as it burned inside her. Sweet agony coursed through her body, and the knowledge that he was equally affected only made it worse. She dragged her mouth away with a great effort.

"*That's* the only thing I need to know," she told him fiercely. "That you want me." She closed her eyes and clamped her mouth shut to keep from telling him that she loved him. It was the hardest thing she'd ever had to do. She wanted to say it so badly that she ached with it. "Beau," she moaned. "My darling..."

"You and your damn rose-colored glasses," he muttered. Then he fiercely pulled her close and kissed her. "I think we'd better go up," he said roughly. "While we still can."

They got up, and for a moment Elaine looped her arms around his neck and they enjoyed just holding each other.

"Merry Christmas, Beau," she said softly.

He smiled and released her. Arm in arm, they walked upstairs and went to bed. He in his room. She in hers.

To their cold, lonely beds.

Chapter 15

On Christmas Day Kitty Deverell cajoled them all into taking a short stroll over some of the snowy trails that laced the area. Eloisa Lamond clung tenderly to her husband's side, and Elaine felt profound sympathy for the poor woman. She obviously adored her husband and was distraught at the polite estrangement of her husband and her son. She smiled affectionately at Beau and kissed him on the cheek, her eyes shining with maternal joy, but only when Carter Lamond's attention was firmly fixed elsewhere and he wouldn't notice what she was doing.

Elaine knew that both the Deverells and the Lamonds were wondering exactly what her relationship with Beau was, but they were too polite to ask. Ever since Kitty Deverell's awkward introduction of her as Beau's "friend," no one had asked anything of a personal nature. From the slightly odd looks she intercepted when they thought she wasn't looking, however, she knew the unvoiced question was in the backs of their minds.

Since she wasn't sure what their relationship was herself, she gamely played the role of polite, supportive friend or, as was twice necessary, the mistress of the estate where he worked. Elaine was as relieved as the Deverells and the Lamonds when Kitty eventually suggested they amuse themselves by playing a few games. It offered them all something safely neutral to enjoy together. They promptly went through canasta, charades and several board games that Elaine had never heard of before and hoped not to again.

When it was finally time for them to return to Foxgrove on the day after Christmas, she was beginning to feel exhausted. It wasn't that she was sleeping badly or exercising too much. The problem was having to be utterly charming and very careful not to inadvertently say something that would unleash a bitter comment by one of Beau's relatives, while spending unrelieved hours at a time confined in the same house with them.

The morning they left, Elaine cheerily waved goodbye, and as soon as they were out of sight of the house, she leaned back against the seat and groaned. "Have they *always* been like that?" she asked, mildly horrified.

Beau glanced at her sideways. "Like what?" he asked dryly.

"Critical. Condescending and nasty to you. Politely rude."

"Were they rude to you?" he asked with a frown.

"No..."

"I didn't think so. I wouldn't have brought you if I'd thought they would be."

Elaine sighed in exasperation. He was sidetracking her again. She brought him back to her original worry. "They were impeccably polite to me," she agreed. "Surprisingly so, since they clearly couldn't figure out if we were sleeping together or not and therefore weren't sure how to treat me, as a nice young woman or as one of your bed warmers."

Beau's eyebrows lowered precipitously.

She laughed softly. "You needn't look so threatening," she teased him. "I'll say what I think whether you like it or not."

"I never doubted that," he said. He didn't like her to categorize herself as merely a sexual partner. He'd never thought of her like that. "Bed warmer," he muttered darkly.

He bit off the denial he would have made. He was going to protect her from himself, from the profound depth of feeling that he hadn't believed himself capable of until he'd met her. She deserved much more than he could give her, and she was going to get it, damn it.

"It wasn't their discomfort about what I am to you...that wasn't what I was talking about," Elaine explained. "It was their rudeness to *you* that angered me. That's what I meant by 'polite rudeness.'"

Beau turned the steering wheel slightly, and the Mercedes made a smooth curve. Beau's face was still less than cheerful.

"If you had a son whose poor judgment resulted in your losing everything you'd spent a lifetime acquiring, you might find it the height of personal strength to be even civil to him," he pointed out bitingly.

Elaine shook her head vigorously. "Your ego's getting in the way, Beau," she chided him gently.

He glanced at her in anger. "What the hell is that supposed to mean?" he demanded, then whipped his attention back to the snowy road ahead.

"You are not responsible for what happened," she said firmly. She ticked off her reasons on her fingers. "First of all, your father laid the groundwork himself. If he hadn't made the initial mistake and then added to the problem by trying to cover it up, there wouldn't have been any truth to the accusation at all."

He kept his eyes straight ahead, but his hands were gripping the steering wheel more tightly.

Elaine held up a second finger and continued. "Second," she said, "the criminal in this mess is Enoch Carlton and anyone he convinced to forge, fabricate or lie about accounting information for him. You are not responsible for his breaking the law. He did it on his own." When Beau looked as if he were going to interrupt, she hurried to add, "And if he so readily framed your father and had the audacity to go through a trial, lying under oath, he's probably done illegal things like this before."

Beau frowned. "That doesn't free me of responsibility," he growled.

Elaine drew in a breath and nodded. "Perhaps not completely," she agreed quietly. She looked out her window at the countryside, covered as if in powdered sugar, a Currier and Ives portrait come to life. The pristine beauty was a painful contrast to the almost sordid picture in her mind. Beau and Babs Carlton. In bed. "You made the mistake of being interested in the wrong woman...." Her voice faded. This was the part she purely *hated* to think about. She closed her eyes. God, how she wished she could wipe that out of her mind.

"I slept with another man's wife," he said mercilessly. If she wouldn't punish him, he would punish himself. He wasn't looking at her, but he'd heard the pain in her voice, and that had been worse by far than if she had said something harsh and lecturing to him. He'd been a fool. And he'd more than paid the price for his idiocy.

Elaine couldn't look at him. She blinked her lashes to keep the jealous tears at bay. "Yes," she said in a soft, twisted voice. "And having met her, I can't... I just can't imagine you..." She let out a ragged breath. "God, whatever did you see in her?"

Beau was looking at her; she could sense it. "At the time, it seemed the easiest way to get rid of her," he said evenly.

He wanted to tell her how he honestly felt about having done that, and exactly how he'd been manipulated by Babs Carlton into bedding her. But that might make it easier for Elaine to forget his sins, his stupidity. And he wanted her to have this last chance to be free of him. God knew, if she didn't take it soon, he wouldn't be able to let her go. No matter how much he knew he should, he simply wouldn't be able to let her leave him. He clenched his jaw as if that would somehow strengthen his resolve.

Elaine did look at him then, searching for the truth in his face. "You know," she told him, her soft voice revealing raw emotional strain, "you've been so honest with me, so gentle, so tender, so selfless and kind, I really hate to think of the way you must have been with her. It's so hard to imagine that you would have done that...." She sighed in frustration. "I keep wishing I could have been there to tear you away from her before you did what you did. If I could have saved you from that one mistake, perhaps you wouldn't be so single-mindedly dedicated to punishing yourself. Perhaps..." *Perhaps you could let yourself love me,* she added in her aching heart. *Because we could be so good for each other.*

Beau swore softly and switched on the radio. "You haven't learned anything from this visit," he muttered in exasperation.

She smiled at him in tender sadness and tightly folded her hands in her lap to resist the urge to fling her arms around him and kiss him into a better mood. He was trying to keep her at arm's length again. She didn't know why, but she tried to respect his need.

"You know me," she said, managing to regain a light tone. "I always prefer the view through my good old rose-colored glasses. I don't leave home without 'em."

"I've noticed," he said succinctly. "Believe me, I've noticed."

It was late when they arrived at Foxgrove, and Beau muttered something unencouraging about checking on the horses and going right to sleep. There was a funny look in his eyes, though, that suggested he had to wrestle with himself to say that.

Elaine, encouraged that he might be finding it hard to keep away from her, smiled her most femininely provocative smile, slid her arms around his neck and kissed him warmly on the lips. She thought he swallowed a groan, and then he was kissing her so fiercely that she didn't think at all for a while. When he finally pulled away, his arms were unsteady, and his eyes were the stormy color of thunder.

She led him by the hand to the table where she'd left the small present she'd bought for him. Solemnly, she handed it to him.

"Why don't you open it now?" she suggested.

He frowned slightly and removed the wrapping. "I wish you hadn't," he muttered. Then he stopped speaking and simply stared at the box in his hand. It held a small figurine, handcarved by an artisan in the nearby mountains. The fine pecan wood was smooth and warm. It was the figure of a man riding a horse at a gallop. He lifted an eyebrow and smiled at her. "Is this me?" he asked in husky amazement.

Elaine laughed and looped her arms comfortably around his neck.

"No," she replied with a smile. "You're warm and strong and very real to me." She blushed a little at the flare of desire in his eyes. She closed her eyes and gave him a tender kiss, which he returned in full measure. "But it reminded me of you..." she murmured.

Regretfully, she drew away from him. Their fingers clung until she reached the staircase. As she stepped up, their hands separated completely. It made her feel bereft.

"Thank you," he said quietly, lifting the graceful carving in a small salute.

Elaine smiled down at him. "You're welcome." She climbed the stairs quickly, not stopping to look at him again until she'd reached the top. He was still standing there, staring up at her. "Good night," she said softly. She blew him a kiss and smiled. "Thank you for taking me with you. I wouldn't have missed it for the world."

His expression went from one of torture to resigned frustration. "You took the words right out of my mouth," he said. He looked for a moment as if he were about to say something more. Then he apparently thought better of it, because the look faded, and his mouth tightened into a stubborn line. "See you tomorrow," he told her quietly. He ran a hand through his hair and turned on his heel, striding to the great front doors while muttering to himself. He shut the door so hard after him that it could only have been described as a slam.

Elaine smiled in delight and turned to run smack into her dishevelled brother in his pajamas and robe.

"Did you have a nice time?" he asked.

She thought about that for a moment before replying. She waved a finger in the air, saying, "I think it was more enlightening than nice," she told him.

"Enlightening?" he exclaimed in surprise.

But she was drifting happily in the direction of her bedroom, recalling how delightfully enlightening that war of emotions on Beau's face had been and treasuring the sweet memory of it. He *did* love her. He was just too darned stubborn to admit it. She would simply have to find a way to get him to tell her.

For the first time she was sure that he was holding her away not because he didn't love her, but because he *did*. The noble idiot was trying to protect her from himself.

She stood at her window and looked down at the stable, where a light burned in the office. Her lips curved in a tender smile, and her eyes were lit softly with love.

"Now how can I get you to tell me?" she wondered softly. "There's got to be a way...."

They fell into a new pattern after Christmas, however, and Elaine soon realized that Beau was trying to disengage himself from their previously intense relationship. He would bury himself in office work for hours at a time, or go into town to take care of stable business that wouldn't normally have been done for weeks, or even months. He had her work with horses while he was busy in the stable, and he made sure he was working with the horses when she couldn't go with him.

If she hadn't seen that look on his face, Elaine might have believed that he didn't want her anymore. Eventually she would have had to let everything fall apart, as he was clearly trying to force her to do. But she *had* seen his face, had seen the naked longing that flashed like an eternal fire in the depths of his eyes. She'd seen the agonizing force of will it had taken for him to wrestle that longing back into the oblivion of his heart. And she clung to that sweet memory to find the courage to fight him.

"You can't get rid of me so easily," she murmured after him on New Year's Day as she watched him drive off to Bradley's to look at a hunter that the other man was having problems with. She leaned her forehead against her forearms along the fence, oblivious to the chilly winter air nipping at her cheeks.

She didn't know whether it was five seconds or five minutes later that the sounds of an approaching car drew her back to reality. She looked up to see a nondescript dark blue Chevrolet pull up in the driveway, stopping fairly close to her. The engine was cut off, and the lone man inside the vehicle opened the door and got out.

He was slightly stocky, about five foot ten, with an unremarkable face and an affable expression. And he was walking toward her with the clear intention of introducing himself.

"Miss Faust?" he asked. He didn't sound as though he doubted for a minute that that was who she was. He extended his arm and smiled diffidently as Elaine took his hand.

"Yes," she acknowledged. He seemed to know who she was, but for the life of her, she couldn't recall ever having laid eyes on him before. "I'm sorry, I don't think I recall your name," she apologized.

"Not at all surprising," he admitted with an engagingly disarming smile. "We've never met. I recognized you from a picture I once saw in the newspaper," he explained. "Your wedding picture."

Elaine hated to be reminded of that, but she smiled and murmured the expected, "I see."

"Besides," he added, "you look just the way Beau described you."

"Beau described me to you?" she asked in surprise. She eyed him more closely. "And who exactly are you?"

He laughed. "Midford Blane." He glanced around. "Is Beau here?"

She recovered from his announcement and took him toward the house, where they could talk more comfortably. "No. He's out, but he should be back in a while."

"Hmm. Perhaps I should come back later."

"Don't be silly, Mr. Blane. Have you come all the way from Arlington?" she asked.

"Yes."

"Then you must be planning to spend the night?"

"Yes."

Elaine beamed. "Then I insist you stay here at Foxgrove. We'd be honored."

"Well..." He looked around, clearly flattered to be invited and not personally averse to accepting. He was a little hesitant, however. "I'm not sure how Beau would feel."

"I'm sure Beau would be the first to say you should accept," she declared, crossing her fingers behind her back and hoping God didn't strike her dead for such a bald-faced lie.

Blane abandoned his doubts and smiled. "Well, in that case, I accept."

By the time Beau returned two hours later, Elaine had a fairly good idea of why the private detective had come. He'd respected his client's confidentiality enough not to say directly, but she'd shared enough of her own knowledge about Beau's battle with Enoch Carlton for Blane to realize that she knew a great deal about what was going on.

Midford Blane rose to his feet and grinned broadly as Beau strode past an elegant pool table to join them in the game room. The private detective withdrew a long, thickly stuffed envelope and waved it triumphantly in the air. "I've got something you've been wanting to see for a long, long time. I came to hand it to you in person." He glanced at Elaine, whose eyes were fixed on Beau's face. "Elaine has been kindly entertaining me while we waited for you to return."

Beau took the envelope from the detective and stared at it. Then he looked up at Blane and held the man's eyes for a long hard minute. "Will this do it?" he asked enigmatically.

Blane was grinning and nodding his head. "Yep. Fogarty's had it since this morning, and he's got half his staff working on the legal papers to get everything in motion." The modestly built man walked over to Beau and gave him a congratulatory pat on the shoulder. "It's just a matter of grinding out the legal details before a judge. Unless Carlton chooses to settle out of court, and you and your family were to agree to that."

Elaine wanted to put her arms around Beau and hug him as hard as she could. There were tears of joy threatening her, and yet she wasn't sure how Beau would react to such an open display of affection. He had been distancing himself from her for days. Of course, this news could change things, she thought hopefully.

She did what she wanted to do, deciding to face the consequences later. She went over to him and put her arms around his neck and laid her cheek next to his. "I'm so glad for you," she whispered unsteadily. She hugged him tightly, aware that his arms were only halfheartedly encircling her. She kissed him on the cheek and withdrew, turning to give Midford Blane a blazing smile through the shimmering tears she was now having to literally choke back. "I'm sure you two have a lot to talk about," she said. "And I've no doubt you'd rather do most of that in private. If you'll excuse me..." She turned at the door and said to the two men staring at her, "Dinner will be served in about an hour. If you'd like it brought in here... just use the intercom on the phone. We'll see to it."

Then she shut the door behind her with her last ounce of dignity, before she walked, then ran, through the halls to the kitchen.

Mrs. Adams was perusing a cookbook when Elaine burst in on her. "What in the world?" the older woman exclaimed, seeing the emotion on Elaine's face. The breath whooshed out of her plumpish body as Elaine wrapped her arms around her and laid her head on her old confidant's shoulder. Mrs. Adams's mystification turned to sharp concern. "What's the matter, dear?"

"Nothing, Mrs. Adams," Elaine said, bursting into tears. "I'm just so happy I don't know what to do."

"Well, for heaven's sake!" exclaimed the thoroughly confused cook. She awkwardly patted Elaine's shoulders as the sobbing became worse. "Happy? Is that what you call this?"

"Oh, yes," Elaine choked. "And by the way," she said, getting a grip on herself and stepping back to vigorously brush away the tears. "We have a guest for dinner. A Mr. Blane. Richard knows him. And he's also an acquaintance of Beau's."

Beau left with Midford Blane the following day, having revealed no details about what Blane had told him. If he hadn't said goodbye the way he had, Elaine would have wondered whether she might have been wrong about how he felt about her. But as she'd stood by the car, gazing at him with her heart in her eyes, he'd reached out and touched her cheek, sliding his warm palm along her soft skin. That warring look had erupted in his gray-blue eyes, and his jaw had tightened as he'd pulled away, as if it had taken every ounce of his strength to do so.

With Beau gone, Elaine was overwhelmed by a sense of loneliness. To comfort herself, she went to the stable office, where she could be surrounded by Beau's work.

She was casually looking over some of the schedules for the horses when she began to realize what she was seeing. "Why, you wretch!" she cried out angrily. "All the time I thought you were in here working on boring paperwork, you were scheduling your life away for the next year. If you ride in all these things, we'll be seeing each other about once a month! Probably in a state of utter exhaustion."

Fuming, she paced around the office like a caged tigress. "You're not going to get away with this!" she exclaimed. "Not even if I have to ride in all those shows myself, you stubborn man!"

She stared at the sheaf of papers in her hand. Ride in the shows herself. Compete. She'd always shied away from it, largely to protect Meg. What had Beau said? Meg was perfectly capable of competing without any protection from her friends. And he'd also said that he thought she could successfully show some of the Faust horses herself. Irish Mist, for example...

Elaine sat down, put her head in her hands and closed her eyes. When she raised her head a long time later, she'd left her past behind her for good. She lifted the telephone and dialed Bradley File's number. When he answered, she felt as if she were beginning her life all over again.

"Bradley, this is Elaine. Could you tell me how to go about getting some entry forms for a few shows? And how to arrange the details?" There was a long silence, and for a moment she thought he might have passed out. She grew worried. "Bradley? Are you there?"

Bradley cleared his throat and managed to get out, "I'm here. And I heard what you said. It just...takes a little getting used to. I don't suppose you'd like to tell me why, at the age of thirty, you've decided to take up competition?"

"Not right now, Bradley," she said.

"Somehow I didn't think so," he said mournfully. "You two clam-mouthed—"

"Bradley! The forms!"

"All right," he agreed. "What horses are you thinking of entering and in what shows?"

Elaine had the complete listing of places where Beau was going to be. She put her finger at the top of the list and started there.

Beau had called Richard to say he would be back the following day. When Richard casually mentioned it over dinner, Elaine stared at her brother as if he'd grown two heads. He managed to keep a straight face, but Meg was half choking on her fruit salad.

"Wasn't that nice of him?" Elaine said much too pleasantly.

Richard swirled his wine and added with the greatest innocence, "I asked him if he had any messages for you...."

Elaine held her knife suggestively. "Richard," she said warningly. "I told you to keep out of this."

He feigned profound surprise. "Sorry. He did ask me to tell you something."

She dropped her knife and blushed at her own silliness.

He was grinning openly now. "He said that you shouldn't wait up for him. He'd be back very late."

"Oh, he did, did he?" Elaine said, her eyes blazing with anger. She smiled sweetly at her brother and then, more honestly, at Meg. Then she got up and excused herself. "In that case, I think I'll accept an invitation to a party tonight. I've been debating about it."

Meg was laughing now, too. "Not to the open house at Pamela Longacre's!"

Elaine's expression was that of a cat about to play for an extended period of time with a very much disliked mouse. "Precisely," she confirmed. "I understand that the Carltons will be there. And about half the boys we dated when we were young and didn't know any better."

Richard was laughing so hard he didn't pay much attention to the first part of Elaine's reply. And the gleam in Elaine's eye when she mentioned the boys they'd dated made Meg worry more about the boys than Elaine.

"Do you need chaperones?" Richard asked, regaining control of himself after something of an effort. "Meg and I could go along with you."

"If you want to come and watch the fun, that's fine with me." She glared warningly at her older brother. "Just stay out of my way."

He held up his hand in surrender. "No problem," he swore, beginning to grin again. He turned to Meg. "Shall we?"

When they met at the front door an hour later, Richard wasn't laughing anymore, and neither was Meg. Elaine was wearing a strapless drop-dead black evening dress that clung to her shapely body like a second skin. It swathed her legs to the ankle, but there was a slit up one side that reached her thigh. She'd put on her diamonds, and the glittering teardrops at her ears, throat and wrist made her look positively dangerous.

"Who are you planning to kill?" Richard asked in amusement as he helped the ladies in his life on with their wraps.

"A number of people," Elaine murmured silkily. She took one of Richard's impeccably clothed arms, and Meg took the other. "It's just a pity that the person I'd most like to sharpen my claws on isn't going to be here."

Meg and Richard looked at each other.

"Uh-oh," Meg said softly.

Pamela Longacre was standing near the front of her elegant country home when the Fausts walked through the door. She was instantly wreathed in smiles and stepped forward to greet them.

After the opening hugs and kisses, Elaine looked over the elegant crowd. Music provided by a three-piece combo drifted in from the ballroom, while people stood in small groups, holding drinks and talking charmingly to one another. As Elaine met their eyes, she smiled coolly. Nerves were no problem this time. Ice water flowed through her veins tonight.

"Pamela," Elaine asked engagingly, "are the Carltons here yet?"

Pamela paled. She'd obviously heard enough gossip to connect Babs with Beau. Nervously, she glanced through the clusters of people in evening dress. "Uh...yes," she said hesitantly. She glanced pleadingly to Richard before returning her attention to Elaine. "I think they may be in the ballroom...."

Elaine kissed Pamela on the cheek and smiled brilliantly. "Thank you, dear." And she turned on her slender three-inch heels to march determinedly in the direction of the music.

Pamela held Richard back just as he and Meg started to follow Elaine. "She wouldn't do anything rash, would she?"

Richard grinned. "I'm afraid she might."

Pamela watched in distress as Richard and Meg followed Elaine.

"Mrs. Longacre," asked a male voice from over her shoulder.

Pamela Longacre recognized the voice instantly. Knowing who else was already at her open house, she felt her heart skip a beat. "Oh, my..." she murmured faintly. She lifted another glass of wine from a passing waiter's tray and closed her eyes as she swallowed.

Elaine quickly realized that the Carltons were not in the ballroom. She had no idea where they *had* gone. Since it was still relatively early, she presumed they would probably reappear. The ballroom was the place where most of the people seemed to be concentrating their efforts. She noticed one of the "old boyfriends" and smiled at him as if she'd been thinking of him for years and couldn't believe her good fortune in actually finding him in front of her.

He gave her a startled smile and automatically came over and asked her to dance. That got her partway around one side of the room. When she smiled affectionately at another old suitor, she got another pleasingly stunned partner who was only too happy to dance her farther through the crowd. She managed two more before the first old friend came forward to claim a second dance. Within forty minutes she had a half a dozen "old friends" taking turns dancing with her, telling her jokes and falling over one another to gain her rapt attention.

Richard was enjoying the sight of his sister holding court and discreetly searching the dancers for her quarry from time to time. "She's got her confidence back," he murmured to Meg as they slow danced in a two-foot square in a secluded corner of the room.

Meg smiled and nodded her agreement. Then she happened to look toward the entrance, and what she saw made her stumble.

Richard held her a little more tightly and laughed. "I'm not *that* hard to follow, am I?" he teased.

"Uh-oh," Meg whispered.

"You already said that once tonight," Richard pointed out in amusement. Then he noted the shocked look on her face and sobered. He looked in the direction she was gazing and grinned. "Well, well. Look who's here. Won't Elaine be surprised to see him?"

Meg looked at him in mild horror. "Look at the way he's watching her dance with poor Larry. This could be serious," she whispered fiercely.

"It could be," he agreed. "But my money's on Beau." He glanced at the man standing in the doorway, who looked as if he were contemplating murder. Then Richard looked at the object of the man's ire and grinned even more. "And the rest of my money's on her," he laughed. He maneuvered his wife over a few feet and danced slowly with her there. "I think this ought to afford a fair view of the fireworks."

Meg groaned and closed her eyes "I don't think I can watch."

The dusky blond man with murder in his eyes threaded his way purposefully through the moderately crowded dance floor until he was directly behind the woman in the chic black dress. He looked over her exquisitely bare shoulder, nailing her partner's eyes. The man blinked, stumbled and gradually stopped dancing altogether.

Mistress of Foxgrove 239

Elaine looked into her old beau's wide-eyed expression. She was puzzled when he slowed down, and when he stopped dancing altogether, she wondered what was wrong.

"Larry?" she asked. To her complete amazement, his arms slipped away from her, and he stepped back. She hadn't seen anybody tap his shoulder to cut in, but he was acting as though someone had. She gave him a perplexed look, but he was backing away and smiling weakly.

"Go right ahead," he was murmuring faintly to someone behind her.

She tried not to be irritated by his ridiculous behavior, and turned, preparing a blinding smile for her silent new dance partner. But when she gazed into his eyes, her heart came to a complete halt. "Beau!"

He took her in his arms as coolly as if they were in a dancing class, but there was nothing cool about the expression in his eyes.

As she recovered from the initial shock of seeing him, she turned her stunned gaze to his shoulders and chest. He was wearing a very nice-looking dark blue suit. She'd never seen him in one before.

"You're not in jeans," she said in amazement, shaking her head furiously as she realized how idiotic that must sound.

He didn't look the slightest entertained by her startled observation. "I keep several suits for special occasions."

"This is a special occasion?" she asked in amazement. Her anger began rushing back full force. "Wait a minute! You aren't supposed to be here. You're not coming back until tomorrow." Her voice became ominous. "Late, I believe you told Richard to tell me."

His lips were almost white with anger. "The special occasion was some formal legal procedures that required my appearing as a responsible citizen. I just kept the clothes on to see a letter delivered here tonight."

"That makes no sense!" she objected, glaring at him. "And why did you say you weren't going to be home tonight if you were?"

He looked heavenward for strength. "I'm not going back to Foxgrove tonight, if that's what you mean by home. And

I never said I wasn't in the area. I said I wouldn't be at your estate until late tomorrow night."

"Why aren't you sleeping in your own bed if you're in town?" she asked in angry frustration.

Beau had maneuvered them into a deserted alcove. Most of the crowd was out of earshot unless they raised their voices. Before he could answer her question, however, a movement in the room drew his attention. He looked behind Elaine, and a cold mask settled over his features.

A female voice murmured in amusement, "If he's not sleeping in his bed, he's undoubtedly sleeping in someone else's." Babs Carlton stepped out of the shadows and smiled at them. "Mine, for example."

Chapter 16

Elaine felt the muscles in Beau's arms become steely, and the anger in his eyes faintly alarmed her. She instinctively tried to soothe him, to divert him from being baited by the spiteful beauty.

She moved a little, putting herself between Beau and Babsey Carlton. "Whatever his plans are," Elaine said distinctly, "I'm absolutely sure they don't include you, Mrs. Carlton."

Babs laughed and directed her fire exclusively at Elaine. "How can you be so sure?" she asked provocatively. "Why, he's broken more hearts than any man I've ever met. He's as cool as they come, and he never looks back." Realizing that Elaine was unimpressed, she shifted tactics a little. "You have a blind spot where men are concerned, I've been told. You're too trusting. Naive. You believe what they tell you until their nasty betrayals are thrust under your nose. Wasn't that what happened with your marriage? Haven't you heard that people tend to repeat their mistakes in their choice of lovers?" She smoothed the sleek silk of her dress and moved to pass Elaine, then hesitated, letting her gaze slide toward Beau and begin to smolder. "In his case, I understand why you might be tempted. *I* certainly am."

Beau moved slightly, and Elaine was afraid he might actually hit the woman. Automatically she turned and flung her arms around him, trying to physically restrain him from doing anything he might later regret.

"She isn't worth soiling your hands on," she told him passionately. "I know she's lying, trying to create more trouble. Don't let her bait you."

She looked up at him and realized he was no longer paying any attention to Babs Carlton. He was looking at her as if he couldn't believe what he'd just heard.

"I don't believe her. I *know* you," Elaine told him softly. Her eyes softened tenderly, and she lifted her hands to lovingly cup his face. "You are tender, noble, loyal and self-sacrificing. You endured the most awful things and never complained. You've had the courage to fight on when the odds against you were overwhelming. Only the tiniest pieces of what she said were ever true, and those a long time ago. But who doesn't make mistakes? It's part of being human. And they're what we learn from. Beau...I know you. I trust you."

He closed his eyes and pulled her into his arms, "For once," he said roughly, "I don't think I object to your rose-colored glasses." He nuzzled her hair and whispered, "Thank you. I would have understood if you'd believed her, you know. You would have had reason enough to be tempted to believe that garbage. But you're right. It isn't true. And it never will be."

Babs made a distasteful noise and left them alone.

"What are you doing here, anyway?" he asked as he gazed down at her, his anger washed away by her loyal defense of him.

"I'm socializing with my neighbors and old friends," she teased. She glanced around the room then and noticed Midford Blane and another man walking circumspectly around the ballroom. That was odd. "What are *they* doing here?" she asked.

He preferred to pursue her original comment. He moved her back into the ballroom, putting his arms around her to resume dancing.

"Old friends?" He cast a look of pure dislike at each of the men who'd been dancing with her for much of the past hour, and his arm tightened around her possessively.

"Yes," she declared. He sounded jealous, which both delighted and infuriated her. If he wasn't so determined not to get involved with her for the ridiculous reason that she had money and he didn't, they could have been spending the evenings dancing and doing a lot of other very pleasant and stimulating things together for the past two weeks. They could be cheerfully planning to spend the rest of their lives together. "If you just weren't so *stubborn*," she muttered in frustration.

"Do you always wear dresses like this to dance with your *old friends*?" he asked in annoyance. He'd been looking at her graceful body, all-too-exposed by the chic dress, and growing more and more irritated that she'd come here to flaunt her beauty before other men when he wasn't around to keep them at a safe distance. She was ruining his well-laid plans again, he thought. He was supposed to go to Bradley's tonight, but he'd be damned if he'd leave her to her "old friends." Not when she was wearing this dress, he wouldn't. Why couldn't she have stayed home like he'd thought she would?

"I would have preferred to wear this beautiful dress for the man I love. Since he wasn't going to be here, I had to make do with the men who were," she snapped.

The minute she had angrily spoken the phrase *for the man I love*, he stiffened as if she'd slapped him. One of her old beaus tapped him on the shoulder, wanting to cut in. Beau snarled at him, "Forget it."

"That was very rude," Elaine exclaimed indignantly. Poor Herbert. She gave him a sympathetic smile as he melted into the crowd.

"Compared to what I wanted to do, that was *extremely* polite," he corrected her. "And stop encouraging that jerk," he added sharply.

He was *very* jealous, she realized then. And he sounded distinctly like a man whose self-control was wearing fatally thin. She melted against him, instinctively wanting to mold herself close to him. She'd missed being in his arms. He tightened his hold on her. He'd missed her, too, she thought with a smile.

Beau noticed Midford Blane and the other man closing in on their quarry, and he stopped dancing to watch what happened.

"What's going on?" Elaine asked him quietly.

"Enoch Carlton is being notified that the court has a few hundred questions it would like answered, starting with a little matter of perjury. And my lawyers are prepared to sue him for every penny he cost us as a result of his fraudulent charges against my father."

"*That* is Enoch Carlton?" Elaine asked in surprise. He was a mildly stooped, balding, pink-faced man with a slight paunch. And he looked as if he couldn't believe what was happening. He scanned the room, his eyes narrowing into black dots of hatred when he located Beau.

Beau stood there without visible emotion, watching as the man who'd ruined his family faced the beginnings of his own end.

"That's why I came here," he told her. "I wanted to see it done. To know that he knew." He looked at Elaine. "They were afraid he might leave the country on a pretext of business and make it difficult even to start proceedings. This way, the foot-dragging will have to be for some other reason."

Beau looked at her, and there was a flash of such deep longing in his eyes that Elaine felt the pain in her own heart.

"I was planning on staying at Bradley's tonight," he told her slowly, lifting his hand to touch her cheek. He ran his fingertip over her soft skin. Then, almost regretfully, he withdrew. "Why the hell did you have to wear that damn dress?" he asked in frustration. "I might have been able to walk out of here and leave you to your 'old friends' if you just didn't look like..."

Elaine looked at him, and her heart beat faster at the heat in his eyes. "Like what?" she demanded provocatively, shamelessly winding her arms around him and pressing her advantage.

"Never mind," he said darkly. He looked around them. "We can't talk here. Come on." He grabbed her hand and pulled her after him through the crowd, threading a path by Richard, to whom he handed an envelope from the inside of his jacket. The two men's eyes met.

"I had originally intended to give this to you tomorrow," Beau said. He glanced at Elaine in exasperation. "But I think maybe I'd better deliver it to you right now."

Richard looked at the envelope curiously. "Shall I open it now?" he asked.

Beau nodded. "Yeah. The sooner the better." He glanced at Elaine. "I'll take her home. We have a few things to discuss," he said ominously.

Richard was grinning as he started to open the envelope. "Don't wait up for us," he said in amusement. It was obvious, of course, that they wouldn't.

Elaine gave her brother an offended look.

Beau pulled Elaine through the clusters of partygoers while she craned her neck to watch Richard's reaction as he read the letter he'd removed from the envelope. Meg looked surprised and a little uncertain, but Richard, after a moment's contemplation, began to grin again.

"Good luck!" Richard called out after them.

"What's he wishing you good luck for?" Elaine asked suspiciously.

"I'll explain later."

"Why don't you explain now?" she demanded in exasperation.

"Because I don't intend to have this discussion at Pamela Longacre's party!" he growled. He helped her on with her mink coat and firmly pushed her out to the parking area.

He had the keys to Midford Blane's car. Midford hadn't needed it tonight, which turned out to be fortunate.

Twenty deathly silent minutes later they were back at Foxgrove and walking through the front doors of the main house.

Ambrose greeted them with his customary restraint. "Could I bring you some coffee? Tea? Cognac?" he asked, following them into the main lounge.

"Nothing," Beau said, running his hand through his hair and pacing across the room nervously.

"Cognac, please, Ambrose," Elaine said.

She let the fur slide off her shoulders and Ambrose removed it. Then he disappeared down the hall to fetch the cognac Elaine had requested, and they were left alone.

"If you keep pacing like that, you're going to wear your legs down to nothing," she murmured teasingly.

He gave her a furious look. "If I stop pacing, you'll have a worse problem," he warned her.

She strolled over to one of the lamps and turned it down to the lowest setting.

"I want to tell you what happened between Babs and me," he told her, frowning as he settled on a spot across the room from her and forced himself to stand still. "Stop turning down the lights, damn it."

"All right," she said softly. She sat on the side of a sofa, and the slit in her dress parted, revealing a long expanse of very shapely leg. "Tell me."

Beau dragged his eyes away from the tempting sight of her thigh and forced himself to continue. "I met her at one of the post-horse-show parties one night. She was alone and attractive, and most of the other people there seemed to feel very sorry for her. Enoch had...has...a reputation for keeping a mistress and ignoring Babs. The mistresses would change every so often, but Babs kept having to endure the insult. She honestly hadn't known that when she married him, and she had finally realized that he wasn't going to change his ways when she ran into me."

Elaine listened, wishing he would let her put her arms around him while he confessed. It felt so lonely having to hear it, having to watch him struggle to admit it, with an entire room separating them.

"Go on," she told him gently.

Beau expelled a breath he'd been holding and shoved his hands into his trouser pockets. "She cried on my shoulder a little that evening, then came to watch me work with one of my horses the following day. I felt sorry for her at first. She wasn't as hard then as she is now. She was sort of a sad woman, really. Hurt, vulnerable and wanting to escape from her husband's sadistic indifference to her." He looked straight at Elaine. "She made it fairly obvious that she wanted more than my ear. For a while I laughed it off and told her no. I also made it plain that I wasn't interested in sleeping with another man's wife. I'd never done that, and I had no intention of starting with her."

Elaine felt a small sense of relief at hearing him admit that. She'd suspected that he'd felt that way, but he'd been so ruthlessly critical of himself that she hadn't been sure.

"How did she manage to maneuver you into sleeping with her?" she asked evenly, repressing a sharp twinge of jealousy.

He sighed angrily. "She lied to me. And I was so sick of her plaguing me day and night, I was willing to believe her. She told me she'd filed for a legal separation and that she was divorcing him. She said he was moving in with his current mistress, and as far as she and her lawyer were concerned, she was a free agent. It had already occurred to me that if she got what she wanted, she might find other sources of amusement and leave me alone. Unfortunately, she pushed her sad little self on me late one night after I'd spent the evening drinking myself under the table with a bunch of old friends. Whatever common sense I ever had was too inebriated to be of any use."

Elaine looked at him sympathetically, but her eyes were glittering jealously. "She was very clever," she noted. "And very determined to get you." She smiled a little at that. "Much as I dislike her, I can understand how a woman could be driven to underhanded and unprincipled methods of getting you to touch her."

The thread of amusement in her voice made him look at her sharply. "Is that so?" he said.

She raised her delicate brows innocently. "Oh, yes," she went on lightly. "Take me, for example..."

"I've been doing my damnedest not to," he pointed out in a growl.

"How much longer do you think you're going to keep...not taking me?" she inquired cautiously.

"I was planning on a year...." he admitted. He pulled his hands out of his pockets and began pacing again, frowning furiously.

"A year!" Elaine exploded. "You are the *stubbornnest* man on this planet!" she exclaimed in frustration. "Your family will be vindicated. You'll recoup much if not all of what you've lost financially. You can't keep pushing me away from you because you're on the Foxgrove payroll, for heaven's sake! You'll have your own independent income, if that's so important to you."

He glared at her, but kept pacing. "Of course it's important to me! Do you think I've enjoyed having nothing to give you? How the hell do you think I feel, anyway? Don't you understand?"

Elaine snapped to her feet. *"Nothing to give me?"* she exclaimed, so amazed that she was nearly rendered speechless.

Ambrose chose that moment to walk into the room and place a silver tray with cognac and glasses on a small table halfway between the two combatants. He restrained an urge to smile. "I imagine that will be all?" he said.

Since they barely seemed aware that he'd entered the room, he left quietly, closing the doors after him.

Elaine's voice ached as she repeated his words for the second time. "Nothing to give me? You idiot! How can you believe that? You've given me warmth when I was cold. Tenderness when I was lonely. Loyalty without asking for it in return. Self-sacrifice bordering on torture to both of us... You keep yourself away from me because you want to protect me. Do you think I didn't know that's what you were doing?"

She closed her eyes against a rush of emotions so strong that they were bringing tears to her eyes. She saw him standing there as if making a last heroic effort to keep his hands off her. The tension stretching between them hurt.

"I fell in love with you, and you knew it, didn't you?" she said brokenly. "You've known it for a long time now. You've bent over backward not to use that knowledge. And you didn't turn me away when I sought you out. You made me realize how wonderful making love truly is. You gave me passionate love, if not the words or the commitment. You gave me companionship and encouragement.... And you kept your own needs away from my sight, trying to keep us from becoming so emotionally entangled that I couldn't leave you if I wanted to." She blinked away the tears trembling on her dark lashes. "Well, I don't want to leave you. And I don't want you to leave me. I know all about your plan to spend the next year competing." She sniffed and gave him a blazingly defiant look. "Well, go right ahead," she told him testily. "Because I'm going to be competing in most of those events myself. I think Irish Mist and I may do stunningly well, if I do say so myself."

He was looking at her as if she'd grown another head. "You're competing on Irish Mist?" he managed to ask at last. "I thought you intended to avoid that at all costs?"

She looked at him helplessly. "I would have," she admitted. "But this time the cost would have been too high. It would have meant that I wouldn't see you for weeks at a time. I just..." Her voice dropped to a tortured whisper. "I couldn't stand that. The past couple of weeks have been bad enough. I've missed you so...." She caught a sob just in time and angrily brushed away a lone tear that had the audacity to drop onto her cheek.

She took the small glass of cognac that Ambrose had poured and was about to drink it, but Beau strode across the room and stayed her hand with his. Their eyes met, and she felt herself caught by his compelling gaze. She barely felt him remove the drink from her fingers and put it back down on the tray.

He pulled her into his arms and tilted her face up to look at him. "Don't cry," he said huskily. "I can't stand to see you cry, you know."

That only made the tears well up more. She looked up at him helplessly. "I'm sorry," she said in a watery voice. "I can't seem to stop it."

He looked as if he were being tortured. "Elaine," he said, pleading with her. "I wanted to give you this year to be sure. God only knows how I'll survive it, but you need time...."

"No, I don't."

"It'll take months before Fogarty begins twisting the money back out of Carlton. Until then, I have to earn my own. That's why I'm practically killing myself and everybody's horses in that schedule you unearthed. It's my way of making enough money to ask you to marry me at the end of the year...if you still feel the same way then."

The tears really got bad then, and Elaine began to sob.

"What did I say, sweetheart?" he asked in an anguished voice. "Is it marriage? Forget I mentioned it. Hell, I'll do whatever you want if you'll just stop crying. Please..." He started swearing softly and running his hands over her shoulders and back, kissing her damp cheeks and nuzzling her.

"Forget it!" she exclaimed between hiccups. "I most certainly will not. I accept. I hold you to your proposal."

He sighed. "I wasn't going to say this to you tonight, you know."

"I know. You've never been going to say anything!" she sobbed in frustration. She looped her arms around his neck and kissed him on the mouth. "But I love you anyway."

"Oh, God, Elaine," he muttered. Something gave way inside him, and everything he'd been holding back burst from behind the dam. His arms locked around her, and he returned her kiss by opening his mouth and ravaging hers.

Sweet, poignant, stinging pleasure blossomed within Elaine's mouth. She welcomed his tongue and caressed it with hers, moaning as he pulled her up against his chest until she was on her toes. His hands cupped her bottom and drew her against him, and she could feel his rising need for her. A rush of desire went shooting through her, leaving her shaking violently and feeling as weak as a kitten.

He tore his mouth away from hers and began placing erotic openmouthed kisses over her throat, neck and the exposed flesh of her shoulders and breasts. He stopped when his tongue slid against the edge of her black evening dress, and he lifted his head to stare into her eyes.

"I swore I was never going to make love to you again until I was a free man and not working for your brother. And for you, for that matter."

Elaine looked as if she might burst into tears of frustration. She sank her hands into his dark blond hair and glared at him. "You have two choices," she told him breathlessly. "You can quit. Or, if you like, I'll fire you on the spot. But if you dare leave me now, Beau Lamond, I'll...I'll..." She broke off futilely. She couldn't think of anything awful enough to do to him in retribution.

He began to grin then, and slowly swept her off her feet and into his arms. He made his way to the staircase and climbed it, as he had once before with her in his arms. But this time he knew which door led to her rooms, and he went there unerringly.

When they were inside and he'd carried her into her bedroom, he kissed her long and tenderly. Then he lifted his lips from hers and stared down into her beautiful dark blue eyes fringed with wet black lashes.

"That paper I handed to Richard..." he explained huskily. "It was my resignation. I had a sinking feeling I might not be able to keep my hands off you."

"Thank God," Elaine moaned gratefully as he lowered them both to her soft bed.

"Now," she gasped as they fumbled with their clothes between increasingly urgent kisses and caresses. "Could...you just tell...me? Ooh, do that again...."

They were sprawled together, nakedly entwined, clothes cast all over the place, their hands running rampant over each other.

His mouth found hers, and his hard body filled her at the same heartrending moment. They were both groaning at the exquisite relief of the intimacy that had been denied for far too long.

Weeks of unrelieved frustration drove them both, and Beau thrust into her again and again, as she eagerly met him. He writhed against her in his desperately aching need. Nothing had ever been so exciting to her as this, and she felt the pressure tighten and threaten to explode just as his body began to convulse against hers. The explosion was overwhelming, and they both cried out, clutching each other, and she heard him say, over and over against her mouth, her neck, her breast, "I love you. I love you. I love you."

* * * * *

Silhouette Intimate Moments®

COMING NEXT MONTH

#313 TIME WAS—Nora Roberts
When Caleb Hornblower comes to after the craft he was piloting crashes, he doesn't understand how very far from home he is. He has traveled not only through space, but through time, only to discover that home is what he finds in Libby Stone's arms.

#314 TENDER OFFER—
Paula Detmer Riggs
Alex Torres returned to southwestern Ohio to help his ex-wife, Casey O'Neill, fight the takeover of her company. But in the ruthless corporate world, it was not the only battle to be waged—he also had to regain the respect and trust of the woman he'd never stopped loving.

#315 LOVE IS A LONG SHOT—
Joanna Marks
Laura Reynolds's testimony had been crucial in sending Quinton Jones to prison for a crime he didn't commit. Now Quint was back, and Laura desperately wanted to set the record straight. But she knew that once he found out who she really was, he would be bound to break her heart.

#316 FLIRTING WITH DANGER—
Linda Turner
Someone was trying to drive beautiful heiress Gabriella Winters insane. So she fled her family mansion—only to run headlong into the arms of Austin LePort. There was more to this handsome hobo than met the eye, and soon Gabriella found herself truly mad...madly in love.

AVAILABLE NOW:

#309 THE ICE CREAM MAN
Kathleen Korbel

#310 SOMEBODY'S BABY
Marilyn Pappano

#311 MAGIC IN THE AIR
Marilyn Tracy

#312 MISTRESS OF FOXGROVE
Lee Magner

Available now from

SILHOUETTE® Desire™

TAGGED #534
by Lass Small

Fredricka Lambert had always believed in true love, but she couldn't figure out whom to love... until lifelong friend Colin Kilgallon pointed her in the right direction—toward himself.

Fredricka is one of five fascinating Lambert sisters. She is as enticing as each one of her four sisters, whose stories you have already enjoyed.

- Hillary in GOLDILOCKS AND THE BEHR (Desire #437)
- Tate in HIDE AND SEEK (Desire #453)
- Georgina in RED ROVER (Desire #491)
- Roberta in ODD MAN OUT (Desire #505)

Don't miss the last book of this enticing miniseries, only from Silhouette Desire.

If you missed any of the Lambert sisters' stories by Lass Small, send $2.50 plus 75 cents postage and handling to:

In the U.S.
901 Fuhrmann Blvd.
Box 1396
Buffalo, NY 14269-1396

In Canada
P.O. Box 609
Fort Erie, Ontario
L2A 5X3

SD528-1R

You'll flip ... your pages won't!
Read paperbacks *hands-free* with

Book Mate • I

The perfect "mate" for all your romance paperbacks

Traveling • Vacationing • At Work • In Bed • Studying • Cooking • Eating

Perfect size for all standard paperbacks, this wonderful invention makes reading a pure pleasure! Ingenious design holds paperback books OPEN and FLAT so even wind can't ruffle pages – leaves your hands free to do other things. Reinforced, wipe-clean vinyl-covered holder flexes to let you turn pages without undoing the strap...supports paperbacks so well, they have the strength of hardcovers!

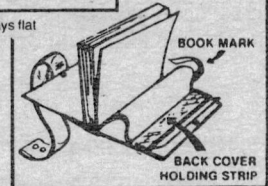

Pages turn WITHOUT opening the strap.

SEE-THROUGH STRAP

Reinforced back stays flat

Built in bookmark

BOOK MARK

BACK COVER HOLDING STRIP

10" x 7¼", opened.
Snaps closed for easy carrying, too

Available now. Send your name, address, and zip code, along with a check or money order for just $5.95 + .75¢ for postage & handling (for a total of $6.70) payable to Reader Service to:

Reader Service
Bookmate Offer
901 Fuhrmann Blvd.
P.O. Box 1396
Buffalo, N.Y. 14269-1396

Offer not available in Canada
*New York and Iowa residents add appropriate sales tax.

BM-G